FORTUNE'S
FOOL

ALSO BY ALBERT A. BELL, JR.

FORTUNE'S FOOL

A SIXTH CASE FROM THE NOTEBOOKS OF PLINY THE YOUNGER

ALBERT A. BELL, JR.

MMXVII

PERSEVERANCE PRESS · JOHN DANIEL & COMPANY

PALO ALTO / MCKINLEYVILLE, CALIFORNIA

A Perseverance Press Book
Published by John Daniel & Company
A division of Daniel & Daniel, Publishers, Inc.
Post Office Box 2790
McKinleyville, California 95519
www.danielpublishing.com/perseverance

Distributed by SCB Distributors (800) 729-6423

Book design: Eric Larson, Studio E Books, Santa Barbara
www.studio-e-books.com

Cover painting: "Fortune's Fool" © by Chi Meredith
Egg tempera on panel
www.sites.google.com/site/meredithchiartist

10 9 8 7 6 5 4 3 2 1

LIBRARY OF CONGRESS CATALOGING-IN-PUBLICATION DATA
Names: Bell, Albert A., 1945- author.
Title: Fortune's fool : a sixth case from the notebooks of Pliny the Younger
/ by Albert A. Bell, Jr.
Description: McKinleyville, California : John Daniel & Company, 2017.
Identifiers: LCCN 2016046131 | ISBN 9781564745873 (pbk. : alk. paper)
Subjects: LCSH: Pliny, the Younger—Fiction. | Tacitus, Cornelius—Fiction. |
Family secrets—Rome—Fiction. | Murder—Investigation—Fiction. |
GSAFD: Historical fiction. | Mystery fiction.
Classification: LCC PS3552.E485 F68 2017 | DDC 813/.54—dc23
LC record available at https://lccn.loc.gov/2016046131

FORTUNE'S
FOOL

I

Fortune makes fools of those she favors too much.

—Horace

"YOU'RE GOING TO make me get *married?*" My servant Aurora, usually so gentle with horses, drew hers to such an abrupt stop that he stumbled. She jerked the reins and turned him to face me. "Why?"

We were out for a ride along the shore of Lake Comum, at the foot of the Alps. My mother had asked me to bring my *familia* here, to the smallest of my villas, one which I inherited from my natural father. We hadn't been here in several years, and I knew she thought she was coming to see, for one last time, the place where she began her married life and to say good-bye to people she has known most of her life. She appears to be in good health, but the disease that I'm not supposed to know she has—a *karkinos* in her breast—is a death sentence, whether it takes a few months or a couple of years to be carried out. My great fear is that she might have come back here to end her life where it began.

This was where I was born and lived until my father died, when I was quite young. The house sits on a small rise on the peninsula ten miles north of the town of Comum, giving it an unequaled view down the length of the narrow lake and up into the mountains. At this time of year, on a perfect morning in mid-July, no place in Italy is cooler or more lush. Aurora had been quiet, as though she had something on her mind.

"Answer me, Gaius. Why are you making me get married?" Aurora gripped the long reins tightly, as though she was thinking about slapping me with them.

My horse whinnied and shook his head as I reined him in. He had been fighting me for control since we rode out of the stable. "Livia says I have to. I've put her off for several months, but she's given me an ultimatum. Her exact words were, 'Either have that girl married before I come to Comum or get rid of her.'"

"'That girl'? Does she even know my name?"

"I assure you, she knows it well enough to curse it."

"And you feel you have to do everything Livia tells you to?" She put a defiant hand on her hip.

"She is my wife."

Aurora snorted derisively. "We both know what *that* means."

"It means nothing except that I have to keep peace with her, for your sake as well as mine."

"Gaius, why don't you just divorce her?" The pain she showed on her face was as profound as what I felt. "You only married her to please your mother. You don't love her and she doesn't love you. When you got married she seemed to accept our relationship, as long as we didn't flaunt it."

"She seems to feel that I am doing exactly that."

"How?"

I patted my horse's neck, trying to calm him, the way I've seen Aurora settle an animal down. My touch had little effect, but then I know how different—how wonderful—it feels to have *her* hands on any part of one's body. Something magical passes through those hands into whatever she's touching. "You have to understand. We've been married for barely six months. If I were to embarrass her by divorcing her like that, there's no telling what sort of revenge she would—"

"Do you still think she killed her first husband?"

Fortunately there was no one in sight at the moment. Still, careless words have an uncanny knack for worming themselves into the wrong ears. "Be careful what you say. I have no way of knowing what happened to the man, but nothing would surprise me, given the fits of rage I've seen from her. At the very least I'm sure Livia would spread stories about us—you and me—and cause my mother great distress. *That* I will not allow, so I cannot divorce her, at least as long as my mother is alive."

"You know I could never wish her death." Aurora's face darkened. As beautiful as she is—with her olive complexion, long brown hair, and dark eyes—she can also be alarming when she gets angry. I think it's her Punic heritage, the visage that enabled Hannibal to terrify us Romans for nearly twenty years. "Gaius, you're a brave man. I've seen you stand up to all kinds of danger. And yet you cower before these two women like a…"

"I believe 'coward' is the word you're searching for. Or perhaps 'craven coward,' just for the alliteration. I truly would rather face a man with a sword in his hand. Then I could judge what my opponent was capable of and have some idea of how to counter his blows. I once saw a fox gnaw off one of its legs to get out of a trap. In the last few months I have come to understand that degree of desperation."

Aurora let out a long breath. "So I'm to be sacrificed, like Iphigenia on the altar at Aulis. Why now?"

"Livia and her mother are coming up here. They'll arrive in a day or two."

"Oh, wonderful!" She threw her head back, as if raising a protest to the gods, or looking to be whisked away, the way some versions of the story say Iphigenia was, to be replaced by a deer. "This was such a pleasant holiday. I should have known it was too good to last."

Her reaction was precisely why I had decided to break this news to her while we were away from the house. There was no way to make it sound good. She was right. We had been enjoying ourselves for the last five days. My friend Tacitus and his wife, Julia, had come up with us, stopping over for a few days on their way to Tacitus' estate in Transalpine Gaul. They know the nature of my relationship with Aurora and are happy with it, so we can all relax and enjoy one another's company, as long as my mother isn't in the room.

At times Julia even seems to forget that Aurora is a slave. They sit in the garden, talking and laughing with their heads together, like the women in a Tanagra figurine. Julia isn't as well-educated as Aurora— not even as intelligent, I suspect—but the experience of losing a child before birth almost two years ago has given her a different type of wisdom and maturity to complement her lively personality. If I were to let myself, I could imagine what it would be like to be married to Aurora and have Tacitus and Julia as our closest friends.

But I can't let myself.

Clicking her tongue, Aurora tapped her horse's sides with her heels and we resumed our ride, now turning back to the villa. I wasn't ready to go back, but it was clearly futile to hope for any more pleasant conversation today, or some time alone in the woods. I hadn't really expected any intimacy, knowing what I had to tell her. She looked out over the deep blue of the lake and the houses lining the opposite shore. Without turning back to me, she said, "So, who is to be my husband? He won't be a happy man. I'll guarantee you that, and I doubt you will be, either."

I reached over and put a hand on her arm. "Please, let me explain. I've got the perfect solution to this problem."

"Perfect" might have been too optimistic a word, but I did believe I had found an answer to our dilemma that would satisfy Livia and not impose too great a burden on Aurora.

I've never admitted to Livia that I've coupled with Aurora, but I've never denied it. She hasn't asked, just assumed, correctly. Merely to satisfy Livia, I wasn't going to marry Aurora to some young, virile man in my household. But, if I married her to my oldest, doddering, gray-haired slave, Livia would see through the subterfuge at once. Although our own marriage might be a sexless sham, at her insistence, she would never let me get away with putting Aurora into a similar relationship.

"Which of us should be wearing the Tyche ring now?" Aurora asked. When we were children we had found the ring—bearing an image of the goddess Tyche, or Fortune—in a cave near my house at Laurentum. Now we passed it back and forth between us, depending on who most needed the luck it was supposed to represent. At the moment it was on a leather strap around my neck.

"I think I'm going to need a good deal more fortune than you are over the next couple of days."

"Don't let Livia get her hands on the strap. She might strangle you with it. No, wait, a blow on the head is more her style, isn't it?"

"I wish you would stop talking like that. There's no evidence she did anything to her first husband."

"But you think she did."

I couldn't deny that, and I couldn't squelch my fear that she might harm Aurora, so we rode in silence for a while. We arrived back at the villa as several people were stepping out of a *raeda*.

"You said Livia wasn't due to arrive for a couple of days," Aurora said, not trying in the least to suppress her annoyance.

"That's not Livia. Come and meet your husband."

The people getting out of the *raeda* were servants from my estate in Tuscany. I had ordered several of them—three men and four women—to be moved up here permanently. And the moves were justified. This house at Comum, I now realized, was not being run efficiently. The income was adequate, but I didn't understand why it wasn't making more money. I had paid too little attention to it, and the *familia* here had gotten lazy. I thought these people from Tuscany had talents that would inject life into this place, but there was one man for whom I had a special assignment.

"Ooh, I hope it's him," Aurora said, pointing to a tall, blond Gallic fellow who was helping one of the young women down from the *raeda*. His name was Brennus, and I had brought him here to oversee the vines and wine-making on the estate. He had a most remarkable nose.

"I thought you were angry about this."

Aurora gave me a mock-serious expression. "Well, if I'm to be forced to bed down with some man I don't know, maybe I should make the most of my chance. You can think about that while you're not doing whatever it is you don't do with your wife."

"Don't get your hopes up," I said as we dismounted. "Or your gown either."

Her shoulders sagged. "I was only teasing, Gaius. You don't have to talk to me like I'm some whore."

"I'm sorry," I said in little more than a whisper, hiding my face against my horse's shoulder. "I'm truly sorry. I hate having to do this. I hate being married to Livia. I hate that my mother is dying. And, most of all, I hate that I can't be with you."

Aurora stepped closer. The anguish and the love on her face told me that she wanted to embrace me, and I wanted her to, but it couldn't happen, not with all those people around.

"My lord," my scribe Phineas said, drawing closer to us and raising a hand to interrupt us, "these are the people you sent for."

"You've made good time to get here early in the afternoon."

"Last night we stayed with your friend Caninius Rufus, my lord, as you suggested we do. I pushed us yesterday so we wouldn't have too many miles today. Caninius was most gracious and sent you this." Phineas handed me a sealed note.

"It is still a bit of a trek from his house." I had brought Phineas with me on this trip because this house doesn't have a scribe of his caliber and also to accompany his mother, Naomi, my mother's most valued companion. In spite of his youth—he's only a couple of years older than I am—I had placed him in charge of the trip to Tuscany because I knew I could trust him with any task.

"Thank you, Phineas. Please get the others settled and send Felix to my room."

"Certainly, my lord. Will you need anything else?"

"No. You can get back to sorting those papers in the library."

"Yes, my lord." He started toward the house, obviously happier to be set to a task involving ink and papyrus, especially old papyrus. The small library on this estate has been neglected for years, and the estate's elderly scribe had recently died. I had assigned Phineas the task of getting the library in order and picking out someone who could be trusted to maintain it.

I turned to Aurora. "You need to find something to do until I send for you. Put on a nice gown and that necklace of your mother's that looks so good on you."

"I thought I was about to meet my husband."

"I need to talk to him first. He doesn't know yet that he's going to be your husband."

─────⊱⊰─────

Felix had lived on my uncle's estate in Tuscany since before I was born. I knew little about him because he made himself so inconspicuous. Although he was about fifty, he looked younger, with barely any gray in his hair. The only sign of his age was that he had begun to gain weight in recent years. Working under the steward in the house, his primary responsibility was to keep track of our food and other household supplies and to procure things as needed. I knew he had done one other important task for my uncle. That was why I had chosen him to play the role of Aurora's husband.

He knocked on my door and I told him to enter. "Close the door behind you." I wished I could leave the door open. The rooms in this old-fashioned house are particularly small. It makes them easier to heat in winter, which is colder here than in Rome, but oppressive to someone, like me, who dislikes confined spaces. The frescoes were done in a dark, heavy style, popular some years ago, which only added to the gloom.

"Yes, my lord." He was tentative, uncertain, as he had every right to be, looking around as though trying to comprehend where he was and why he was here. A slave who has served as long and as well as Felix has in one position would not be summarily moved somewhere else without a serious reason.

"Welcome to Comum," I said, remaining seated at my writing table, crammed into a corner of the room.

"Thank you, my lord, but, if I may be so bold as to ask…why am I… here?" His intonation on the word "here" made clear his instant dislike for the place. I could sympathize. This villa was older and much smaller than the one in Tuscany. Because I seldom come here, I haven't spent any money on updating or remodeling it. Even though I was born here and am fond of the area, the house itself doesn't appeal to me the way several of my other estates do. In fact, it has an ominous feel to it, like the story I've heard of a house in Athens that was haunted by the ghost of a man who'd been murdered and stuffed down an abandoned well in the garden.

"Don't worry," I said, "you won't be here long."

Instead of consoling him, that statement caused his eyebrows to rise and his breathing to quicken. "My lord, am I to be sold? Have I done something to displease you?"

"No, not at all." I held out my hand to calm him. "I want you to do something else for me—a different task but, I think, a not unfamiliar one."

"And what would that be, my lord? All I've ever done in your household, and your uncle's before you, is watch over your stores."

I touched the pointed end of my stylus to my lip, as though warming it so I could write something. "That's not entirely true. At one time you were married to my uncle's servant, Delia."

He nodded, his eyes growing wary. "Yes, my lord, I was. She was a sweet girl."

"She had a child, didn't she?"

"Yes, my lord." He looked down.

"And it wasn't yours, was it?"

"No, my lord," he said without looking up.

I tapped my stylus on the table. "Delia, I assume, was my uncle's lover. Am I correct to think that the child was his?"

"As far as I know, it was, my lord." He studied his feet as though he had never seen them before.

"So my uncle married her to you to divert someone's attention from his affair."

"Yes, my lord. His wife's. She strongly disapproved of his affair with Delia, as I suppose any wife would."

Was that statement as insolent as it seemed to be? But I had to let the comment go because I needed his help. I was beginning to wonder if the Stoic doctrine of a recurring cycle of events might not be true. I had almost forgotten that my uncle had ever been married, to a woman named Tullia. It lasted less than a year, and nothing was ever said about it in our family. If only that part of the story could be repeated in my own life. I could endure another six months with Livia if I knew there would be an end to it after that and the whole fiasco could be forgotten.

"And that was...thirty-five years ago?"

"Yes, my lord. As soon as Delia realized she was pregnant, your uncle married her to me. I was eighteen at the time. Delia was a year younger."

"Was there any particular reason he chose you?"

Instead of answering the question, Felix raised his tunic. He was wearing a loincloth, unusual for a man who wasn't doing hard work, but not unheard of. He lowered the cloth enough for me to see that he had been castrated. I couldn't help but recoil from the sight.

"When was that done?"

"When I was sixteen, my lord." He shivered at the memory and I motioned for him to cover himself again.

"Did my uncle do it?" I had never heard of my uncle doing such an unspeakable thing to a servant. Enough owners, wanting male servants whom they could trust around their wives, have done it that Domitian recently issued an edict against the practice.

"No, my lord. It was done by my previous owner."

"Why?" Before I put any man in close proximity to Aurora, I had to know his full story, and there was apparently more to Felix's story than I had suspected.

"My owner's daughter got pregnant. I was not the father, my lord," he added quickly. "But another servant in the house was. The girl accused me, and her lover swore that he had heard me boasting about it. He even said I told him about a mole on her body in a place that only a lover would see. He, of course, had seen it. My master…did this to me and made his daughter watch." His voice caught and he paused. "He swore he would do the same, or worse, to any man who touched her. Once I had recovered, he sold me to your uncle."

I ran my fingers on the edge of the table while I considered this astounding development in my plan. "Men who have been castrated are sometimes still able to couple, even if they can no longer father a child."

"Sadly, my lord, I am not one of those."

I tried not to show my relief. "So my uncle knew you would not be able to couple with Delia."

"Yes, my lord."

"Does anyone else in the household know you've been castrated?"

"I don't think so, my lord." He seemed to be trying to decide what to do with his hands. He clasped them in front of him, then lowered them to his sides. "It's not something one boasts about. I act as though I'm overly modest and that's why I wear a loincloth and prefer to bathe alone. There's a rumor that I'm a Jew, ashamed of my circumcision. I'd rather be teased about that than about…this."

"Your voice isn't unusually high."

"No, my lord. For that I am thankful."

"So Delia's child really was my uncle's?" That would confirm what I had learned over the past few months as I considered who among my servants would make a suitable—that is, safe—husband for Aurora. I had a cousin I'd never heard of.

"I'm sure he was, my lord, although your uncle never acknowledged the boy. I raised him as my son until your uncle emancipated him and found him a place as an apprentice with a goldsmith in Comum."

"What was the boy's name?"

"He was called Marcus Delius, my lord."

Another point confirmed. I had seen one reference to that name in a letter. "Where is he now?"

"I don't know, my lord. I was told that he ran away."

That would have made him no better than a fugitive slave. Although he had been freed, Delius still had an obligation to my uncle and to the goldsmith who was feeding him and training him for a respectable profession. "When did that happen?"

"Not long after he was apprenticed, my lord. Twenty years ago."

I was barely four at the time. I could not recall ever having heard the name Marcus Delius until I was looking through some of my uncle's letters and notes earlier this summer. When I saw the name and guessed his relationship to me, I felt some impulse to know more about him. As the only surviving child of an only child, I have no circle of relatives, so even a bastard cousin piques my curiosity. But if no one had seen or heard of him in twenty years, it seemed unlikely that I would ever learn anything. It would be like trying to track an animal days after it has passed through a forest and the trail has grown cold or been washed away.

"What else do you know about him?"

"Just that he was a difficult lad, my lord. His mother died when he was eight. After that, there was little anyone could do with him. He ran roughshod over the other children in the household—even older ones—and you could never get the truth out of him. He took great delight in sneaking up on people. He had no respect for me as his father. Sometimes I felt he had guessed the truth. I think your uncle freed him just to be rid of him."

"Or to remove evidence of his indiscretion."

"That could well be, my lord. But that was the last anyone in our house heard of him or spoke of him."

I paused to think what I was going to say next. Although I had known from two comments in my uncle's letters that Felix was married to Delia, I hadn't been able to learn why he was picked to play the role of her husband. I thought it must have been because my uncle believed he could count on the man to restrain himself and be content to pretend to be a husband or that he had hung some dire threat over his head, like the sword of Damocles. As it turned out, the blade had been hung a bit lower, but it meant that Felix was the best possible candidate for the role of Aurora's husband.

"My lord, you said I wasn't going to stay here. Do you have some task for me? At my age I hope it's one I will be able to carry out."

"Yes, and I don't think you'll find it onerous." I paused and took a breath before saying the words that would commit me. "I want you to marry my slave Aurora."

Other than blinking a couple of times, he showed no surprise. "Is she pregnant, my lord?"

"No, she's not. But otherwise the situation is the same as the one my uncle faced."

"May I ask if you love her, my lord?"

I slapped the stylus on the desk and Felix stepped back as much as the small room allowed. "No, you may not. That is most impertinent."

My outburst didn't faze him. "If you do love her, my lord, then the situation is not the same as your uncle's."

I stood without moving any closer to him, but Felix, who was somewhat taller than I am, leaned back anyway. "What do you mean?" I demanded.

"Your uncle did not love Delia, my lord. He treated her well and was affectionate to her, but she told me that he did not love her. He had told her so himself. She was not to expect love from him, he said. It broke her heart. More than that, it broke her will to live when she became ill."

I was surprised to hear that. From what I had seen of my uncle with Aurora's mother, Monica, I would have said that he loved her. He grieved deeply when she died. But this was not a conversation I wanted to be having with a slave.

"You understand your role then."

"Yes, my lord. Your uncle made it clear that I was not to touch my 'wife' except to show a bit of affection in front of others—holding hands, a peck on the cheek perhaps. I assume those rules will apply in this case."

"Yes, but don't overdo it." It galled me to think of any man being allowed even that degree of intimacy with the woman I love.

"Will we be sharing a room?"

The question stopped me for a moment. "I'll have to work all that out, but I suppose you will." Livia wouldn't stand for any other arrangement, I was sure, even though we do not share a room ourselves.

"So your wife will think it's a real marriage?" His tone was more kind than accusatory.

"That is my hope."

"When will this marriage begin, my lord?"

I sat back down at the writing table and picked up my stylus. "This afternoon." When something is inevitable, there's no point in delaying it. The dread is usually worse than the actuality.

He nodded his understanding. "Will I have any other duties in the house, my lord?"

"Yes, you'll be doing in Rome what you were doing in Tuscany. My man in Rome is sixty. Keeping supplies in order for such a large house is starting to wear on him."

"I'd best work with him for a while, my lord. It will take me a month or two to get acquainted with the people you buy from and to see who's cheating you."

I looked up at him in surprise. "Why do you think someone is cheating me?"

"Did the sun rise this morning, my lord? As surely as that, merchants are always cheating you. There's a reason why Hermes is the god of travelers, merchants, and thieves. It's merely a question of how much cheating your servants allow or are aware of, and how deeply they're involved in it."

"How much cheating goes on at my estate in Tuscany?" That estate has always been the most profitable of my properties.

Felix straightened his shoulders, like a soldier coming to attention. "Only the little bit that I simply cannot ferret out, my lord. There's always that little bit, no matter how diligent one is."

"Aurora dear, may I come in?" Julia's voice sounded from the other side of my door. I was too angry to have company at the moment, but I couldn't refuse her. Sometimes I wonder what it would feel like to be able to say no, even to Gaius. Not that he's ever forced me to do anything I didn't want to—until today.

"Yes, my lady."

I stood as she entered my room and closed the door. She's shorter than I am, as most women are, with a round, fair face and the impish smile of a child who's always planning some mischief. She was carrying something in a bag.

"First of all," she said, "let's have none of that 'my lady' business when there's no one else around. We're friends and we have to get you ready for your wedding. Gaius is telling everyone it will take place today."

"Today?"

"Yes, in a few hours, I think."

"Damn him!"

Julia twisted up her mouth as though she had tasted something sour. "Aurora, you know I won't tell anyone anything you say, but you need to be careful how you talk about him. You never know who might be listening."

I had crossed the boundary between servant and friend. "Yes, of course, I'm sorry."

"Now, you want to look your best for your wedding, don't you?"

"I don't even know who I'm being married to. Why would I want to look my best for him?" I folded my arms over my chest. I knew I looked and sounded like a petulant child, but I was hurt, deeply hurt. Gaius should have told me. It was as simple as that.

Julia touched my hair. "It's not your husband you're trying to impress, silly girl. We're going to make Gaius Pliny regret he ever decided to do this."

I stamped my foot and could hardly keep from crying. "Why did he do it, Julia? Why can't he stand up to Livia and his mother? Tell them to—"

"You should count yourself lucky that he doesn't." Julia hugged me for a moment, then sat me down. "That shows you he's a man who cares about those around him and how they feel."

"What about how I feel?"

"Gaius knows how you feel. And you know he loves you. You two have told each other that, haven't you?"

"Yes, but—"

"Then trust what he's told you. Men like him and Tacitus don't always have a choice about what they do. What Gaius is arranging is his best option in this situation. If he didn't find you a husband, he'd have to send you somewhere else. This way, he is actually standing up to Livia. She wants you gone, but he's keeping you here, where he wants you to be."

I sighed heavily. I hadn't seen the situation in those terms. "I guess you're right. But what am I supposed to do tonight? Am I to couple with my 'husband'?"

Julia looked at me, with her head cocked, like I was the stupidest person she had ever met. "Do you honestly think Gaius is going to put you in a room with a man without making it clear to him that he's never to touch you? If he could find a eunuch for the job, I'm sure that's who would be your husband."

I laughed in spite of myself.

"That's the spirit. All you'll have to worry about is how much he snores or farts in his sleep."

"I hope you're right."

"Of course I am. I assure you, it's not going to be easy for Gaius to marry you to another man, even if it's only a pretense. And, by the time we're done here, he's going to be on his knees begging your forgiveness."

Opening her bag, she pulled out a white tunic—the traditional bride's dress. Motioning for me to stand, she held it up against my cheek.

"This was my wedding gown. I added the filigree. With my pale skin, I would rather have worn something darker, but it will look stunning on you. I let down the hem."

"Wait. You brought your wedding dress? Did you know Gaius was going to do this?"

"Oh, well...he said...something about it."

"He told you and Tacitus before you left Rome but didn't tell me?" My voice was rising, just like my anger.

The look of surprise on Julia's face seemed genuine. "He didn't tell you?"

"Not until this morning."

Julia held the dress away from me. "I'm sorry. I didn't know—"

"Oh, that man!"

"Don't get yourself worked up. You don't need a lot of distress now."

"You mean, distress like being forced to marry some man I've never met." I sighed and tried to calm down.

Julia patted my belly. "Have you told Gaius yet?"

"No." I put my hand over hers. "I was going to tell him this morning, when he asked me to go riding with him. But then he told me about this marriage."

"So you've told me—"

"Only after you suspected."

"But you admitted it. And yet you're angry at Gaius for not telling you something important."

It wasn't fair of her to inject logic into the conversation. "You haven't said anything to Tacitus, have you?"

Julia gave a quick shake of her head. "No. I promised you I wouldn't. But a man has every right to know when a woman is carrying his child."

"Because it's his property, I know, just like I'm his property, to be married off whenever he sees fit."

"Aurora, you know Gaius doesn't think of you that way."

Before I could say anything—and what could I say? I sounded ridiculous to myself—we heard a knock on the door. A woman's voice that I didn't recognize said, "My lord Pliny would like to speak with Aurora."

Julia, who was standing closer to the door, opened it just a crack and said, "He'll have to wait. We're getting her ready for her wedding. He wants her to get married, so that's what we're doing."

I finally had a few moments to open the note from Caninius Rufus that Phineas had handed me. Caninius is a fine poet, and we've known one another since childhood. This note was short, but not pleasant to read. He was writing a poem in which he wanted to make an allusion to the eruption of Vesuvius and the death of my uncle almost six years ago. "Would you mind," he asked, "describing what you saw? I know those memories are painful, but I hope enough time has passed that you can think back on them more calmly now."

I dropped the note onto my writing table. Fortune had spared my mother and me from that catastrophe. Now it seemed determined to keep the memory in front of me.

II

*The man who has planned badly, if fortune is on his
side, may have a stroke of luck, but his plan was
a bad one nonetheless.*

—Herodotus

TACITUS, MY MOTHER, Naomi, and a few other servants
gathered in the garden that afternoon for the wedding of Felix
and Aurora. A bride is supposed to be accompanied by a woman who
has been married only once and whose husband is still living. Even
though this wasn't a formal wedding, Julia, in that role, came out of
Aurora's room with her and stood beside her.

Everyone in the garden held their breath as Aurora walked along
the winding path, past the fountain, and came to a stop in front of me.
I couldn't look at her, partly because she was more beautiful than I'd
ever seen her—her hair swept up and pinned in a way that made me
ache to kiss her neck, makeup applied with just the right touch—and
partly because I thought she was going to bore a hole through me with
her eyes. The rest of her face betrayed no emotion, but I had never seen
such anger in her eyes. I fixed my gaze on Julia, who had more than her
usual half smile playing on her lips.

As Aurora took her place beside Felix and nodded to acknowledge
him, my mother patted her on the arm and said something to her,
but so softly I couldn't hear her. Aurora smiled modestly in return
and kissed my mother on the cheek. The second best thing that has
happened to me in the last six months is that my mother's animosity

to Aurora—which had its roots in her resentment of the relationship between Aurora's mother and my uncle—has softened.

Slaves cannot legally marry in the sense that free persons can, but I do allow my servants to establish what amounts to marital relationships, which I recognize as binding. I also allow them to make wills, something very few masters do, and I act as executor of those wills when the time comes. Since a marriage between slaves is not legally binding, we did not engage in the offerings and oaths that solemnize a marriage. The way Aurora was dressed surprised me—the white gown and orange veil with matching shoes and the knotted belt around her waist. She could not have known in advance to procure the traditional dress for a bride—the *tunica recta*.

Then I understood Julia's smile and Aurora's anger and knew that I had made a serious mistake in not saying something to Aurora earlier.

Felix and Aurora held one another's right hands in the traditional manner, but we made no sacrifices and invoked no gods. Aurora would not say to her husband the age-old vow, "Where you are Gaius, I am Gaia." She had said that to me during the Saturnalia when we went to the cave where we had found the Tyche ring. The words had no legal effect, of course, unlike when Livia said them a few days later in the atrium of my house in Rome, but they meant more to me than all the pomp associated with my wedding to Livia.

She had dropped thinly veiled hints—threats, to be more precise—about not wanting Aurora present at our wedding. I had refused to comply. As a member of my household, I had pointed out, she had an obligation to be there. Her absence would cause more comment than her presence. Because of her own good sense and her pain over what was happening, Aurora had remained on the edge of the crowd. I was certainly aware of her, but I'm not sure Livia noticed. At least she never said anything, and if Livia is unhappy about something, she lets me know about it, quickly and loudly.

I realized everyone was looking at me in anticipation. I couldn't put it off any longer.

"I've called you here today," I said, "to acknowledge that…Felix and Aurora are…husband and wife." I had never had to work so hard to force words out of my mouth, even though I knew they had no meaning. I could feel Tacitus trying to hold me up with his eyes as I said a few more innocuous platitudes. I like to write my speeches down and revise them for possible publication. These words I wanted to be utterly forgotten. The only thing that enabled me to proceed with the ceremony was my awareness of Felix's secret and my knowledge that not even Aurora knew it. "Let's join in congratulating them and wishing them every happiness," I concluded.

Tacitus stepped forward. "Good fortune for the newlyweds," he said. "A cheer for Felix and Aurora. *Talassio!*"

The others joined him in the traditional shout for a newly married couple, so ancient that no one knows anymore what it means.

I couldn't eat, but while the others enjoyed a meal in the garden, another bed was moved into Aurora's room. Then it was time to accompany the couple to their quarters with obscene jokes and ribald songs, a part of Rome's wedding traditions, regardless of the couple's class or wishes, that I particularly despise. It was the one thing Livia and I agreed on at our wedding but could do nothing about. We sat on opposite sides of my room after the wedding until the noise subsided outside the door. I had stashed several of Musonius Rufus' treatises under the bed before the ceremony, so I had something to do. Like Socrates, Musonius won't write anything himself, but his students and friends take down his teachings and circulate them among a small group. While I read, keeping my voice down, Livia just sat and fumed. Stoic philosophy held no charm for her, as I had hoped when I selected those books.

My mother ran her arm through mine. "You've done the right thing, Gaius. And she looked absolutely beautiful."

"Well, I hope everyone else is happy with the arrangements." I turned my back to the celebration and fixed my gaze on one of the columns on the other side of the garden. It was cracked and no longer straight.

"I'm sure we all are. I wish you could be, too." The way she patted my arm told me she understood more than she was saying.

Even though I knew now that none of the crude suggestions would be carried out in Aurora's room, I couldn't stand to listen to any more of the buffoonery. Stepping away from my mother, I told Tacitus, "I'm going to inspect the vineyards."

"I'll ride with you." He clapped a hand on my shoulder.

I nodded. "I would appreciate that."

The servant who oversaw the stables on this estate went by the name Barbatus, because of his affectation of a beard. I didn't know his real name. He claimed to be descended from a Gallic prince captured by Julius Caesar. Even as a child, I had never much liked the man because of his habit of stroking his beard and because he talked so much, always asking so many questions about where I was riding to. I could never seem to find the nerve to tell him it was none of his business. All I could do was keep my answers as brief and uninformative as possible.

Time had not changed his mannerisms or made him any less annoying. When I requested horses for Tacitus and me, he asked, "Where will you be riding, my lord?"

"Away from here. Why does it matter?"

"Some horses are better for distance, my lord," he said with studied indifference. "Others can give you speed. If I know where you're going, I can give you the best horse for your ride."

"We're going out to the vineyards," I said.

"I see. Should I be expecting you back at any particular time, my lord?"

"Why does that matter?"

"I just want to be sure someone is here to assist you, my lord."

"We're perfectly capable of dismounting and unharnessing the horses by ourselves. Just see to your business and don't worry about us."

Barbatus stroked his beard. "As you wish, my lord." He brought two horses from the stalls and helped us mount.

"He's an inquisitive fellow, isn't he?" Tacitus said as we turned toward the vineyards. "I'd expect that sort of nosiness from a female slave, not a stable hand."

"He's always been like that. I should give him the benefit of the doubt, I suppose. Perhaps he's just being solicitous of my welfare."

"Or perhaps he's one of Regulus' spies and wants to know your every move."

I groaned. "This day is bad enough. Don't start—"

"Sorry. That was an ill-advised attempt at humor. The man's obviously just a congenial blabbermouth. Forget I said anything."

We rode in silence—companionable on Tacitus' part, morose on mine—out to the vineyards on the east side of the estate. Lake Comum is long and slender, splitting into two branches, like a capital Greek upsilon (*Y*), only inverted, from a Roman point of view. The house sits halfway up the peninsula. The mountains rise quickly on either side of the lake. We dismounted, tied the horses to a tree, and walked among the vines.

"How did you settle on Felix?" Tacitus asked. "I know you were thinking about this problem back in the spring, but I've seen so little of you the last couple of months, I feel like I've missed an important part of the story."

I held a vine in my hand, rubbing the leaf between my fingers with no interest whatsoever. "I had Phineas compile a list of all of my male servants—slaves and freedmen—over the age of forty. Then I eliminated those who were already married. I narrowed the list down to the oldest ones who might pass Livia's inspection. I kept coming back to Felix because of his age and because he was married years ago to one of my uncle's mistresses."

"So he should understand how the game is played," Tacitus said.

"After talking with him, I'm sure he does."

"But do you think you can trust him absolutely? Aurora is a stunningly beautiful woman. Even as much as I respect our friendship, I'm not sure you could trust *me* with her."

"It doesn't matter. He turned out to be the best choice for a reason I never could have anticipated." I paused.

"Well, come on, man. Out with it! Does he prefer other men? Is that it?"

"No. Even better, actually. I found out just before the wedding that he's a eunuch. Castrated when he was sixteen and completely unable to couple."

"A eunuch?" Tacitus doubled over with laughter. "By the gods, it's like a comic play. Does Aurora know?"

"I didn't get a chance to tell her. She's hardly speaking to me."

"Oh, that's even better. I would love to know how *that* conversation goes when they're alone together for the first time."

"Damn you!" I turned on him abruptly and shook my fist in his face. "This is no joke. I don't care if he is a eunuch. I wouldn't care if he was blind into the bargain. I cannot stand to think that another man can go into a room with her and close the door." I had to pause to keep my voice from breaking. "Did you see how beautiful she looked? Like Hesiod said of Pandora, 'a face like a deathless goddess.'"

Tacitus covered my fist with his larger hand and pushed it back. "She's always beautiful, but as spectacularly gorgeous as she was today—that was Julia's doing, not a bunch of gods. My wife is adept at that sort of thing. She may not be able to parse a line of the *Aeneid*, but she knows what color eye shadow a girl should wear and exactly how much. The outfit Aurora was wearing was what Julia wore at our wedding."

"I suspected as much. She just brought out what was already there." I put my hand to my head, which was aching. "Oh, dear gods! That dress means Aurora knows that I told you and Julia well ahead of time what I was planning but didn't tell her until the last minute."

Tacitus' shoulders slumped and he shook his head. "Gaius, to be so intelligent, you can do some stupid things when it comes to women. You don't understand how they think unless they've killed somebody."

That point I couldn't argue. "I rue the day I ever came up with this scheme."

"It's the only choice you had."

"I know, but that doesn't make it any more palatable."

"You need to take your mind off the whole business. It doesn't really change anything between you and Aurora." Tacitus took me by the shoulders and turned me toward the vines. "I know you didn't actually come out here to inspect your vineyards, but as long as we're here, we might as well."

I took another leaf between my fingers. "They remind me of the filigree on Aurora's wedding dress."

Tacitus sighed. "You're hopeless, my friend. You should remember Horace's advice in one of his poems: 'Xanthis, don't be ashamed of love for your serving-girl.'"

"Xanthis was Greek, not a Roman of the equestrian class. I'll bet he wasn't married." But Tacitus was right. What hope did I have? Certainly none of ever being truly happy. The best I could do was to distract myself by devoting full attention to running my estates and keeping up my literary work. As Cicero said, "If you have a garden and a library, you have all you need." At the moment I would have been willing to debate that claim with him and was confident I would have run him off the Rostra. I wondered if he had a favorite girl aside from his wife.

"Your vineyard isn't exactly impressive," Tacitus said, drawing me back to the harsh light of reality. "Didn't your uncle write about grapes and the best places to grow each variety?"

"He did, extensively. But this property belonged to my father, not my uncle." Tacitus was right, though. Nothing about the vineyards, or anything else on the estate, suggested prosperity. "This estate produces less income than any of my other properties."

"That doesn't surprise me in the least."

"That's why I'm bringing in some people from Tuscany to look things over. I've not spent enough time here in the last five years to know just what's going on. I've been paying more attention to my place at Misenum in the aftermath of Vesuvius."

"Whatever profits you're making here," Tacitus said, "they certainly aren't coming from your vineyards." He plucked a grape and squeezed it between his fingers. "It ought to be a lot plumper by this time of the summer. You grow more olives and wheat on your other estates, don't you?"

I nodded. "But, considering how pathetic the plants in this vineyard look, I should reread what my uncle says about vines in his *Natural History*. If I can't improve the output here, I should switch to growing something more suited to the land and more profitable... You may have noticed the tall, blond fellow I brought up here."

"Yes. I thought I was going to have to restrain Julia when she saw him."

"His name is Brennus. He's quite good with vines, and his sensitive nose is the most remarkable I've ever seen in a human being."

"He'll have his work cut out for him here."

We walked among the vines, studying drainage and the angle of light. "You inherited this property from your father," Tacitus said, "but your mother and uncle also grew up around here, didn't they?"

"Yes, my uncle's family owned the estate on the lake at the foot of this property. That's where he and my mother grew up. He sold it not long after she got married. I've made an offer to buy it back. I'd like to have access to the lake."

"Why? You can't stand to be on a boat."

"But I enjoy looking at the water and listening to the rhythm of it. That's why I like my estate at Laurentum so much. I've been so involved in restoring my property around Naples that I've neglected other places. I want to correct that oversight and some others. Did you know that my father started work on a temple to Rome and Augustus outside Comum?"

"No, I didn't."

"He never finished it before he died, and he left no funds for the work. I want to look into finishing it."

"If you could let Domitian think he's the Augustus you have in mind, it wouldn't hurt."

"I'll make it clear that I mean the first one. Domitian can't publicly object to that."

"I suppose not." Tacitus looked up at the sun and said, "We'd better be getting back."

"Must we?"

"Do you plan to live out here like some savage? What was it Aristotle said, 'Anyone who finds delight in solitude is either a wild beast or a god'?"

I folded my arms across my chest and put my chin in my hand, the classic pose for statues of orators and philosophers musing over something. "Or the husband of a shrew like Livia."

"When is she due to arrive?"

Tacitus might as well have thrown a pail of cold water in my face. "Tomorrow or the next day. They went to Narnia first, to drop off Livilla at their house there. For obvious reasons, she doesn't want to be around me."

"Do you think Livilla's told her sister what she knows about you and Aurora?"

"If she had, I would probably be a dead man by now."

"Just like Livia's first husband."

"We have no way of knowing what happened," I reminded him, although Livia had stopped just short of admitting to me that she killed the poor man. I took her all-but-confession as a veiled warning.

"I wonder why a woman would do that, when divorce is so easy."

"An ex-wife has to endure all the whispering, and she doesn't get anything but her dowry back. A childless widow gets sympathy and everything her husband had. And Liburnius had a lot of everything."

"So do you, my friend. So do you."

What he said was true. My father's estate and my uncle's together had made me one of the wealthiest men of my age in Rome. But now I was wondering why my uncle had left my adoption to his will. He wasn't the only man to do so. Julius Caesar had adopted his grand-nephew, Octavian, in his will, but he also named Brutus a guardian of any son he might have. Had my uncle, like Caesar, hoped to have a son? Considering his age and his lack of a wife, he hadn't been trying very hard. Or was he hoping to find his illegitimate son, Marcus Delius, and recognize him?

I was surprised and a little relieved when I walked out into the garden and saw who my "husband" was to be. I don't know Felix well, but I had met him on visits to Gaius' estate in Tuscany. When we were children, he used to let Gaius and me explore the storerooms in the house and usually had some small treat for us. All I knew about him was that he seemed to be a nice man who kept to himself. He had an air of resignation—even of sadness—about him, which I sometimes feel when I'm around older servants.

But, no matter how nice he might be, I still didn't want to share a room with him. When he closed the door, I scooted across the bed, as far away from him as I could get. For reassurance I touched the knife I had strapped to my thigh, a knife Gaius gave me, with his dolphin seal embossed on the handle. Julia had gasped when she saw it while she was helping me dress, but I wouldn't take it off.

"You don't have to be afraid of me, dear," Felix said, sitting down on the far end of the second bed and making no movement toward me. Because of that bed there wasn't much floor space left. "I know I'm not really your

husband. I couldn't be, even if I were lucky enough for this to be a real marriage."

"What do you mean? What did Gaius…Pliny say to you?" Gaius had sent someone to ask to talk to me before the wedding, but Julia sent back word that we were too busy preparing for the ceremony. Maybe that hadn't been such a good idea.

Felix shook his head. "It's what I said to him. It's something you should know, but I hope I can rely on your discretion not to tell anyone else."

"Of course you can." I could hear the crowd of servants outside the door, still wishing us well and singing every bawdy song they knew to encourage us.

"All right then." He paused for a moment, as though gathering his courage. "You see, my first owner…castrated me when I was sixteen."

I could see on his face how hard it had been for him to admit that. That look stirred up a twinge of sympathy. "Why…why did he do that?" Castration could be punishment for…things I hated to think about.

"For something I was accused of but did not do. That's all you need to know."

I could make a guess. Probably something involving his owner's wife or daughter. "Did Gaius Pliny know this when he sent for you?"

"No. He knew I had been married a long time ago to his uncle's earlier mistress—meaning no insult to your mother—and he assumed I knew how to play that role. He didn't know his uncle chose me because I would be unable to couple with her."

I relaxed enough to move closer to him, but not too close. "Felix, I'm so sorry, but do you mind if I say I'm relieved?"

"I wouldn't take advantage of you, even if I could. You know that. You've known me since you were a child. I've been treated well by this family and I will repay that kindness by doing what's expected of me."

"Does anyone else know about…your condition?"

"No. I've tried hard to keep it a secret."

I could tell that people were pressing their ears to the door. "They're expecting to hear something soon."

Felix glared at the door. "Well, I guess they'll have to be disappointed."

"Not necessarily. Come here." I took his hand and we stood next to the door. "Just don't look at me," I whispered. "You'll make me laugh."

Starting slowly at first, I began to moan, remembering Gaius' hands *on my body, his lips on my neck. Felix's eyes brightened as he followed my lead and made a few appropriate noises.*

"Oh, yes. Yes, Felix. Yes! Yes!"

Outside, the crowd cheered.

Felix smothered a laugh. "That will certainly give them something to talk about."

And it will give Gaius something to think about, damn him.

As Tacitus and I drew close to the villa, we saw three wagons approaching from the south, from the direction of the town of Comum. The first two were an open style of *raeda*, with leather curtains that could be drawn against bad weather. On both wagons the lower half was painted blood red and the posts that supported the roof were a yellow that did not exist anywhere in nature—two garish colors that Pompeia Celerina favored. The third was a closed *raeda*.

"Are you expecting company?" Tacitus asked.

"It's Livia and her mother," I said with a groan. "Damn them! I thought I had another day."

"Do you have any other vineyards that need inspecting? Somewhere in Greece, perhaps?"

I glared at him with my mouth screwed up.

"You have to greet them, Gaius. You have no choice."

"I'm getting very tired of hearing that. I'm a free man. I'm supposed to have choices."

"No one but the emperor is really free," Tacitus reminded me with a tired philosophical commonplace. "And then only if you believe there are no gods waiting to exact retribution for his numerous crimes."

"Yes. As Ovid says, 'Gods are convenient to have, so let us concede their existence.'"

We reached the front of the house at the same time as the wagons. I dismounted and went to help Livia and her mother out of the first wagon. They were accompanied by a few favorite servant women. The rest of their retinue rode in the second wagon. The third, I was sure, held their baggage.

"Welcome to Comum, ladies," I said, trying to inject civility into my voice, since I couldn't quite manage warmth. "We weren't expecting you until tomorrow at the earliest, so I'm afraid things may not be entirely ready for you."

"Oh, we'll manage." Pompeia dropped her considerable bulk to the ground with a grunt and offered me a hug and a perfunctory kiss on the cheek. She wore a blue gown and had her hair done up in the style of women of the Flavian court, with crimped curls piled up high toward the front of her head. Given her size and the color of her gown, the effect was like waves on the ocean. "We got far enough yesterday that we just decided to push on and finish the trip today, rather than make another stop."

Livia's hair was done in a simpler style, pulled back into a bun on her neck. She wore a soft green gown, with gold bracelets on each arm and a brooch pinned over her heart. In a rare moment of tenderness she had told me that her father gave it to her. *He was the only person who ever loved me*, she said. Standing in the wagon as though not certain she would get out, she looked down her nose at the villa. "How old is this place?"

"My grandfather built it," I said, "during the time of the deified Augustus."

"It's a nice place," Pompeia said. "I visited here when I was a girl." My mother and Pompeia are cousins. Her family's home was south of Comum, but she and her brother sold it after their parents' deaths. She claims to prefer the sophistication of Rome, but she's just a pretentious snob.

"It's ancient then," Livia said, wrinkling her nose.

"My father did some work on it. It's smaller than my other houses, but quite comfortable," I assured her.

"And the servants have finally learned not to scratch their bottoms in our presence," Tacitus said over my shoulder.

"*Hmpf*," was all Pompeia said. Livia just gathered her cloak around her and reluctantly stepped down from the *raeda*.

My mother, Julia, and several servants emerged from the house, laughing about something.

"Pompeia dear, how lovely to see you," Mother said, stepping forward. "I hope the trip wasn't too tiring for you."

"Aren't all trips tiring?" Pompeia said, embracing my mother and kissing her lightly on the cheek, a gesture which my mother returned.

"Well, you're here now. That's all that matters."

The noise from the servants in the garden drifted out to us.

"What's going on?" Livia's simple question sounded like an accusation.

"Oh, Gaius arranged a marriage for Aurora," Mother said. "We've just finished celebrating it. If we'd known you were arriving today, we could have waited."

Livia questioned me just by the tilt of her head and the arching of an eyebrow.

"We'll talk later," I said abruptly. "You thought Aurora ought to get married. Now she is."

"Who is her husband?"

Before I could repeat my admonition that we talk later, my mother said, "His name is Felix. He's a servant from our house at Tuscany."

"Is that where Aurora will be living now?" Livia asked with a hint of hope in her voice.

"Well, I don't know," Mother said. "What is your plan, Gaius?"

"Yes," Livia echoed, "what *is* your plan, Gaius?"

It's odd how the same words, spoken by two different people one right after the other, can convey simple curiosity on the one hand and a direct challenge on the other. And it all depends on the meaning of "is," or at least the emphasis given to that little word.

"My plan is that Felix will come to Rome with us. He'll be in charge of buying supplies for the house there. Arcturus, who does that job now, is getting old."

"And how old is Felix?" Livia asked.

I shrugged, trying to show my indifference, but my mother spoke up. "He's older than I am. That's all I know. Isn't he at least fifty, Gaius?"

The curl of Livia's lip let me know that, when we did talk later, it would not be a pleasant conversation, and probably not a short one.

Julia stepped up beside my mother and extended a hand to Pompeia. "There's food set out in the garden. You must be famished after your trip."

Pompeia needed no other encouragement. Given her girth, I doubt she has ever been anywhere close to famished.

"Perhaps we can still extend our good wishes to the happy couple," Livia said.

As we passed through the small atrium Livia's eyes rolled at the frescoes which, I had to admit, were badly dated. The place had last been painted when my father was a young man, probably early in the reign of Claudius. The only time I had suggested repainting, my mother had strongly objected. The decorations had been done shortly after she married my father and she was loath to change them.

"You can't receive many clients in here," Livia said.

"I save a lot of money that way."

"But people can't see how important you are."

"Around here, everybody who needs to know does, and nobody cares." That lack of pretension was one of the great charms of Comum.

As we entered the garden the servants moved away from the door of Aurora's room, still laughing and making noises and gestures like a couple engaged in love-making. Our presence put a damper on their fun, as I was glad to see. I wanted to play out this scene without an audience.

"Back to work, everyone," I ordered. They shuffled off to their various tasks, with a few backward glances.

"Bring them out here," Livia said. "I'd like to offer my congratulations."

"Do we really need to disturb them right now?" Tacitus asked.

Livia drew herself up. "As mistress of any house which belongs to my husband, I have a right to know who will be working in it."

"Of course you do," my mother said. She knocked on the door. "Aurora, you and Felix come out here for a moment."

The door opened and Aurora and Felix emerged sheepishly, smiling at one another. Aurora had unpinned her hair and shaken it loose. All I could think about was Ovid's line about reaching across the table at a dinner party to claim his mistress from her husband. I had a momentary fear that Felix had lied to me, as Aurora looked into his eyes with adoration.

"Here's the blushing bride," Livia said, taking Aurora's chin in her hand and turning her head back and forth. "Perhaps your new husband can nip a bit off your other ear, to even things out."

Aurora flushed, but in anger. The tip of her right earlobe had been cut off when she was almost killed in one of our recent misadventures.

Livia patted—almost slapped—Aurora's cheek, then turned to Felix. "And you're Felix."

"Yes, my lady." Livia had not yet been to my estate in Tuscany, so Felix had never met her. Even though he had no idea who she was, her dress and arrogant manner made it clear how he should address her.

"You do look as happy as your name implies."

"I am, my lady. This is a joyous day." He took Aurora's hand.

"I'm Livia, wife of Gaius Pliny."

Felix bowed his head. "I'm honored to meet you, my lady. And may I offer you belated congratulations on your marriage and the utmost good fortune."

"I suppose you may, and I'll return the same."

"Thank you, my lady."

"How old are you, Felix?" Livia touched his shoulders and felt the muscles of his arms.

"I'm fifty-three, my lady."

Livia sneered at me. "That's no surprise. Have you been married before, Felix?"

"Yes, my lady."

Aurora had not met my eyes yet. She leaned close to Felix, her shoulder touching his. I would have to tell her not to overplay her role.

"Was she a servant in this house?" Livia asked.

"Her name was Delia, my lady, another servant in my lord Pliny's household, and I mean your husband's uncle."

"So that was some time ago. Did you have any children?"

"My wife gave birth to a son, my lady."

I silently applauded Felix for his logical dexterity. He must have practiced saying something like that to divert attention from his castration. It stopped Livia for a moment, the way a charging animal is stunned when it hits an unseen net.

I took Livia by the arm before she could lower her horns for another charge at the obstacle. "Will you come with me, please?"

Livia followed me to the far corner of the garden, as far from the others as we could get. "What more do you want?" I said, lowering my voice.

She answered me in an angry whisper. "I'm still not sure that this is a real marriage and not a sham."

"You mean, like ours?" I gave her an opportunity to reply and her mouth moved, but what could she say? "You wanted Aurora married. She is married."

"But can someone that old even service her?"

"His wife had a child." I was as careful in arranging my words as Felix had been.

"Years ago. That doesn't mean he can still—"

"You heard the servants. It sounds like Aurora was...serviced quite well. Or do you want them to perform in front of you, like Tiberius' sexual acrobats on the isle of Capri?"

"Well! You don't have to—"

"Aurora is married, as you...requested, *and* before you arrived in Comum, as you requested. I don't want to hear another word on the subject."

III

*As the blessings of health and fortune have a beginning,
so they must also find an end. Everything rises but
to fall, and increases but to decay.*

—Sallust

OUR CONVERSATION was interrupted by Livia's servants bringing the women's trunks and bags into the garden. No wonder the four horses pulling the closed *raeda* had been straining so hard.

"Take the lady Livia's things to her husband's room," my mother said, pointing the way.

"Let me look at the room first," Livia said. Everyone came to a halt as she poked her head into my room, then pronounced her judgment. "It's much too small for two people. What other rooms do you have?" She directed the question to my steward, a freedman named Decimus, who looked to me in consternation.

"There are two rooms on the other side of the garden," I said, "which are not currently in use. Perhaps you'll find them more satisfactory."

Livia gathered up her gown like a woman does when she's afraid she might step in something disgusting. "Let's take a look."

As Decimus led her and Pompeia across the garden, my mother edged closer to me.

"Aren't you going to share a room?"

"Apparently not." We had slept in the same room a few times since our marriage—even in the same bed on two occasions when we absolutely could not avoid doing so—but neither of us preferred that arrangement.

"But, Gaius, you're husband and wife."

"Mother, many couples have their own individual quarters. You know that."

She lowered her voice to a sharp whisper. "Yes, many childless couples. Pompeia and I didn't arrange this marriage so you and Livia could wave to one another across the garden."

"Then you should talk to Livia. As you saw, this is her choice, not mine."

Mother pointed across the garden. "Are they going to take *those* two rooms?"

The rooms Livia and Pompeia were looking at were separated by a stretch of blank wall where an opening used to lead to a vegetable garden. My father had walled up the space some years ago.

"What's wrong with them?" I asked.

"The servants here told Naomi that they sometimes hear strange noises in those rooms. Things even fall off the shelves for no reason."

Perhaps something will land on Livia's head, I thought.

"There's always an explanation for that sort of thing," I said. "Something probably was done incorrectly when that opening was closed up, so the stone work is shifting."

While the women got unpacked and got their servants settled, I retired to the library, where I wished I could spend the rest of the day, if not the rest of the time we were on this estate. Tacitus and Julia had gone to "bathe" and everyone knew by now to let them have the bath to themselves for the next hour.

I paused at the door of the library, letting my soul—whatever that is—soak in the calm. I had asked Phineas to sort and arrange the books. The scribe who had had charge of the library until his recent death had become careless toward the end of his life, as his mind began to leave him. Even if I didn't come here often, I wanted the library to be useful, and I hoped we might hit on some rarity, a bit of Ennius or

Naevius perhaps. Looking over the piles of scrolls on several different tables, I asked him to tell me what he had done so far.

"Well, my lord, this table is the Greek books." He waved his hand over the table closest to us. "Those two tables are the Latin books, and that far table is personal correspondence and business documents."

"Have you found anything of unusual interest?"

"No, my lord. I'm afraid your father did not have your, and your uncle's, exquisite and wide-ranging taste in books. Judging from what I've seen so far, the collection is quite pedestrian, if you'll forgive me for saying so. And, even if you won't forgive me, it's still quite pedestrian."

Phineas is three years older than I am. He still bears resentment about the destruction of Jerusalem fifteen years ago, where he and his mother, Naomi, were captured, but he does such excellent work that I can tolerate a certain degree of abrasiveness in his personality. My mother has reminded me that he and I have more in common than we might realize. Our mothers both lost daughters before we were born. We were both raised by an uncle whom we lost tragically. We've both been known by other names—my uncle named him Peleus and his mother Niobe because he didn't like the sound of their Jewish names. A few years ago my mother insisted that we respect them enough to call them by their real names.

"As you can see, my lord, I'm about halfway through." He raised a hand toward the boxes of scrolls lining the back wall of the room. "I've still got that section to clean out."

"I'll take a look at it." *Anything to pass some time and stay away from everybody for a while.*

"I would appreciate the help, my lord. None of your people here has shown much aptitude for this kind of work, I'm afraid."

"That's a pity. Is there anyone in my *familia* in Rome who could do it?"

Phineas didn't have to think long at all. "Xenobia, my lord, has shown a keen interest."

"That blond girl I've seen you working with?"

"Yes, my lord. I've been teaching her. She's even picking up the Tironian notation."

I smiled to myself. "I thought there was some connection between you two." It was obvious Xenobia was more interested in him than in the scrolls.

He blushed. "She's an apt pupil, my lord. Nothing more."

"*Pssht*. I'm not blind. The attraction between you two lights up the library. I'm surprised the scrolls don't catch fire."

His back stiffened. "She's not Jewish, my lord. I could never hurt my mother by taking a Gentile as my wife."

In this brief moment we'd found two more points of similarity: Phineas and I both respected—or feared—our mothers too much to hurt them, and he was also in love with a girl he could never have. Fortune makes fools of us all. I touched the Tyche ring. Do we build temples to this most fickle of goddesses to seek her favor or just to keep her away from us? Does anyone get what they want? Or do we have to figure out, after we have something, that we want it? Tacitus didn't particularly want to marry Julia but now he's falling so madly in love with her that he sports with her in the bath like most men enjoy their mistresses.

"Would it be…easier for you if she were somewhere else?"

"I think she would do a fine job here, my lord."

"That's not what I asked you."

"I've given you the only answer I can, my lord."

I could see that he was going to break into tears if I pursued the matter any further. His eyes were pleading with me to change the subject. I cleared my throat. "But a woman as the chief scribe in a household? It's unheard of."

"If you'll forgive my crudity, my lord, she doesn't need a *mentula* to dip into an inkwell."

I couldn't help but laugh. "I'll also forgive your audacity."

"Thank you, my lord."

"All right, then." I clapped my hands. "Write a letter for me, assigning her to this household."

"Could she bring some books, my lord, to improve the quality of this library?"

"Certainly. Why not? Tell her to bring whatever you think suitable. I'll seal it and we'll send someone off with it today. Have her come up

here right away. You'll need a few days, at least, to show her what needs
to be done."

"Thank you, my lord," he said, sharpening a pen.

"And you may need to come up here regularly, just to oversee her
work."

Dinner in the *exhedra* was a chilly affair, and not just because a light
breeze was blowing down from the mountains. Since the house has
a small kitchen and a cook unaccustomed to company, the meal was
simple, featuring fish from the lake and vegetables grown on the estate.
My appetite, along with my spirits, was dampened by Livia's presence
on the couch beside me and Aurora's absence from behind me. Livia
had insisted on having a meal packed for Aurora and Felix and sending
them down to eat on the shore of the lake.

"The 'newlyweds' need some time to themselves," she said.

The girl who served me did the job adequately, but she didn't touch
my foot when no one was looking or kiss the cloth she used to wipe
the rim of my cup when she refilled it.

"Are your rooms comfortable, dear?" I asked Livia.

"They'll do for a short visit," Livia said. "I gather they're not used
much. One of your servants said some unusual things have happened
in there."

"Allegedly. You know how those stories get started. One jar falls
off a shelf when no one's around and before you know it the room is
'haunted.'" I wanted to put her mind at ease to insure she stayed in
the room.

"Perhaps you'd feel safer," my mother put in, "if you moved to
another room, Gaius' for instance."

"I'll be fine where I am," Livia said as she dipped another piece of
fish into the *garum* sauce.

Julia, her cheeks still rosy from her "bath," asked Pompeia, "Do I
remember correctly that your family is from this area?"

Pompeia nodded and swallowed a large bite. "My father and Plinia's
mother were cousins. Our families have lived around here since Julius
Caesar established the new town."

"The Pompeius family has as many branches as our own Cornelii and Julii." Julia laid a hand on Tacitus' shoulder. "Are you related to any of the more distinguished ones? Pompeius Magnus by any chance?"

"No one that famous," Pompeia said. "I don't think I would claim it if I was. There are some people you'd just as soon not be related to."

"Seneca's wife was a Pompeia, wasn't she?" Tacitus said. "Pompeia Paulina, if I recall."

"I believe you're right."

"But no connection to your branch of the family?"

"I hope not."

"Why wouldn't you want to be related to her?" Livia groused. "Everybody's heard of Seneca."

"And everybody's heard about the plot," Pompeia said, obviously sorry the whole subject had come up.

"What plot?" Livia was sitting up on the couch now. Apparently there was at least one person who hadn't heard of it.

"There was a plot to assassinate Nero," Tacitus said. "Seneca was implicated, though no one is sure he was actually involved. Nero ordered him to kill himself. Pompeia Paulina tried to kill herself alongside him, but Nero forbade it. She lived several more years and is much admired for her loyalty to her husband and to his philosophy."

"But they tried to kill a *princeps*?" Livia looked down her nose.

"Well, it *was* Nero," Julia said.

"Still—"

"There's no evidence that Pompeia or any relative of hers participated in the plot," Tacitus said. "In a case like that, though, Nero always cast a wide net."

"And anyone to whom my cousin Pompeia is related," my mother said, "has some connection to us. Remember that."

"It's the sort of thing," Pompeia said, clipping her words, "that one hopes is never talked about so it can be forgotten."

"Then let's talk about something else," Julia said. "Where is your family's home?"

Pompeia sighed in relief at the opportunity to change the subject. "They lived closer to Comum. My brother and I sold the property after the deaths of our parents. He prefers his place on the shore of the lake, just south of here. I haven't been back here in some time. Rome is so much more an interesting place to live, and my husband left me a beautiful property at Narnia."

Julia nodded. "Certainly much closer to Rome and yet far enough away from the city."

"One never wants to be too far from Rome," Pompeia said. "And being back here at this time is painful."

"Why?" Julia asked.

"It was twenty years ago, almost to the day, when my husband drowned in this lake. The last time I saw him was in this garden. They never found his body."

Julia picked up an apple that a slave had sliced. "They never found—"

"Let's not dwell on the misfortunes of the past, dear," my mother cut in. "We can't change anything. Such memories only intrude on a pleasant evening."

A fleeting expression on my mother's face made me think she wasn't concerned only with Pompeia's feelings, but the conversation quickly degenerated into banalities—the new hairstyle worn by Domitian's wife, Martial's latest book of salacious poems, and so on. The only reason I didn't excuse myself was because I didn't want to leave Tacitus and Julia to endure the company of my wife and mother-in-law without reinforcements. I need not have worried about Julia, though. She answered Livia's every insult about the provincial character of the house or the food with a wit worthy of one of Martial's epigrams.

At one point Pompeia excused herself to use the *latrina*. Livia got up to join her. "Is there room for two?"

"There's plenty of room," Julia said. "But we use the bushes at the other end of the garden. Mine's the one with the yellow flowers on it. They were white when I arrived."

I turned my head to cover my chuckle and noticed Naomi, sitting at my mother's feet, with her hand over her mouth. My mother, on the other hand, was clearly appalled.

Upon their return the two women brought the dinner to a mercifully early conclusion by professing to be tired from their travels and ready for bed.

As we watched the two short, stubby women wend their way across the garden my mother said, "Really, Gaius, how are you and Livia going to have a family if you don't share a room?" Since she discovered her illness she has been pushing the subject of children like a man setting the pace for the oars in a trireme. I wondered how she would feel if Aurora provided her with a grandchild.

A miracle could happen, I wanted to say, *like a god impregnating the mother of Romulus and Remus.* "Mother, we've had this conversation. You heard Livia say that my room was simply too small for two people. She could never be comfortable in there."

"Then why don't you build some larger rooms?"

"I suppose I could do that." Anything to keep up a pretense that made my mother happy for whatever time she had left. I looked around the garden and pointed to the west wall. "The land on the other side of that wall is open and flat and overlooks the lake. We could break through there and add a wing."

"It wouldn't be difficult," Tacitus said. "You don't have to worry about a neighbor's house being in the way, as you would in Rome. There would be a lovely view."

"Yes, the view was quite lovely," my mother said.

A vision, or a memory, arose in my mind of walking in that garden. "Do you know why my father walled it up?"

"He said he was concerned about you wandering out there and falling into the lake."

"Was that a real concern?" Surely I was too sensible a child to do something like that.

"It certainly was. The old vegetable garden extended from the house to where the land drops off into the lake. And you were an adventuresome child. One of the servants once found you on the very tip of the land. One more step and you'd have been in the lake."

"I could have walked through the rear gate just as easily," I pointed out.

"We could lock that, and there was no gate at all on this opening."

"Why didn't he just put up a gate?"

"I think he was concerned about the political situation, too," Mother admitted. "It was near the end of Nero's reign, twenty years ago. There were rumblings of trouble on the frontiers. That opening in the wall left us vulnerable. He seemed to decide to do all this rather suddenly and did not consult me." She took a long sip of her wine. "He rarely consulted me on anything."

I fell silent as I looked at the space where the opening had been. I was warming to the prospect of enlarging the house, for reasons other than my mother's impossible dream for a grandchild. "You know, it wouldn't be a bad idea. To run this place more efficiently I need to bring in a few more people. The ones I've brought up here will need space. We might add eight or ten rooms." I was envisioning a rectangular addition with four rooms on each side and two at the end, a space that Xenobia and Phineas might share.

"Just make sure one of them is large enough for you and Livia. It's not natural for a husband and wife to spend so much time apart."

"Well, as she said, the rooms here are small."

Mother raised herself on both elbows and leaned toward me. "But it's not just here, Gaius. You two are hardly ever together. She spends so much of her time on her estates."

For which I thank the gods. "Her family has their property, Mother, and she inherited a large estate from her first husband. These places don't run themselves. With her father dead, she has to help her mother manage things. Give us time." *An eternity, perhaps.* "Meanwhile, we'll get started tomorrow on an addition."

"An addition to the family is what I want," Mother groused. "You ought to get started on that tonight."

"We're young," I said. "There's plenty of time."

"There may not be," Mother said quietly. "You never know."

"As long as we're talking about building," I said, "I'm thinking about finishing that temple my father began." I had ridden past the site but it was far enough off the main roads that I had never taken the time to examine it. By now it was badly overgrown.

"I wish you wouldn't," Mother said.

"Why not? It puts our family in a bad light to leave it unfinished, as though we don't have the will or the resources."

Mother turned her eyes on me with what I recognized as her pleading look. "Please don't, Gaius. Please."

The ride down to the shore of the lake took only a few moments. Neither Felix nor I said much, since the path was narrow and the horses unfamiliar to us. I could see that Felix was uncomfortable with the whole idea of riding. He sighed in obvious relief when we dismounted and tied the reins to a tree.

"That looks like a good spot," I said, pointing to a place where the shore jutted out enough to offer an uncluttered view of the mountains across the lake and a few boats still on the calm water. "Shall we eat there, husband?" We had agreed to call one another "husband" and "wife," in part to mock ourselves and in part to make people think we were getting accustomed to the idea.

Felix untied the baskets containing our supper which had been strapped across his horse behind him. I unfolded the blanket I'd been riding on and spread it on the ground.

"Yes, very pleasant, wife," Felix said as he began unpacking the baskets. "I suppose we can thank the lady Livia for being so jealous of you that—"

"That she would send me to Lusitania or Armenia, if she could, not just to this shore."

"She has good reason to be jealous. You are a beautiful woman and my lord Gaius Pliny is obviously in love with you. Perhaps I should be jealous."

"You are a kind and gracious man, husband. Neither of us asked to be put in this situation, but it's certainly not the worst situation a slave ever faced."

"That's true, wife. We couldn't ask for more considerate masters, both the elder and the younger." He set out a plate of fish, some bread, a block of cheese, and a wineskin.

"The old man was certainly good to my mother."

He looked out over the lake and sighed. "How did you become a slave?"

"When I was six my mother and I were sold to pay off my father's debts." The memory was still painful—being dragged away by men who were saying things I didn't understand, my mother in tears. "I came into Gaius Pliny's household when I was seven. Somehow Gaius and I became friends right away. And the last couple of years…"

"Rather more than friends?"

I could feel myself blush. "That's one way to put it."

Felix scrounged in one basket, then the other, and looked up in frustration.

"What's the matter?"

"They forgot to pack a knife. I guess we'll just have to tear things apart with our hands."

I reached up under my gown and unsheathed the knife strapped to my thigh. "Don't tell anyone you saw this, husband."

Felix scooted away from me. "By the gods, Aurora! Do you always carry that?"

"Only in situations where I'm not sure how safe I'll be."

"Do you not feel safe with me?"

"I barely know you. I think you're a good man, but—"

"Are you going to slice the bread and cheese or use it on me?"

I began slicing the bread. "I'm sorry, Felix. But we're out here alone. We don't even have a kitchen knife to protect ourselves."

"No, you're right. You just caught me by surprise. You know a slave can be punished for carrying a weapon. You could be accused of plotting your master's death. Where did you get it?"

"My master gave it to me." I handed him a piece of bread and started to slice the cheese. He uncorked the wineskin.

"My wife is a woman of many talents, it seems. With horses, for instance. Where did you learn to ride?"

"My father bred horses, near Carthage. I was on a horse as soon as I could sit up. But my mother said he lost money on the races. A lot of money. After he sold the horses…he sold us." I needed to talk about something else. "What about you?"

"Nothing so glamorous. I was born the son of a slave. I've never known any other life. You at least must have some memory of not being a slave."

"I barely remember anything else. I do recall a farm on the edge of the desert. My most vivid memory is the way the sand would sometimes blow into the barns and the house. I've often wondered if it has covered them by now."

"In spite of everything, wife," Felix said, "Fortune has certainly smiled on you, and I guess she's given me a wink, to make up for…"

The next morning, as soon as it was light enough, Tacitus and I walked around the area where the addition would be built. I had brought a hammer, some stakes, a knife, and a coil of thin rope. Two ladders were already set up against the wall.

"It's entirely feasible," Tacitus said, scuffing an outline in the dirt. "Probably only three rooms on each side, though, and two across the back wall."

"Or perhaps one large room across the back wall, to mollify my mother." I drove stakes in the ground to mark the corners of the new work.

"Do you really want to build a room that Livia might actually share with you?"

"I doubt she'll ever set foot on this place again." I handed Tacitus one end of the piece of rope and strung it around the stakes to guide the men who would dig the foundation, squaring it off as best I could. Phineas and Xenobia might enjoy a larger room.

"Does that mean you'll become a more frequent visitor here?"

Before I had to answer that question the servants whom I had chosen as a work crew the previous evening began to assemble. Being a rural estate, this house had more male servants than my house in Rome, so we could do a good part of the work ourselves. Taking up a knife, I scratched two lines down the plaster on the wall.

"I've measured from the corner of the building, inside and out," I said. "This is where the opening used to be. As long as we stay within these two lines, we won't damage any of the rooms around the garden. The older servants say this wall is like the rest of the house, two rows of finished stone with rubble in between."

"My lord," one of the men said diffidently, "none of us is stoneworkers."

"Oh, I realize that. We'll need to hire a crew of masons to finish the walls of the addition, but we can begin knocking this down ourselves. You'll take down the finished stone on the outside and begin to dig the foundation of the addition. You can see where we've staked the outline, so a couple of you start digging." I handed shovels and picks to several of the stronger-looking men. "The rest of you, take out this side of the wall. Be careful so we can reuse this finished stone. It won't be enough, but I've sent Felix to the quarry down the road to order more."

I planned to have Felix running back and forth to the quarry for as long as it took to get enough stone to complete this project. I'd even given him money to stay overnight in the village near the quarry and encouraged him to do so if he felt it necessary to oversee the shipping of the stone. He seemed to understand me. He had left at dawn. I hadn't seen Aurora yet today.

The men climbed the two ladders and began hacking at the wall. Removing the plaster raised a cloud of dust. Tacitus and I stepped back as the workmen began to cough.

"Let's go get something to eat," I suggested. "We can check back in a while to see how they're doing."

We went into the garden through the rear gate and found Julia and Aurora looking at the dust rising over the wall.

"It's going to be a dirty job," Julia said.

Aurora met my eyes but then looked down as though we were just master and slave. Felix had given me short, polite answers to my questions about their dinner on the lake. I'd like to hear Aurora's version.

"Are the other women up yet?" I asked.

Julia shook her head. "They soon will be, though. It can't be easy to sleep through that."

I took Aurora by the elbow and turned her toward my room. "While we have a chance, let's talk."

She resisted being led but didn't go so far as to pull her arm away from me in front of other people. "What do you want to talk about, my lord?"

"I know why you're angry at me. I was stupid."

As soon as we were in my room, Aurora did jerk her arm away from me. "If you'll forgive me, my lord, 'stupid' doesn't begin to describe it. You didn't trust me."

"I didn't trust myself."

"In either case, I'm not ready to talk. I will be, I'm sure, but not now." She got halfway out the door and stopped. "By the way, I enjoyed my supper by the lake with my husband last night. We talked until well after dark. Felix knows how to listen to a woman."

"What else can he do?"

Anger flared in her eyes and she stepped toward me. "Don't talk like that, Gaius. Masters do cruel things to slaves. We don't have any control over what happens to us. Like Medea said about women and their husbands, if Fortune gives us a good one, we should be thankful. Otherwise death is better. Felix is a gracious and thoughtful man. I may end up thanking you for arranging this marriage."

"Even worse. You'll have to thank Livia. She insisted on it."

She looked out toward the garden. "Perhaps I should do that now. Here she comes."

Accompanied by my mother and Pompeia, Livia stalked—that was the only word I could find to describe her gait—across the garden. Aurora bowed to me and left before the three women stood before me.

"I see no ghosts or monsters got to you during the night," I said to Livia.

"Do I detect disappointment in your voice? I did hear a scraping noise in the wall."

"Rats, most likely," Tacitus said. "As much as I hate to think about it, they're probably in all the walls in a country estate like this."

Pompeia took in a quick breath. "Do you think we have them at Narnia, too?"

"I'm sure you do. Who knows what we'll find when that wall comes down."

We were beginning to eat and discussing the size and arrangement of the addition when a cry of surprise went up from the other side of the wall. Not the surprise of delight, but more like fear.

I stood. "We'd better see what that's about."

Before I could take more than a step one of the workmen came running in through the back gate. "My lord, my lord! Come quickly. Please."

He turned around and ran back through the gate. All we could do was follow him.

We turned the corner of the house and I could see that the top courses of the finished stone had been removed from the wall. The rubble had begun to tumble out. The workmen were standing around something, all looking down at the ground.

"All right, fellows," the man who had summoned us said. "Move aside."

The workers stepped back and I saw, lying on the ground amid the rough stones, a jumble of bones and a human skull.

IV

Fortune raises up and fortune brings low both the man
who fares well and the one who fares badly.

—Sophocles

STEPPING AROUND the pile of rubble, I climbed two rungs
up one of the ladders and looked into the interior of the wall.
When I investigate a crime—and a skeleton in a wall certainly implied
"crime"—I have to see the scene before anyone starts moving things.
A lot can be learned from where things are lying and what is next to
what. But, in this case, I hadn't seen it until things had already been
moved. I stepped off the ladder.

"Pull out the rest of the bones," I ordered my servants. The women
standing behind me gasped.

"But, my lord," the head of the crew said, "do you want to disturb
him…them? The dead don't like—"

"He's already been disturbed, and I certainly don't intend to leave
him in there. Get him out." I agree with Epicurus that the dead know
nothing, but I didn't want to say that in front of a group of supersti-
tious servants.

In a few moments the rest of the skeleton had been extracted and
laid on the ground in a jumbled pile. The paleness of the bones glared
against the gray stone as the sun rose full over the horizon. Tacitus and
I knelt beside the skeleton. When I touched one of the bones, Livia,
Pompeia, and my mother all gasped.

"I don't want those hands touching me," Livia said with a shudder.
"Not ever again."

I quickly picked up another bone, rubbed my hand up and down it to clean it off, and began laying the bones out in their proper arrangement. Tacitus assisted me.

"You saw him," Livia screeched. "He touched it! You all saw him." She made a retching sound and ran back toward the rear gate, followed by her caterwauling mother.

"Gaius, what...what are you doing?" my mother asked in shock.

"What I have to do, Mother." I hoped she didn't realize that I was talking on two levels. "You'd best go back inside. And the rest of you, get back to your duties," I said to the other workmen and servants who had come out to gawk. "Put someone on guard at the front and rear of the house and don't let anyone come out here. We'll call a halt to this work for now." It was one order they were all eager to obey.

That left only Julia and Aurora standing behind us. I knew I didn't have to caution Aurora, but I asked Julia, "Are you sure you want to be here?"

She seemed no more bothered than if she were watching us lay out pieces of a mosaic floor before cementing it in place. "Oh, I wouldn't miss a chance to watch you two work, not after all Tacitus has told me. That's part of an arm, isn't it?" She ran a finger over the bone Tacitus had just picked up and then squeezed her own arm.

"The upper part." Tacitus held it beside his own arm and then placed it where it belonged. "There are two bones in the lower part. That's why you can turn your wrist." He ran his hand over Julia's arm. I wondered what they would do when we found the leg bones or the pelvis.

When we were finished, I lay down beside the skeleton we had reconstructed. "He was a little bit taller than you," Tacitus said. "Of course, a lot of men are taller than you."

I ignored the jibe as I got up and dusted myself off. Tacitus is a full head taller than I am, as he likes to remind me every chance he gets.

"How do you know it's a man?" Julia asked.

"We don't," Tacitus admitted. "I just said 'he' to avoid saying 'it.' Given the height, I think it's more likely a male, but, without clothing or jewelry or any hints of that sort, we can't tell."

"Wouldn't there be some bits of cloth left?" Julia asked.

Tacitus looked into the wall. "I would expect so. I think he must have been stripped before he was put in here."

"Possibly to make it more difficult to identify him," Aurora said. "How do you think he died?"

I wasn't sure to whom the question was directed. I pointed to several cracked ribs. "Those could be injuries received from a beating."

"Or they could have been broken by stones being dropped on top of him after his body was placed in the wall," Tacitus said.

Getting to her knees, Aurora shook her head. "Stones dumped on top of him wouldn't have hit with enough force to do that much damage, my lord. He was beaten." She still wasn't talking to me.

"I agree. This is different, though." I picked up the skull and pointed to a spot I had noticed on the side of it. "This hole is deeper. He was hit here by something with a point on it."

Aurora got up and stepped around us, paying close attention to the pieces of rock that had fallen out of the wall along with the skeleton. She picked up one and examined it like a woman looking over a jewel her lover has given her.

"Have you found something?" I asked.

"I think he might not have been dead when he was put into the wall." She held the rock up in Julia's direction and pointed to dark stains on it. "Isn't that blood?"

"It could be," I said. "Probably where one of his wounds brushed against the rock."

Aurora peered closely at the stone. "My lord, I believe these are letters."

"We need a chest or basket to put these bones in," I said.

"I'll get something, my lord," Aurora said before I could tell her to.

"I'll go with you." Julia shook the dust off her gown and caught up with Aurora as they turned the corner of the house.

"'My lord'?" Tacitus arched his eyebrows. "Oh, you really are in trouble, Gaius."

"What do you mean? That's the appropriate way for her to address me, especially out in the open like this, where someone might overhear us." I was bluffing. Aurora's coldness cut me deeply. I ached to take her aside and try to set things right between us.

Tacitus waved his hand dismissively. "Well, you're going to need all the luck that Tyche ring can bring you to sort this out." He grabbed the strap around my neck and gave it a tug. "But we've got another problem here." He knelt beside the skeleton.

I was glad to turn my attention to something that I could deal with logically. "All right, what do we know?"

"We know when the wall was built—twenty years ago—so we know when this person died. He, or she, was hit several times, including the blow to the head, then dumped between the two finished courses of stone. He was near the top, and rubble was thrown in on top of him."

I looked up at the wall, as though it could tell me something. "It must have happened when the wall was almost complete, or somebody would have noticed the smell as the body decayed. We need to find out exactly when the wall was finished—to the day, if possible."

"Your mother or some of the older servants must know."

"I'm not sure how reliable my mother's memory is right now." I picked up a leg bone and examined it more closely. "These marks look like something gnawed on the bone."

"Rats, I'm sure."

"Could they get in between the pieces of rubble?" I looked at the broken wall, afraid to visualize what might be going on inside it and the rest of the walls of the house.

"Rats can squeeze in anywhere, my friend. As I said last night, I'm sure they're scampering around in your walls right now. The scent of anything they can eat draws them. And they can eat almost anything."

I held the bone reverently. Being in the presence of a victim of a heinous crime—and murder is the most heinous of all crimes—I couldn't help but feel the terror that must have come over this man when he realized what was happening to him. I closed my eyes and could feel the shock of a stone crashing into my head. If he was still alive when he was thrown into the wall, he must have seen—or felt, if it was dark—the rocks piling up on top of him, crushing him. Did he try to push them aside? Did he cry out? My breathing grew more rapid.

"Gaius Pliny," Tacitus said, "are you all right?"

I took a deep breath. "Yes. I hope the poor fellow was dead before the rats went to work on him."

"He must have been killed at night, don't you think?"

I nodded. "He must have been. And I doubt that he was killed here. He was struck several times, in the head and the ribs, so there obviously was a struggle. That would have created some noise. Surely someone would have heard."

"It wasn't someone in this house then, was it?"

"I've never heard of anyone going missing, but I'll certainly ask the older servants."

"But he must have been killed near here." Tacitus looked round as though he could identify the spot where the murder had taken place. "Somebody wouldn't have killed him in Comum, for example, then hauled him all the way out here to dispose of the body."

"No, that wouldn't make any sense. But who would have been out here at night, near the time the wall was being finished? And why?"

"It could have been somebody that people here would have known. That might be why there's no sign of clothing or jewelry that someone could recognize."

"He might have been wearing something worth stealing." I put the leg bone back in its place and climbed one of the ladders again, peering into the rubble between the two walls. "We need to pull more of this stone out. The rats might have carried something away from the body."

"They are attracted to shiny objects. Shall we call some of your servants?"

"No, let's do it ourselves, and carefully. The fewer people who know what we find, the better."

We dislodged some more of the rubble, coughing in the dust, and examined the stones for blood stains or any other markings.

"Is that a nest of some sort?" I asked, pointing to a dark wad of material about an arm's length below where we had found the skeleton.

"I think it is," Tacitus said from the other ladder. He reached down and dislodged the thing. "It's made mostly of human hair. Black hair. There's nothing in it. I don't think it's been used in a long time."

"Do you see any more rocks with bloodstains on them?"

We turned over a number of the rocks, but they had gotten so jumbled when they started falling out of the wall that it was hard to tell what came from where.

"Here's one more," Tacitus said, brushing dust off a rock and holding it up to the full light of the sun. "That could be a C, couldn't it?"

"It just looks like a smear to me."

Julia caught up with me as we turned the corner of the house and slipped her arm through mine.

"Slow down," she said. "Those bones aren't going anywhere."

I let her stop me. "I just need to get out of Gaius' sight. I am so angry at him right now."

"You've made that abundantly clear. You obviously were talking to anyone but him."

"I can't talk to him, not yet." I squeezed her hand.

"You have to be careful, Aurora. You know he loves you and he's caught in a very difficult position. He didn't want to arrange this marriage. Be patient with him. Don't say or do anything you can't make up for."

I knew she was right. And he had picked the perfect husband for me, a man who was incapable of coupling with me but was gentle and considerate. What upset me so badly was that he didn't trust me enough to tell me before we came up here.

"From what I saw of him," Julia said, "Felix seems a nice enough man."

"He is. I actually enjoyed spending an evening with him."

"Do you think he understands what's expected of him? I mean, about—" She made a gesture with her hands mimicking the act of coupling. I was surprised to see a noble woman doing something I would have expected from a slave. But Julia is full of surprises.

I had promised Felix that I wouldn't reveal his secret to anyone. As much as I felt the urge to talk to someone and as much as I liked Julia, she was not a person who could keep such a secret. "Yes," I said, "he understands. There won't be any problem about that."

Julia winked. "Too old, huh? Well, if he can't get aroused by you, he must be almost dead."

I decided just to leave it at that.

I expected Julia and Aurora to return with a container of some kind. After a while they did come back carrying a small wooden chest between them, the sort of thing we use to store clothing or blankets. What I didn't expect was for Naomi to accompany them.

"Will this do?" Julia asked as they set the chest down in front of me. Aurora looked up at me with an expression that seemed softer than any I'd seen so far today but still not warm, like embers buried in ashes, waiting to be fanned to life again.

"That's fine. It will even make it easier to burn the bones when we're ready to do that. Whoever this was, I want to give him a proper funeral."

"My lord," Naomi began, then paused.

I turned to her. "Does my mother need something?"

"No, my lord. I wanted to ask a favor of you."

"What sort of favor?"

"It's what you just said—about burning the bones. I'd like to ask you not to do that."

Having a Jewish slave in my household—and one who holds a prominent place as my mother's closest confidante—I've learned some things about their customs. Instead of burning their dead, they place them in a tomb and come back a year or so later to gather the desiccated remains and place them in a container, usually a carved stone box. When my mother dies, I am determined that she will have a Roman burial. I will not let her suffer the indignity of rotting and having her body gnawed by rodents. A funeral pyre is final and purifying.

"Why not?" I asked. "We have no reason to think this person was a Jew. We certainly can't tell if he was circumcised."

"It's highly unlikely that he was Jewish," Tacitus put in.

"But not impossible, my lord," Naomi said. "It would cost you nothing to keep the bones. In fact, it would cost you much less than the expense of a funeral pyre for a person you don't even know."

"We're not going to do anything immediately," I said. The bones were all the evidence I had of whatever had happened. "I'll keep your request in mind."

"Thank you, my lord."

I knew she was going to talk to my mother about this, if she hadn't already. Over the last couple of years my mother has shown an increasing sympathy to Jewish customs. I might as well resign myself to finding some place to store the bones, but I wasn't going to admit that yet.

"Have you learned any more about him?" Julia asked.

"We think he had black hair." Tacitus pointed to the remains of the rats' nest lying next to the body.

"Around here a lot of people have brown or blond hair," Julia said, running her fingers through her own light brown locks. "The Gallic influence is strong."

Both of Julia's parents were from Gaul on the other side of the Alps. My hair, while a bit darker than hers, would still be called brown, as would my mother's. Romans—especially our women—seem taken by blond hair. They dye their dark hair or buy wigs made from the hair of captive German and Gallic women.

"Most Jews have black hair, my lord," Naomi said as she turned back to the house.

"Your son's hair is red," I reminded her. Like an opponent in court who has been presented with an irrefutable argument, she offered no rejoinder.

We put the box of bones and the bloodstained rocks in my bedroom, which we could lock.

"You don't want to use the treasure room?" Tacitus asked.

"No." The house did have the traditional "treasure room," but in this case it was a grandiose term. It was just the smallest of the bedrooms off the garden. Beyond enough money to meet expenses and a few of my father's most personal documents, there was nothing of particular value in it.

"This will serve as a private place to talk," I said, motioning for Tacitus to light the two lamps sitting on my work table. As I started to close the door, Julia, who had been standing just outside it, stepped in and brought Aurora with her.

I blinked in amazement. "I didn't think—"

"That we would be interested?" Julia said. "You know Aurora is, and you won't get rid of me as easily as closing a door in my face."

I looked to Tacitus, but he could do nothing except raise his hands, palms up.

"Well, it's a small room," I said.

Julia pulled the door shut. "That makes it all the easier to keep our secrets."

The room's only furniture consisted of my work table, two chairs, and the bed. I motioned for the women to take the chairs. Tacitus slipped into one and took a giggling Julia on his lap. He gestured for me to take a seat on the bed. I would much rather Aurora and I had imitated him and Julia, but nothing in Aurora's face told me that she would react as Julia did—and I didn't think I could blame the poor light.

When we were all settled I said, "I think we should begin by summarizing what we know. A person—probably male, slightly taller than I am, with black hair—was killed twenty years ago by a blow to the head and dumped inside the wall being constructed on the other side of the garden. He might have lived long enough to scrawl letters in his own blood. Beyond that, all I can see are questions."

"Lots of questions," Tacitus said. "How could someone have done this without anybody hearing or noticing? Your entire household would have had to be deaf not to hear something."

"Or maybe they weren't here," Julia said. "You could see if they remember a specific time when most of them were out of the house."

"That's one of the questions I want to ask my mother and the older servants."

"How are we ever going to identify him?" Tacitus asked. "Except for the color of his hair, we have no clues at all."

"Can we take another look at the bones?" Aurora asked.

I stood up and opened the box containing the bones. "Certainly, but I don't see what good that will do."

"We were in a hurry earlier, and people were watching. Your wife was making such a scene. We might have missed something."

"Is there any particular bone you want to see?"

"The skull, I think. A person's face is the most identifiable thing about him."

Glad that she had at least dropped the "my lord," I handed her the skull. The lower jaw had gotten separated from it. "Do you want to see both parts?" I asked.

"This will do for now." She held it close to the small lamps, turning it one way and another. "He must have been hit in the face," she said. "A couple of teeth are broken, on the top on the right side, and one is missing entirely. I think someone hit him in the face, then on the side of the head."

As I took the skull from Aurora our hands brushed. She looked up at me and, for the first time in two days, I saw hope of restoring our relationship. "You're right. I'd say he was hit in the mouth, then, as his head turned, he was struck again. Like this." I took advantage of the opportunity to touch her cheek and turn her head to the side.

"No," she said. "He was struck on his right side. That means the person who hit him was left-handed." She brought her hand up fast to my cheek, stopping just before she struck me.

"Probably, but not necessarily," Tacitus said, holding out a hand to take the skull. "If someone was swinging a weapon, this fellow could have ducked but then got hit by the second effort." He swung his right arm from right to left, then back in the other direction.

Julia took the skull in her turn. I was amazed at how matter-of-fact she was. I would have expected a noble woman to react to such a thing the way Livia had, with revulsion. Tacitus once told me that Julia insisted on seeing and holding their stillborn child. In such cases the infant is usually spirited away, to spare the mother's feelings. Julia must be made of sturdier stuff than I realized. But then her father is Julius Agricola.

"Let me see," she said. "His other teeth look pretty good. They're clean and healthy. He must have come from a household of some standing. We encourage our servants to use a chew stick to clean their teeth. I don't think people from poorer houses always do that."

Most upper-class households follow Julia's advice. I certainly do. A toothache can develop into more than a minor nuisance, disabling a servant as much as an injury to a limb and much more difficult to treat. Some of the cures suggested for a toothache in my uncle's *Natural History*—such as rubbing it with a hippopotamus tooth—make it clear why people have to finally have a sore tooth pulled. But my uncle's accumulated wisdom isn't as bad as the folk tale which says that a person with a toothache should, by the light of the full moon, catch a frog, spit in its mouth, and tell it to take the pain away.

"It's curious," Julia said, as though she were addressing the skull, "that just last night we were talking about the disappearance of Livia's father, and now this."

"How could one have anything to do with the other?" I asked. "Livius drowned when his boat capsized in a storm. His body was never found."

"I'm not suggesting that this is Livius," Julia said. "I'm just saying his disappearance at the time this person was killed is one of those coincidences you dislike so much, and a remarkable one at that."

"Well, that's all it is."

"But this wall was built about the time Livius disappeared, wasn't it?" Julia asked tenaciously.

"I believe so."

"So this man must have been killed right before the wall was finished, therefore, at the time Livius drowned. Another coincidence?"

"Those are two unrelated facts," I said. "If we're going to make any sense of *this*"—I pointed to the skeleton—"we need to focus on what's relevant to this." I was beginning to doubt the wisdom of involving Julia in this inquiry, if she was going to distract us.

"Gaius is right, dear," Tacitus said. "I'm sure somebody else died around here the night Livius drowned. Somebody dies around here just about every night. They don't have anything to do with one another or with this man."

Julia wouldn't quite give up. "This man didn't just die. He was killed."

"Exactly," I said. "Killed by a blow to the head, not by drowning."

"How can you ever know any more about him?" Her voice echoed the sadness lining her face.

I took the skull from her and placed it back in the box. "When we had the bones laid out on the ground, they looked straight, so he wasn't a person who did a lot of heavy work. Both legs were the same length, so he didn't walk with a limp or have any injuries of that sort."

"Do you think he might have come from a wealthy house?" Julia asked.

"There's no way to tell," I said. "As you said, though, the good condition of his teeth makes me think he wasn't a poor man. Even if he was a servant, he could have come from a wealthy house."

"Rich man, poor man, or slave," Tacitus said, "it makes no sense that somebody could have killed him and disposed of his body this way without *someone* in this house being aware of it."

"Are you suggesting that someone in my family was involved?" I was thinking the same thing but hated to hear it said aloud.

"I didn't say that," Tacitus replied quickly.

"You all but said it, dear," Julia put in.

"Well, I don't mean to impugn your family, Gaius Pliny, but—"

"It's a possibility we can't dismiss out of hand," I said. "I know that. But, if something did happen, the secret has been well kept. I never heard even a whisper of anything like this while I was growing up."

"I've never heard any talk among the servants," Aurora said.

I wondered how much other servants talked to Aurora, or talked when they were around her. Everyone knew she enjoyed a special status in the house, even if they didn't know how much more special that status had recently become.

"We'll need to ask my mother. And I want to talk to a friend of mine, Romatius Firmus."

"Who's he?" Tacitus asked.

"Our fathers were friends. He and I went to school together during the periods when I was in Comum as a child." After my father's death my mother and I lived at times with my uncle and—when he was away—with a family friend, Verginius Rufus, whom I still revere as a teacher. "Romatius and I have remained friends. He stayed here and has held a couple of minor offices in town."

"He hasn't tried for office in Rome?"

"I don't think his family has the money to do that. I know he's never qualified for the equestrian stripe."

"But if he's your age," Tacitus said, "how would he know any more about what happened twenty years ago than you do?"

"He might have heard something over the years, just because he's been here all this time, and he's always been fond of gossip. If he doesn't know anything, he might point us to someone who does. He's the only person outside my household I can think of to start asking questions, and his family did have business dealings with my father."

"How soon can we see him?" Tacitus asked.

"It will take us the rest of the day to get to Comum, but we should be able to talk to him tomorrow. There are also a couple of other things I want to check on."

"This sounds like a trip for the men only," Julia said, getting up off Tacitus' lap with a final wriggle and straightening her gown. Tacitus remained seated with his hands folded demurely across his lap.

"It will be. I'd like for you and Aurora to talk to my mother and some of the older servants. See if they recall anything about that summer. Try to do it when Livia and her mother aren't around."

"And I want to take another look at those rocks later," Julia said. "I'm sure those are letters, not just random smears of blood."

V

Jewels are the gift of fortune; character
comes from within.

—Plautus

THE RIDE INTO COMUM, ten miles away, would take the rest of the day. We took only three servants with us—one of mine and one of Tacitus' to attend us in the bath, and another of mine to stay with our horses when we had to leave them on the edge of town. I chose one of the older servants in the house, a man named Nereus, as my attendant so I could question him in relative privacy.

"What do you remember about the building of the wall in the garden?" I asked as soon as we were well away from the house. "How old were you when it was done?"

"I was fifteen at the time, my lord. I helped carry some of the stone off the wagons, but your father hired masons to do the work. No one in our house was skilled in stonework and he said he wanted that new section to look like it had always been part of the house. He didn't want people's attention to be drawn to it."

I glanced at Tacitus and could see that he grasped the contradictory implications of Nereus' statement—someone from outside my household could have been involved in the murder, but my father went to some lengths to disguise the work he'd had done. He'd succeeded.

"I know the wall was built in the summer, but do you recall more precisely when it was finished?"

"The middle of the summer, my lord. Somewhere close to your birthday, I believe."

"Which birthday?" Tacitus asked.

"Let me think, my lord." He appeared to be counting in his head. "It would have been his fourth."

"I'll bet he was a cute little tyke," Tacitus said, with the corners of his mouth turning up in a smile that he could barely keep off his face.

"That he was, my lord. And into everything. That's one reason why his father built the wall—to keep him from roaming all over the place."

"We've heard all that from my mother." I could feel my face reddening.

"Sorry, my lord."

"You know a body was found inside the wall." I could tell my voice was taking on too somber a tone. "Can you remember any time when someone could have placed that body there?"

"I've been thinking about that, my lord. The men hadn't torn down much of the wall when they found him, had they?"

"No. They had barely gotten started."

"Wouldn't that mean he was placed in there close to the end of the work, my lord?"

I nodded. "Tell me what you remember about the day it was finished."

"Well, not much, my lord. You see, I was very interested in one of the girls in the house at that time, so I didn't pay much attention to anything else." He shrugged. "I was fifteen. That's the only excuse I can give."

"Oh, we were all fifteen at one time," Tacitus said.

"Yes, my lord. We all enjoy that blessing from the gods, but it's one I'd want to enjoy only once." Nereus' smile seemed directed to himself.

"What happened to the girl?" Tacitus asked.

"We've been man and wife till this day, my lord."

"What's her name?"

"Leucippe, my lord."

"Well, I hope your happiness continues."

"I didn't say we were happy, my lord, just that we've been man and wife for all that time." He sighed. "But, as for the wall, the main thing I remember about it is that my lord Caecilius seemed in a hurry to have it finished. He hadn't been in any particular hurry until then, but he couldn't seem to get it finished fast enough."

"Why do you say that?" I asked.

"On the last two days, my lord, he paid the mason's crew double to work all day, instead of stopping at noon. There was a storm that kept them from working one day, so your father wanted to make up that time. On the last day, they worked until almost dark, just to finish it."

"Do you know why he did that?"

"No, my lord. I do know that your mother wasn't happy with him spending the extra money. They had a...well, a discussion about it in the garden. Quite a few of us saw them, and heard them."

Suddenly an image flashed into my mind, as clear as a bolt of lightning and just as unsettling. I could see my mother and my father standing in the garden of the house, arguing. As a very young child, I was frightened by the anger in their voices and was hiding behind some bushes. I didn't understand what they were arguing about, but it was one of the earliest memories I had, and one of the few vivid memories of my father.

"It sounds," Tacitus said, "like your mother was just as miserly with your father as she is with you."

I nodded. I sometimes thought my mother could grasp a *denarius* tightly enough to strangle the *princeps* depicted on it. Hardly a day went by that she did not object to the amount of the morning dole I gave my clients. Since she had never known poverty and never would, I found her stinginess difficult to understand.

"Do you remember what reason my father gave for his haste?"

"I'm afraid I don't, my lord. I wasn't close enough to hear what they were saying, just to know that they were both...well, animated."

I was about to enter the latrina *when another servant woman came out. "You might want to wait," she said. "The lady Plinia and the lady Pompeia are in there."*

There's room for four in this latrina, *but I did decide to wait. I didn't want to see Pompeia any more than she wanted me to be around her. While*

Gaius and his mother are gracious in their treatment of servants, camaraderie between servant and mistress has its limits, in my opinion. There was no door on the latrina, just an entryway about three paces long that made a sharp left turn, preserving privacy but also allowing circulation of air. I leaned against the wall, pondering the poor condition of the plaster and paint and wondering how much longer I should carry my grudge against Gaius for the way he had handled my "marriage."

"I thought that girl would never leave." I recognized the voice as Pompeia's. I could tell she thought she was talking softly, but, like everything else about the woman, her voice was outsized. I could hear her easily over the flow of water under my feet. When this villa was built they diverted a nearby stream to supply water. From the bath it ran under the latrina with a soothing babble and out to the lake.

"This is unnerving," Pompeia continued. "Imagine! Last night I slept in a room with a skeleton only a few feet away in the wall. And it was put there twenty years ago."

"That's not the most distressing part of it," Gaius' mother said. "What if it is your husband?"

Plinia spoke even more softly than she usually does. I took a step closer to the opening into the latrina, so I could hear her better.

"It can't be, my dear," Pompeia said. "Poor Livius drowned when that storm capsized his boat. They found his tunic, but they never found his body."

"Are you sure it was his tunic?"

"Of course. I recognized the stitching. It was the way my girls did it."

"But why just his tunic?"

"I'm sure he pulled that and his sandals off so he'd have a better chance of swimming to shore. All that wool soaks up water like a sponge. There's no way Livius could be the man in the wall. I assume his bones are out there at the bottom of Lake Comum. The discovery of these bones is just a coincidence."

"But Gaius says there's no such thing as coincidence. And Livius disappeared at the time the workmen were finishing the wall. The storm even delayed them."

"With all due respect to my clever son-in-law, it has to be a coincidence. Why would we be told that Livius drowned when he was stuffed into a wall? Whoever put that poor man in there murdered him. Nobody had any reason to kill my husband."

Now I was puzzled. The names of the two girls, Livia and Livilla, mean both of them had a father named Livius. But Livilla is only sixteen. A man who died twenty years ago couldn't be her father.

I could tell from the rustling sounds that the women were just about finished, so I stepped back farther in the entryway.

"Well, well," a voice behind me said. "I see Gaius has you spying for him now."

I knew immediately that it was Livia. I couldn't do anything but turn to face her.

"I was just waiting to use the latrina, my lady. Your mother and your mother-in-law are in there. I wanted to give them some privacy."

"That's not what I saw," Livia said. "You were edging closer and closer so you could eavesdrop." She grabbed my arm and dragged me out into the garden.

"Please, my lady. I—"

She slapped me hard on the cheek. I didn't give her the satisfaction of putting my hand on the spot. It was all I could do not to hit her back.

"I guess you can report that to him, too, you brown-skinned whore." Anger narrowed her beady eyes and drew her lip into a snarl. "Someday I'll find a reason to have you strung up and whipped. And don't think I wouldn't do it."

I wouldn't have minded. If she did something like that, I could endure it because I knew Gaius would divorce her in an instant. If I even told him that she slapped me...

Livia unpinned the brooch that she always wears. It's oval, with a large blue stone surrounded by a gold filigree. It has a long, nasty pin on it. I couldn't believe she was going to stab me with the thing, but that clearly was what she intended to do. I crossed my hands over my belly to protect my child.

"Oh, Livia dear, there you are," Pompeia said behind me as she and Plinia emerged from the latrina. Livia pinned the brooch back in its usual place and pushed me away from her. Out of the corner of my eye I saw Julia coming across the garden toward us. An ally!

"Is everything all right, dear?" Pompeia asked Livia.

"Of course, Mother. How could it not be? I'm surrounded by my loving mother and my loving husband and his loving servant. How could everything not be all right?" Livia stalked into the latrina. Plinia looked at my cheek but said nothing and the two older women headed for the kitchen.

I really needed to relieve myself, but now I would have to wait a bit longer or find a chamber pot. If I dared to go in there with Livia, I was afraid she might try to drown me.

"Are you all right?" Julia asked as she reached my side.

I nodded.

"Did I see Livia slap you?"

"Yes."

"We'll have to tell Gaius—"

"No! That's the last thing we can do. If she found out I told him, she'd just look for more reasons to make my life miserable."

"If that's what you want… Come here. Let's sit down."

"No, I need to relieve myself. I have a feeling Livia will take her own sweet time in there. Let's go to my room. I'll use the chamber pot." I set off at a quick pace.

While I got the chamber pot from under the bed and stepped to the far corner of the room, I asked Julia, "Do you know anything about Livia's father drowning?"

"Gaius didn't tell you?"

"No. He doesn't seem to tell me much of anything these days." I lifted my gown.

Julia sat on the bed, facing away from me. Her voice brightened the way it always does when she's about to impart some juicy gossip. "Well, you know Tacitus loves history. He says I like to gossip too much, but he does the same thing and just calls it history. He told me that Pompeia married a man named Marcus Livius, the younger of two brothers. His family is from around here—sturdy equestrian stock, like Pliny and Tacitus. But the poor man drowned, right here in Lake Comum, let's see, it would've been—"

"Twenty years ago."

"Why, yes, that's right. How did you know?"

"That's what Pompeia and Plinia were talking about in the latrina. So he was Livia's father. But how did Livilla get her name?"

"*Because Pompeia then married the older of the two brothers, Quintus Livius.*"

"*She married her brother-in-law? Was there something going on between them?*" It was revolting to think of Pompeia having an affair.

Julia waved a hand dismissively. "*Nothing as interesting as that. In this case it was a matter of keeping property in the family. And there is a lot of property in that family. Pompeia and her daughters have inherited all of it, from both brothers.*"

"*So Livilla and Livia are only half-sisters.*" Finishing with the chamber pot, I slipped it back under the bed, straightened my gown, and sat down beside Julia. "*That explains a lot.*"

"*More than you know. Everyone who sees them thinks of them as 'the pretty one' and 'that other one.' I have to feel some sympathy for Livia. Her own mother treats her like some unloved stepchild.*"

"*I might be more sympathetic if I weren't so afraid of her.*"

Julia turned to me in surprise. "*Surely you don't think—*"

"*I don't think she'll stop with just slapping me.*"

My uncle used to say that, viewed from high enough in the mountains on its western side, Lake Comum looks like the legs and body of a running man, without the head and arms. The town of Comum sits at the foot of the front leg, with my villa just above the bend that resembles the knee. The back leg is stretched out straight.

"That's the house of my friend Caninius Rufus," I said, as our horses trotted past a large villa in the bend of the knee, about two hours into our journey. "He's a poet."

"I've not heard the name," Tacitus said. "What has he published?"

"Actually, nothing. Although he's a good writer, he revises a lot but never seems to finish anything, in spite of my urgings."

"Oh, one of those. From the look of his place I'd say he's rather prosperous. I guess he doesn't depend on his writing for his livelihood."

"No, he's no Virgil or Horace, with a wealthy patron behind him. He received a substantial inheritance. He has no political ambitions, though. He just wants to write."

"Do you think he would put down his pen long enough to greet some unexpected guests?" Tacitus said. "I need to relieve myself, and I could use a drink."

"I'm sure he would. He wants to pump me for information about the eruption of Vesuvius."

"Perhaps we shouldn't stop then. I know how much you hate talking about that."

"Not as much as I would hate having you piss all over one of my horses." We turned onto the lane leading to Caninius' house. "We can't stay long, though, if we're going to reach Comum before dark."

Caninius did give us a gracious welcome. We drank and chatted for about an hour, as long as we could afford. I apologized for the abruptness of our visit, promising to write more about Vesuvius, and he seemed to understand. As we were leaving, he handed me a copy of some of his latest poems. "I would appreciate any criticism you might have time to give me," he said.

I passed the small scroll to Nereus to place in the bag he was carrying with a change of clothes for us. "By all means. You'll have to come to dinner soon so we can talk about them."

"Yes, let's do that. Let me know when it's convenient for you."

As we rode back to the main road, Tacitus said, "Nice fellow."

I gave the house one last glance over my shoulder. "Some days I envy him."

"Pssht. Gaius Pliny, I don't think you could ever be content with the life of a provincial dilettante."

"'Dilettante' is too harsh a word. Caninius is a fine poet. He knows what he wants and is willing to sacrifice a public career to achieve it. I don't suppose I could do that. My uncle and my tutors taught me to value public service. But they couldn't foresee how...difficult that might become."

"In certain circumstances and at certain times, yes."

We both knew we couldn't say any more. One breath of criticism whispered against Domitian—even in the presence of not one but three trusted servants—and we might suffer a fate like that of the poor soul in the wall of my house. But the reason for his murder surely couldn't have been political. Comum is a long way from the intrigues of the capital. Twenty years ago Nero was *princeps*. It was late in his reign, but the revolts that led to his overthrow hadn't broken out yet.

Besides, hiding a body in a wall didn't have the imperial flair about it. An enemy of the *princeps* was more likely to be spirited away to some island and never heard from again. Poison was Nero's preferred method of eliminating his enemies. This crime displayed all the marks of an amateur, an opportunist. The weapon—probably a rock—was what happened to be at hand. The hiding place for the body couldn't have been planned far in advance. The only evidence of any planning was the removal of the victim's clothing and any identifying jewelry— although that might have been an afterthought born of panic.

Then a question leapt unbidden into my mind: what if the blow to the mouth, just one blow, was designed to obliterate some distinctive feature? We've been assuming that the person was struck in the mouth first, then on the head. But the order could have been reversed. I would have to take another, much closer look at the skull when we returned. And I would have to thank Naomi for the fact that we hadn't already placed the bones on a pyre. I wondered how many crimes went unpunished—unnoticed, even—because we Romans are so anxious to dispose of the bodies of our dead.

Maybe that's why our primitive ancestors instituted the practice. Some acorn-belching Lucius killed some equally flatulent Gaius and realized that his best chance to cover up the deed was to burn the evidence, so he said the gods expected it. How convenient the gods sometimes are.

As we rounded a bend in the road we got our first view of Comum and I brought my attention back to the matter at hand.

"Remember," I said to Tacitus and the servants, "we're not to say anything specific about what we've found. We're just going to ask a few general questions about anyone—male or female—who might have gone missing twenty years ago. If somebody does know who killed our victim, we don't want to alert them."

"What office does your friend Romatius hold?" Tacitus asked as we rode up to the point on the outskirts of town where we would have to leave our horses.

"He's an *aedile*."

"What are his duties? Public works? Games?"

"Nothing so glamorous. He's one of those who oversee the markets."

"A bean-counter, eh?"

Once we had stabled our horses we entered the north gate—or the archway where the north gate had once hung. With no worries about defending themselves, the people of the town had removed the inconvenience of an actual gate years ago. I could not remember seeing it hanging in place, even in my childhood. We found lodging just inside the gate, and I sent Nereus to Romatius' house—on the east side of town—to ask if we could see him the next day. Romatius replied to my message with an invitation to meet him at the market at noon.

The town we call Comum is, technically, Novum Comum. The original town—just a village which can still be seen—clung to the hills beside the lake for defensive reasons. Almost a hundred and fifty years ago, with this area pacified, Julius Caesar moved the town to the lower end of the lake and laid out, on a proper grid of streets, a new, regular Roman *municipium*, with a forum, a market, baths, and all the other amenities of civilization. This new Comum was originally encircled by walls, but had long since outgrown them. Now their primary function was to provide solid support for the houses and public buildings springing out beside them like the large mushrooms that sprout from tree trunks.

The next morning I had already eaten something by the time Tacitus and our servants gathered in the dining room of our inn. "While you're eating," I said, "there's someone here in town I want to talk to."

"Go right ahead," Tacitus mumbled, still not fully awake. Then he had a second thought. "Do you want me to come with you?"

To his obvious relief, I shook my head. "This is a personal matter."

When he heard me asking the innkeeper for directions to a goldsmith's shop—the only one in town, it turned out—Tacitus acted puzzled. "Are you going to have some jewelry made for Livia?"

Neither of us could laugh at his joke in front of the servants. "No. My mother's birthday is coming up. I'll be back shortly." I turned toward the door.

"Aren't you going to take someone with you?" he called after me.

"It's not far. And I'm not entirely alone." I patted the short sword I've become accustomed to wearing under my tunic over the last couple of years. It's a bit cumbersome, but it has proved useful on several occasions.

On my way to the goldsmith's shop I took some lightly traveled streets so I could pass a few spots I had known as a boy. My childhood had been spent in various places—part of it going to school here after my father died; part under the tutelage of a family friend, Verginius Rufus; and part living with my uncle, sometimes near Comum, sometimes on one of his other estates. My mother had been the only constant presence in my upbringing. My mother and Aurora, I immediately corrected myself.

Now someone else was near me, I realized as I crossed a street. And I thought they had been there for several blocks. It hadn't rained in a while, so the muck of garbage and waste in the streets was thick. The stepping stones in the middle and at the end of each block were a necessity. Picking my way over them, I caught a movement to my left and behind me. When I glanced over my shoulder, I thought I saw someone step into a doorway. Turning a corner, I flattened myself against the wall and placed a hand on my sword.

When I had waited long enough for anyone following me to turn the corner, I stepped around it, prepared to draw my sword…and ran into two women, carrying their purchases from the market. Excusing myself, I surveyed the street. Except for the three of us and a few women at the next corner, it was empty. Had I been deluding myself? Perhaps my tunic's equestrian stripe, probably a rare sight in this part of town at this time of day, had made someone weigh the risks of a robbery. Tacitus was right. I should have taken a servant or two with me.

It was only two more blocks to the goldsmith's shop, and I didn't see anyone else who aroused my suspicion before I arrived. Traffic was beginning to pick up as the earliest risers—like myself—returned from the market and the second wave—Tacitus' lazy cohort, content with less selection—made their way to it.

The goldsmith's shop occupied a corner on the street level of an *insula* that stood three stories tall, a large building for a town the size of Comum. I inherited two of these apartment buildings in Rome from my uncle and have considered selling them every time I have to repair something—which is practically every month. The only way to make a profit off such properties is to let the tenants live in squalor, which my uncle was willing to do but I am not.

"Good morning, sir," the goldsmith said when I stepped inside. "What may I do for you?"

He was an affable-looking fellow of about forty, with thinning blond hair and carrying burn scars on his hands and one on the left side of his face, perhaps indicating that he was a bit clumsy at his trade. I hadn't started out with the intention of buying anything, but I knew I would get more information from him if I did.

"I'd like a…necklace. For my mother."

"For your mother. Of course, sir." He managed to keep the smirk in his voice off his face. "Let me see what might be fittin'…for your mother."

He obviously thought I was a philandering husband sneaking off by himself to buy something for a mistress. He picked up a box, set it on a stool, and opened it. "Gold? Silver? What do you think she would like, sir?"

I picked up a few pieces and examined them, settled on one, and haggled with him over the price. I let him get the better of me so I could move on to my real objective.

"Will there be anything else, sir?" he asked.

"Yes, a question or two, if I may."

He shrugged, acknowledging that I had bought the right to ask him something.

"Have you ever heard of a man named Marcus Delius?"

From the curl of his lip and the flaring of his nostrils, I thought about moving my hand closer to my sword.

"Be you a friend of that scoundrel?"

I thought, *Even worse, he's my cousin,* but I shook my head quickly. "I've never met him. He was a freedman from my uncle's house. I'm told he was apprenticed here but disappeared. I know it was a long time ago, but—"

"Your uncle? You're the nephew of Plinius Secundus?"

"Yes, and the adopted son."

"It's a pleasure, sir. Your uncle was as fine a gentleman as ever I've knowed."

I nodded to acknowledge the compliment. "I came across Delius' name in some old letters recently and wondered what had become of him."

"He robbed us and run away. That's what become of him."

"When was this?"

"Twenty year or so ago. He worked here for three years. One night he took three pounds of gold that we was supposed to make into jewelry and that was the last we seen of him for almost a year. We had to make good on the loss ourselves. It right near ruined us."

"You reported him to the magistrates, I'm sure."

"Of course. We even told them where we thought he was going."

"Where was that?"

"North. He was mad in love with a girl on the estate of a man named Caecilius."

The only way I could suppress my shock at hearing my father's name was by asking another question. "Do you by any chance remember her name?"

"It were something Greekish. Had to do with horses."

"Xanthippe?"

"No, sir."

"Leucippe?"

"Yes, sir. That's it."

"You said 'we.' Was this your shop then?"

"No, sir. It were my father's. I was learning the trade. Delius and me was almost the same age. My father meant for us to work together and increase the size of the shop."

"What sort of man was Delius?"

"A difficult one, sir. He seemed to resent that he had to work at all. But the odd thing is, he were pretty good at it. He could carve anything. He even made teeth for people what had lost their own. Give him a piece of ivory and he could carve you a tooth that you'd never know warn't the real thing. He had an artist's eye. In fact, your uncle come in and had him design and cast a signet ring. We told him my father could do a better job, but your uncle insisted that Delius do it."

I couldn't believe what I was hearing. First my father's name, now my uncle's. "A signet ring?"

"Yes, sir. It had a dolphin in the center and your uncle's name around it." He made a circle in the air with his index finger.

I held out my right hand with the signet ring up. "This ring?"

"May I, sir?" He drew my hand up closer to his face. "I do believe so, sir."

"Why aren't you certain? He didn't make another one like it, did he?"

"No, sir. But he was a vain fella. He liked to sign the things he made."

I pulled the ring off and looked at the inside of it.

"It reads DEL, don't it, sir?"

The letters were worn but still legible. "I've always thought that meant Delphinus, although I've never understand why someone would write that on it."

"No, sir. It means Delius. That was his mark."

"Where is he now?"

"He's still in these parts, sir. He come back after a year or so and repaid what he had stolen, plus interest. We still had people asking for him to do work, so he comes in from time to time and does a piece or two for us."

"Where would I find him?"

"You don't. He finds you."

VI

The less we deserve good fortune,
the more we hope for it.

—Seneca

ALL THE WAY BACK to the inn I mulled over what the gold-smith had told me. The signet ring I had been wearing since my uncle's death was made by his illegitimate son, my bastard cousin. I ran a finger over the dolphin again.

Even more startling was the news that Delius had disappeared while apparently on his way to my father's house to meet one of my father's servant girls and while carrying a significant amount of stolen gold. Then he had reappeared and restored what he had stolen. Nereus was now married to Leucippe, the girl Delius was apparently going to see. Could she tell me more about Delius and what happened to the man in the wall than Nereus did?

The streets were busy now. I looked around whenever I turned a corner to see if anyone was following me, but the crowds made it impossible to pick out any one individual. I tried to dismiss the feeling as an unreasonable suspicion arising out of events and situations I had been involved in over the past few years.

When I arrived at the inn Tacitus noticed the small bag I was carrying. "So you did buy something. I never actually thought—"

"It's for my mother. Her birthday really is next month."

"Oh. Well, we have a few hours to while away before we see your friend Romatius. What do you propose?"

"Let's go out and take a look at a temple my father began to build shortly before his death. When I suggested finishing it, my mother became upset and asked me to drop the idea."

"You know she doesn't like you spending money."

"I felt there was more to it than that. Before I pursue the matter any further, I want to see the site, to get a sense of how much would have to be done."

We rode, rather than walked, out to the temple just because it was on the other side of town from where we were staying. Someone coming from the east side of town—the more heavily populated part of Comum—could walk to the site in just a few moments.

"Why do you keep looking over your shoulder?" Tacitus finally asked me.

"I had the feeling earlier that someone was following me. I suppose it's nothing."

"When a skeleton falls out of your wall, it can set your nerves on edge, but I don't see anybody."

"We're here now anyway," I said as we rounded a bend in the road.

We dismounted and approached the site, overgrown with bushes and small trees. The foundation of the building, the main floor, and a few courses of stone for the walls showed that it would be substantial if completed. Pieces of finished stone were piled around the building. It reminded me of the temple of Zeus in the forum in Pompeii, which had been destroyed in the earthquake seventeen years before Vesuvius erupted—the year in which I was born—and sat in that state until the city was obliterated. I have heard people argue that, if the city had rebuilt the temple promptly, the gods would have protected them from the volcano. My reaction to such reasoning is that, if the gods wanted the temple rebuilt, they could have provided the money, and done it more easily than causing a volcano to erupt, killing thousands.

I climbed the steps of my father's temple and walked around the floor. One pile of stones sitting off to the side consisted of pieces that had been carved with decorative motifs and the inscription that would go over the front.

"To judge from those tracks," Tacitus said, pointing to a path lead-ing off to the north, "somebody has been helping themselves to some of your stone."

"At least they haven't taken the pieces that were carved."

"They would be too easy to identify." He mounted the steps and began pacing off the dimensions of the building.

I knelt beside the stones that had been inscribed with the names of Rome and Augustus, for whom the temple was being built. That's when I noticed, in smaller letters on one of the blocks, IN THE NAME OF CAECILIA. Had my father intended for this temple to commemorate my sister, who died soon after birth, as well as to honor the *princeps?* Then why hadn't he finished it? Why didn't my mother want me to finish it?

"I'm going to see what's under the floor," Tacitus said.

I followed him down the steps and into a doorway that led to storage rooms under the temple. The door itself had been removed. Small animals scurried away from us in the dark.

"I can't tell much without a torch," Tacitus said, "but it doesn't look like anyone has taken up residence down here."

As we emerged from the doorway Tacitus glanced at the position of the sun, almost overhead. "By the time we get back and stable our horses, it'll be time for the market to close. Your friend Romatius ought to be just about finished for the day. Perhaps we can buy him some lunch, with plenty of wine to loosen his tongue."

"Just be sure it doesn't loosen yours," I reminded him as we mounted our horses for the trip back to the inn. Tacitus has a well-deserved reputation for his eloquence, but, by his fourth cup, even with the wine well diluted, he can become more loquacious than eloquent.

Like any Roman town, Comum was slowing down after a busy morning as we left our horses at the stable and set out for the forum. Some of the shopkeepers had already taken their wares in off the sidewalks and shuttered their doors. With Nereus carrying the bag containing our bathing supplies, we came to an intersection and used the stepping stones to cross to the other side. As we turned toward the forum, a group of children ran in our direction, rolling a large iron hoop, no doubt taken off a broken wagon wheel.

"You were quite good at that game, my lord," Nereus said, "when you were a boy. You and that girl who was always with you. Still *is* always with you."

Tacitus laughed and tousled my hair. Chagrined, I jerked away from him.

"It's more challenging when you play the game in a city street," I said. "You have to maneuver the thing between the stepping stones and around the muck if you can. If it falls, another player gets a turn. When I played on one of our estates, the main challenge was to keep up with the hoop. On an open road it can get up quite a bit of speed."

In spite of the embarrassment of being reminded of my childhood in front of Tacitus, I smiled because I could see myself running after a hoop with Aurora on the estate at Laurentum. It had gotten away from us and rolled over the cliff. As we were climbing down to the beach to retrieve it, we came upon the opening to a cave, and that was where we found the Tyche ring. I put my hand on my chest, touching the ring which hung, under my tunic, on a leather strap around my neck. How much simpler everything was then! The misfortune of losing the hoop had turned into the good fortune of finding the ring—and of giving Aurora a childish first kiss.

We turned another corner and could see the forum ahead of us. The town's market opened onto the street we were walking on, and the morning's last customers were emerging from the market, carrying their purchases. They looked behind them at an eruption of angry voices, then had to step out of the way when a man stumbled through the entrance, as though he had been pushed.

"That's the last I want to see of you here!" a familiar voice said from inside the doorway. My friend Romatius stepped into the light to give the man one more shove, knocking him down on the street. He opened a bag that he carried in one hand and ran his fingers through the small lead weights it contained.

"You've no right to treat me like this," the man said, scrambling to his knees.

"If you bring dishonest weights into my market," Romatius said, "it is my *duty* to treat you like this." He swung the bag, striking the man across the face. "And it'll go much worse for you if you come back again, you thieving scoundrel."

The man got to his feet, holding his hands to his bleeding nose, and hurried past us. When Romatius turned to follow his progress, he noticed us. He tossed the bag to a servant.

"Gaius Pliny, what a delight to see you!" He began walking toward us, his arms extended in greeting.

I stepped forward to meet him. Romatius, although he is my age, has never cared as much for physical activity as he has for a good meal, so he is quite a bit heavier than I am. He also has the misfortune of being one of those men who begins to lose his hair at an early age. But he is a convivial soul.

"I see you're ever the conscientious magistrate," I said as we embraced.

"That rascal comes from a village south of here," Romatius said. "Since I hadn't seen him before, I decided to check his weights. I'm just sorry I was too busy to do it earlier." He stepped back and held me at arms' length. "I was delighted to receive your message about meeting. But what brings you back home, my friend?"

"My mother felt she had been away too long. And my wife's family is from around here as well."

Romatius' jaw dropped in shock. "Gaius Pliny! You're married? Who is she? When did this happen?"

"We were married six months ago. She is Livia, the daughter of Pompeia Celerina."

"The older daughter or the younger?" He cocked his head as though waiting for a very important answer.

"The older."

Romatius' shoulders and voice dropped as if he'd been told that someone had died. "Oh, Gaius—"

"You can offer condolences," Tacitus said. "My wife and I do, every time we see Gaius."

Romatius gave me a consolatory embrace and a pat on the back. "I'm so sorry."

I pulled away from him and turned to Tacitus. "Let me introduce my sardonic friend, Cornelius Tacitus."

"Not *the* Cornelius Tacitus? Sir, it is an honor." Romatius shook Tacitus' hand warmly and bowed his head. "Even in this benighted

corner of the world we've heard of Cornelius Tacitus. Will we have a
chance to hear you speak while you're here?"

"Perhaps we can arrange something," I said. I know that Tacitus is
rapidly gaining a reputation for his oratory in the courts in Rome, but
I didn't realize his fame had spread this far.

"That gives me something to look forward to." Romatius smiled
broadly. "Now, may I buy you gentlemen some lunch?"

"That gives me something to look forward to," Tacitus said.

"There is an excellent *taberna* around the corner there," Romatius
said. "It's not much to look at, but the owner has a little farm just outside of town, so the food couldn't be any fresher if, well, if the chickens
laid the eggs right on your plate."

I found that image less appetizing than Romatius apparently did.

"The owner's name is Lutulla," he said in a slightly rhapsodic tone.
"Do you know her?"

"Should I?"

Romatius hesitated. "No, perhaps not. I just thought you might
have... Well, never mind."

I let him lead us to the *taberna*, where he was greeted as though he
was part of the family. Our servants were seated inside and we were
given one of the tables in a courtyard behind the building which was
formed by the walls of the neighboring buildings. Bread, wine, and
cheese appeared in front of us. Tacitus ran his glance over the serving
girl, as he always does, but she kept her eyes down. Before taking his
seat, Romatius talked with the owner. The conversation seemed to
involve a lot of nodding and glancing in our direction.

I studied the petite blond woman for a moment, since Romatius
seemed to think I should know her. Nothing about her seemed familiar. She was one of those women whose beauty had faded a bit but
still defied the years. I suspected she might be about my mother's age,
and yet her figure and the lack of lines on her face made me doubt my
own judgment.

Waiting for Romatius, I took in the courtyard, which was about
ten paces by twenty. In the center of it stood a rectangular fountain
graced by a bronze statue of a little girl holding a bucket under the
spout where the water flowed out. My attention was drawn back to

Romatius and the owner when a dark-haired young man came out of the building and said something to them. That seemed the signal for the conversation to end as Lutulla followed the young man back inside.

"She prepares a chicken," Romatius said when he joined us, "with a special blend of herbs and spices that no one has yet duplicated. I've offered her a considerable sum for the secret, but she keeps the recipe in her head. She claims she's never written it down."

"That's the best way to keep a secret," Tacitus said. "As Socrates says in the *Phaedrus*, once you write something down, it can speak to anyone. You lose control of it."

The mention of secrets so soon in the conversation unsettled me. I had hoped to work around to the topic, not charge at it in a frontal assault. I had already slammed head-on into one secret today. "So, are you married yet, Romatius?" I asked.

My friend shook his head. "Not yet. There's plenty of time before I have to submit to the harness. I'm still enjoying a romp in the pasture, so to speak."

Tacitus laughed. "Lots of mares and fillies around Comum?"

"Exactly. In fact, I'm planning to meet one as soon as we finish eating."

"Ovid and Corinna, midday?" Tacitus said, arching an eyebrow.

"My very exemplars." Romatius beamed broadly. "'May such afternoons often come for me' is my motto."

"How is your father?" I asked, in an effort to wrest the conversation back to where we might gain some useful information from it.

"He's quite feeble, I'm sorry to say. He keeps to his bed and his mind wanders. He seems to be in the past most of the time."

"That is sad news. But for some of us those were happier days." Certainly for me, days before I was married to Livia.

"I'm not sure they were for my father. He often seems troubled."

We went on to talk about various people Romatius and I had grown up with. As we talked we enjoyed a chicken, served by a buxom young woman, that exceeded even Romatius' hyperbole about it. The wine was a full-bodied Falernian. My uncle used to say, about a wine so rich, that it would catch fire if put too close to a flame. I worried about whether Tacitus was going to ignite.

When Romatius appeared to be getting eager to go romp in somebody's meadow, I decided to broach the topic of missing people. Before
I did, though, I looked around at the other guests, wishing they weren't
there. I could keep my voice down, but Romatius seemed incapable
of doing so. The amount of wine he had drunk was no help in that
regard.

"Coming back here," I said, "has reminded me that my wife's father
disappeared about twenty years ago." It felt like a natural enough transi-
tion to the topic.

"Yes," Romatius said. "I've heard the story. Drowned, didn't he? And
they never found the body."

"That's right. Hearing my wife and mother-in-law talking about it
got me to wondering if there are any records of anyone else who might
have disappeared around that time."

Romatius blinked, suddenly looking more cautious, more sober.
"Why...why would you ask that?"

"Call it my accursed curiosity."

"That's what I call it," Tacitus said, pouring us all some more wine
and sloshing it over our cups. "All the time. Curse your curiosity, Gaius
Pliny. That's exactly what I say. It has gotten us into some serious
scrapes."

Romatius smiled weakly. "Well, just like you, Gaius, I'm too young
to remember anything from that long ago. I must say, it's a most peculiar thing to ask about."

I waved my hand, as though dismissing some minor point. "Thinking about my father-in-law's disappearance—his death, to be blunt
about it—set me off down this path. I was just wondering if you might
have heard stories, since you've lived here all your life. Maybe you've
heard your father and his friends talking."

"People disappear now and then. You know that. Slaves run away.
Travelers fall victim to bandits on the road. Unhappy wives or children
decide they might be happier somewhere else." Romatius took a gulp
of wine and wiped his mouth.

"Yes, I know, but—" I knew I sounded foolish.

"Why twenty years ago? Why that particular time?"

"It's when my wife's father disappeared. We were just talking about it and the question came up of whether anyone else had gone missing around then."

"Not to my knowledge." He put his hands on the table in preparation for leaving. "Now, if you'll excuse me, a lovely filly is waiting to be mounted. Stay as long as you like. The bill has been settled. Cornelius Tacitus, it's been a pleasure and an honor to meet you." Romatius pushed his chair back and didn't wait to receive our thanks for his hospitality.

"He was a very convivial fellow," Tacitus said as Romatius disappeared into the *taberna*, "until you brought up the topic of missing people."

"Or maybe he was just eager to play stud."

"Well, I can sympathize with him on that. He did raise one interesting point. Maybe the man in your wall was a traveler who was attacked on the road and robbed. That could be why we didn't find any clothing or jewelry with him. Somebody took advantage of a place to dump the body."

"But who would have been traveling near my house? And why? The road that runs past my house doesn't really go anywhere. It curves around and goes back down the other leg, as it were, of the lake. Nobody would be passing through there on their way to someplace else. And they would have to know about the wall." Delius and his three pounds of gold kept running through my mind, but I wasn't ready to discuss him with Tacitus yet.

"Why don't we ask the innkeeper?" Tacitus said with a slur in his voice. "Innkeepers know everything and everyone."

"I'm not sure that's such a good idea," I said. "We don't want to attract too much attention."

But Tacitus was already waving to get the innkeeper's attention. I realized he was a little in his cups and hoped he didn't say anything out of place.

Lutulla turned away from a vivacious conversation with two other customers and approached our table, wiping her hands on her apron. Seen up close, she was even more youthful-looking than my first estimate. From the way she'd been flirting with the other customers, I wondered if she supplemented her income with some personal service.

"What else can I get you, gentlemen? I have a lovely cake—honey and dates—fresh from the oven."

I hoped to distract Tacitus. "That sounds like just the thing."

But Tacitus wouldn't be deterred. "As delightful as it does sound, we'd like to ask if you know of anyone from this area who went missing twenty years ago."

"Well, there was that Livius who drowned and was never found."

"Yes, yes. We know about him."

I wondered if Tacitus was as drunk as he seemed to be, or just pretending to be so that she wouldn't take him too seriously.

"Do you know of anyone else? Maybe somebody with black hair?"

The innkeeper glanced at the men at the other table. "From twenty years ago? No, sir, I don't recall anyone from that long ago. I did have a helper in my kitchen once who ran off. Took a good sum of my money, too, he did. And he had black hair."

"Was that twenty years ago?" Tacitus asked too loudly.

"Now, let me see." The innkeeper put a hand to her chin. "No, no, come to think on it, that must have been more like fifteen years ago, not twenty."

The two men at the other table—the only other customers by now—got up and dropped money on the table. One looked over his shoulder at us just before he left the courtyard and stepped back into the *taberna*.

"Well, if the cake doesn't tempt you gentlemen," the innkeeper said, "I'd like to clean up out here now."

"I think we're getting booted out," Tacitus said, standing unsteadily.

"It's not that, sir." The innkeeper wiped her hands rapidly on her apron. "I just need—"

"What is it that bothers people around here," Tacitus said, "when we ask about someone who might have disappeared a long time ago?"

"Well, sir, every town has…things that people…don't like to talk about."

"You mean dirty little secrets?" Tacitus said. The volume of his voice, even more than the slur, told me he wasn't pretending. He had in fact had too much to drink.

"Sometimes very dirty, sir, and maybe not so little." She turned away from us and disappeared into the kitchen.

"What do you suppose she meant by that?" Tacitus said, slurring his words again.

"Let's think about it while we go get a bath." I put my hand on his back to start him moving toward the building. Even if we didn't need a bath, I wanted him to be sober enough to sit on a horse.

"Don't push me."

Nereus and Tacitus' servant, Marullus, joined us at the front door of the taberna. While Marullus was steadying his master, Nereus and I got a few steps ahead of them.

"My lord," Nereus said in a low voice, "I think I should tell you that Marullus was trying to impress the kitchen girl and told her about the skeleton. He even claimed he'd touched it."

"Damn him! Just like his master," I muttered.

We spent less than an hour in the bath, which was small and crowded, but the *frigidarium* in particular did seem to have a salubrious effect on Tacitus. By the time we got back to our horses, he was in good enough condition to ride. We could have stayed another night, but I was anxious to get home, even though we would be late arriving.

At least the trip had been worthwhile. I had learned more about Marcus Delius, my illegitimate cousin, and ruled him out as the person in the wall. If I could get Leucippe away from Nereus, I would see what else she could tell me about Delius and anything that had happened at the time the person in the wall was killed. But it was a long time ago. Would anyone even remember?

We hadn't gone more than a mile when we drew our horses to a stop and stared at the bizarre sight ahead of us.

"Is that what it appears to be," Tacitus asked, "or am I still drunk?"

"It certainly wasn't there yesterday." I edged my horse ahead a few paces and stopped under the branches of a tree which hung over the road. Mounted on a broken branch was a human skull. Beneath it was tied a piece of parchment with a message on it in a large but fine hand: LET WHAT WAS HIDDEN REMAIN UNKNOWN. The document bore a seal—a skull—pressed into a blob of wax.

VII

A shoe that is too large is apt to trip one, and when
too small, to pinch the feet. So it is with those
whose fortune does not suit them.

—Horace

I RETURNED THE BONES *we had found in the wall to the chest*
where Gaius had deposited them, careful to place the skull on top. Now
I had to find Julia and tell her what I had noticed. When I came out into
the garden, though, the first voice I heard was Livia's, so I stepped back
far enough into the doorway to be out of sight but still able to hear and see
when I peeked around the doorframe.

"I'll be back in a couple of days, Mother. I just can't take this place—
and some of these people—anymore right now."

I assumed she meant me. I hoped she did.

"But Tertia isn't expecting you."

"She's my cousin. She has to entertain me. Her house is only an hour
from here, and it's not as though my entire household is descending on her.
I'm just taking a few servants and a driver."

Pompeia raised her hands in surrender. "All right. Do what you want.
You always do anyway. Give me a few moments to write a note to my
brother."

"Well, hurry up. I'm ready to go." Livia headed for the front of the house
with two of her servant women trailing after her.

I stepped out of the room and into the sun. Livia gone overnight and
maybe longer! That was the best news I had heard in two days. Now I was
even more eager to talk to Julia, but she was walking across the garden with

Gaius' mother and Naomi. I picked up a cup and towel that someone had left on a table outside the door and started toward the kitchen. Any servant in a large house quickly learns that, as long as you're carrying something and look like you know where you're going, the masters will assume you're working.

Pompeia returned from her room with a note, folded and sealed. "Give this to my daughter," she told one of our servants. Then she joined Julia and Plinia, who had taken seats under an arbor at the back of the garden, with Naomi sitting behind them. I was going to pass them on my way to the kitchen. I would have to talk to Julia later.

"Oh, Aurora," Julia said, raising a hand to stop me. "There you are. Please bring us something to drink."

I was almost offended by her request, until I reminded myself that we weren't really friends, no matter how friendly we might have been over the last few days. I was a slave, who could be ordered to do anything Julia wanted. I went to the kitchen and brought out a tray with cups and pitchers of wine and water. Placing them on a small table in front of the women, I bowed my head and started to leave.

"Wait," Julia said. "Ladies, would it be all right if she stayed, in case we want anything else while we talk?" She hadn't used my name. I was feeling resentful about that. Did she think slaves should just have numbers, like Trimalchio's slaves in the Satyricon? *Why couldn't Naomi wait on them?*

Both of the older women nodded, barely looking up from filling their cups, mixing wine and water to their own tastes.

"Pull up a stool back here," Julia said, giving me a wink that Pompeia and Plinia couldn't see. I realized she was trying to downplay my presence and was actually making it possible for me to listen to the conversation in the only way a slave could, by becoming part of the scenery. I found a stool near the fountain and situated myself behind Julia, hoping I would soon disappear from Pompeia's and Plinia's awareness.

"Livia certainly has her own mind," Julia said, pouring herself some wine. "Was her father like that?"

Pompeia sighed. "That girl is like her father in every respect. Marcus Livius was a squat, dumpy man with black hair. As I recall, he wasn't any taller than Gaius. Just imagine Livia in a toga and you'll have the perfect picture of him."

Julia and I exchanged a glance. When we had all the bones of the skeleton in place and Gaius lay down beside it, it was just about the same size he was.

Pompeia seemed to be warming to her topic. She leaned back on the bench. "His brother Quintus—my second husband—was taller, more graceful, and far better in bed. I used to think Marcus might have been happier if I'd been a man." She and Plinia chuckled. Naomi blushed. "I'm reminded of him every time I look at Livilla. She and Gaius could have had such beautiful children. I wish I understood what made Livilla change her mind about marrying him."

Did she glance over her shoulder at me, or was I just imagining it?

Julia got her back on track, like a driver in a chariot race tugging on the reins. "What happened the night Livius died? I've heard bits and pieces, but I don't know the whole story."

"No one does." Pompeia looked at the ground for a moment, then seemed to gather the strength to tell the story. "He had sailed across the lake that morning."

"What was he doing over there?" Julia said.

"He and Caecilius and my brother and Romatius had some sort of business arrangement," Pompeia said. "They never did tell us anything more specific than that."

Plinia nodded. "They were very vague about it. All Caecilius would tell me was that they had gotten involved in some sort of investment and needed to see someone in that village near the old town of Comum now and then."

"Livius told me," Pompeia said, "that it was all more complicated than I could understand. He never did think I had a head for business. I just wish he could see what I've made from the estates he left me."

Julia poured herself some wine. "So he was sailing by himself? That's dangerous."

"Yes," Plinia said. "But he was a good sailor. He grew up around here. Caecilius, too, of course. He sailed boats from the time he was a boy. I wish Gaius took after his father in that regard."

Pompeia nodded. "Livius was certainly comfortable in a boat."

I whispered in Julia's ear and she asked, "Did he take any cargo on the boat?"

"Not as far as I know," Pompeia said. "I don't think he ever did. He just *sailed over there, saw someone, and came back. Whatever their business was, Livius was the one who went back and forth across the lake."*

Julia sipped her wine and added a bit more water. "So Livius sailed across the lake that morning and was coming back in the evening?"

Plinia took over the story. "Yes. Caecilius said he tried to persuade Livius not to go that day. Caecilius was concerned about the weather. Livius wasn't. He always was a bit reckless. It doesn't take more than half an hour to sail across the lake. But the storm caught Livius out there and the boat capsized. Caecilius said he became worried when the storm blew up, so he went down to the shore and he saw the boat overturned and sinking."

"Did he see Livius in the water?"

Plinia shook her head slowly. "He said he didn't."

"Has anyone ever tried to find the boat?" Julia asked.

"The lake is much deeper than you might suspect," Pompeia said.

"And that's all either of you know?" Julia asked.

Plinia nodded. "After Caecilius told Pompeia what happened, he refused to talk about it anymore. He said he couldn't bear to be reminded."

As we neared the villa I saw three wagons on the road ahead of us, laden with quarried stone and pulled by oxen. Handing Tacitus the bag containing our bath supplies and the skull and the note from the roadside, I urged a bit more speed out of my horse and caught up with the little caravan. Felix was riding at the front.

"This looks like a good start," I said as I drew up alongside him.

"Greetings, my lord. I certainly didn't expect to see you here. Yes, I was pleased to get this amount on short notice. They should have this much more ready for us by the time these wagons get back there."

"There's not as much urgency about it as I thought," I said. Motioning for Felix to ride with me, I took him far enough up the road that I could explain what we had found in the wall while he was gone, without the drivers of the wagons overhearing us. I ended by cautioning him to avoid spreading the story. "Apparently we've already upset someone just by asking a few vague questions."

"I've had a lot of practice keeping quiet about things, my lord."

"A skill much to be prized." *Especially in a servant.* I waved to Tacitus and our servants to catch up with me. "I don't want to make the rest of the trip at an ox's pace," I told Felix. "Have the men unload at the work site. Given how late it's getting and the way the clouds are thickening up, we should feed them and give them a place to sleep tonight."

"I was going to ask that, my lord."

When we rode up to the stable and dismounted, I noticed that one of Pompeia's *raeda*s was missing. "Has someone gone out for a ride?" I asked. "It's getting late, and I don't like the looks of those clouds."

"The lady Livia went to visit her cousin down the road, my lord," Barbatus said. "I believe she'll be away for a couple of days."

"Did she take anyone with her, a guard?"

"The driver and another man, that tall blond fellow you brought up here."

"Brennus?" I cursed silently. I had brought the man up here because of his skill in wine-making. He was too valuable to waste on guard duty. "You say she'll be gone for a couple of days?"

"That was her plan, my lord."

I had to turn my back to him to keep him from seeing my broad smile, but I couldn't hide it from Tacitus.

"The day suddenly seems brighter, doesn't it?" he said. "In spite of the clouds and in spite of skulls popping out of walls and dangling from trees."

"It's a lovely day," I said, turning my face up to the first few drops of rain. "A lovely day. Only one thing could make it better."

Tacitus put a firm hand on my shoulder. "You have to talk to her, Gaius, and soon. The longer you wait, the more difficult it gets."

It was actually a day that I was glad to see coming to an end—dragging interminably, it seemed, to an end. Conversation at dinner was desultory, the food no more noteworthy. Even Julia's wit seemed diminished by the rain and the events of the day. I knew Tacitus would fill her in on our conversation with Romatius and our discovery on the road back from Comum.

What made me, more than anything, want this day to pass into history, so it could be forgotten like most days, was the lack of Aurora.

The girl waiting on me was adequate, but she wasn't the one I wanted. As soon as I could decently do so, I bid good night to Pompeia and my mother and went to my room.

I knew Tacitus was right. This estrangement, which was my fault, had gone on too long. Any longer and the damage might be irreparable. Tomorrow morning, I resolved, I would take Aurora aside and plead, grovel, or do whatever was necessary to make things right. At least I could do it without Livia being around.

Since I couldn't sleep, I lit a second and third lamp and sat down to study the two skulls which had come into my possession. They were resting, side by side, on my writing table. I had the lower jaw of the one from the wall. Even lacking that piece, the one we had met with on the road this afternoon was still larger. That could mean that person was older. Perhaps I was looking at a man's skull and a boy's. On the other hand, men are generally larger than women, so this could be a man's skull and a woman's from the wall.

I tried to imagine the eyes which had once peered out from those sockets. What color were they? Pressing around my own eyes, I could feel the same bone structure. I had the demoralizing sensation that I was looking at my future. Inevitably, we all come to that end. It's odd to think that our eyes, noses, and ears—which are such important parts of our appearance—are just holes filled with something that disappears when we die. Noses and ears can even be cut off as punishment without taking the life of a person. Aurora could have the tip of one of her ears cut off and still survive. What defines the shape of our heads is something no one sees until we're dead. Then one person's skull is indistinguishable from another's.

The rain was pelting when I heard a knock on my door. I opened it to find Felix standing there, with Aurora just behind him.

"Forgive us for disturbing you, my lord," Felix said. Then he stood aside, put his hand on Aurora's back, and pushed her, stumbling, into my room. "Good night, my lord."

As he closed the door behind her, Aurora, looking more awkward and uncertain than I'd ever seen her, said, "Felix thought it would be more decorous if we were both at your door…in case anyone saw us."

"What…what are you doing here?"

She sighed and looked straight into my eyes. "My husband told me to stop being a silly goose and go back to you. You were only doing what you had to, he said, what you thought was best, even if you were a bit clumsy in the way you did it."

"Felix said that?" The man was certainly taking liberties. Advice to a fellow slave was one thing, criticism of his master quite another.

"I added the clumsy part." She held out her hands to me. "You *were* clumsy, Gaius. You should have trusted me all along the way. I would have understood."

I took her hands in mine. "I know. And I'm sorry, so sorry."

We clung to each other and did not say anything else for a long time.

I awoke at some time during the night to find Aurora sitting on the edge of the bed. I ran my hand up and down her beautiful bare back. She sighed but made no other response. Instead, she kept her gaze fixed on the two skulls on my writing table. When she had removed her gown earlier, she had tossed it over the skulls so the macabre sight wouldn't disturb us. Now she clutched her gown to her, with her arms crossed over her chest.

"What are you thinking?" I asked.

"That we need more light in here so we can get a better look at these things."

We had left one lamp burning because neither of us enjoys making love in total darkness. Now we slipped into our clothes and I lit two more lamps. Picking up one skull in each hand, Aurora turned them at different angles, keeping them facing the same way.

"I thought I had figured out who it was," I said and told her about Delius and the missing gold. "But he's alive and well. Now the second skull and the note seem to reopen the whole question. Why would someone want to warn us off if this is just a robbery victim from twenty years ago? And is this second skull someone we should try to identify?"

"Let's focus on the skull from the wall," Aurora said. "The main thing I notice about it, other than the smaller size, is the spot where some of the teeth are broken." She put the larger skull back on the table and held a lamp up close to the smaller one.

"I suspect whoever killed him," I said, "hit him in the mouth first, then on the head."

Aurora scrunched up her mouth, as though she'd tasted something disagreeable. "But he was hit on the right side of his face. Or *her* face. We do have to remember that it could be a woman, especially given the size of the skull."

"Yes."

"If you were hit on that side, wouldn't you turn your head to the left?" She moved the skull.

"Yes."

"But the hole where this person was struck on the top of the skull is on his left side." She put the skull down and put her finger on the spot of the lethal blow. "Most people are right-handed. A blow to the right side of the face would come from someone's *left* hand. A blow to the left side of the head, like this one, would come from someone's *right* hand. Let me show you."

She faced me and brought her left hand up to the side of my mouth, turning my head. I kissed her hand.

"I doubt *that* happened," she said with a smile. Then she brought her right hand down on the top of my head to demonstrate how that blow could have been struck. If she had actually hit me, I wouldn't have cared. I deserved it. "You see, I could not have delivered that fatal blow to the head in that spot with my left hand, or the blow to the mouth with my right hand."

"Well, that's most likely," I admitted, "but not the only possibility. Maybe the blow to his face was hard enough to spin him around. It was hard enough to break some teeth. When he turned, a left-handed person could have hit him on the head from behind."

She took my hand. "But, if you put a couple of your fingers in the hole—about the size of the rock that must have been used—they slope toward the front." She sucked on two of my fingers and used them to demonstrate. "You see, he was struck on the head from the front, with a pointed object, by someone who was right-handed."

"But you're not taking the cracked ribs into account. If he was hit there first, he would have doubled over or fallen."

"Stand up," Aurora said. "Let's see if we can figure out what happened."

I did as she told me, appreciating the irony of the servant giving the master an order. I don't think she noticed.

"He must have been hit in the ribs," she began, "on his left side, by some weapon. The person who attacked him would have swung like this." She drew her arms back and pretended to strike. "The blow came from a right-handed person."

I bent over as though I had been hit. "Now what?"

"My instinct is to swing again and hit you on the head." Aurora raised her arms high and brought them down on my head. Like a good actor, I fell to the floor.

"This would be where you take my clothes off," I said. When she looked puzzled, I went on. "And this would be where you smile seductively as you think about taking my clothes off."

Instead she looked at her hands, as though she were holding something. "Gaius, I think we were wrong."

I got up, brushing myself off. "About what?"

"About the weapon. We said it was a rock, but I don't think someone would have hit him in the side with a stick or a club and then picked up a rock to hit him in the head."

"You're right. That means he used a tool of some sort, with a long handle and something sharp and heavy on the end."

"Something like that would be easy enough to find on an estate like this."

"If he was in fact killed here," I reminded her. "We aren't at all sure about that."

"Lie down again," Aurora said.

"Why?" I complied as I asked the question.

She glanced at the skulls again and then down at me. "When was he hit in the mouth? And why at that particular spot?"

I got up and stood beside her. "That's as big a puzzle as why he was killed."

Aurora placed the two skulls side by side, both turned to the left. "Two of the teeth in the skull from the wall are broken, but there are still pieces of them in place."

"There's a gap right here, behind the tooth that's shaped like a dog's." I pointed to the spot.

She picked up the skull and turned it so we could see the teeth from the bottom. "You're right. That tooth is completely gone. It must have been missing before this person was killed. I wonder if somebody was trying to cover up something that might have made this person recognizable."

"I don't think the killer was worried about him being found and identified, not once he was sealed up in that wall."

"His—or her—clothes and jewelry were removed."

"We don't know that he was wearing any jewelry," I reminded her.

"Well, he certainly was wearing clothes."

"I can't dispute that. This tooth is far enough back in the mouth that it wouldn't be the first thing you'd notice about this person."

We fell silent as one of the lamps flickered out. I reached under the writing table for the flask that contained more oil but the stopper wouldn't come out. The last servant who filled the lamps had jammed it in tightly.

"Tap it against the table," Aurora said. "That'll loosen it."

After a couple of sharp taps I got the flask open, filled the lamp, and relit it from one of the burning lamps. As I was putting the flask back under the table, I said, "By the gods! What if…No, it couldn't be."

"What couldn't be?" Aurora said.

Before I could reply, we heard a knock on the door.

"It's Felix, my lord," a man's voice said.

I gave Aurora a quick kiss on the cheek. "Never mind. It's just a crazy idea."

I opened the door to see that it wasn't light yet. "What do you want?"

"With your permission, my lord, I think it's time for my wife to return to our room, for the sake of appearances."

The man displayed eminent good sense. I had chosen the right husband for the woman I love. "I suppose it is."

As Aurora came to the door she said, "Wait, husband." She threw her arms around my neck and kissed me, with Felix smiling behind her like a doting father.

—⁂—

"Are you sure this is a good idea?" Tacitus asked as we watched a crew of workmen resume their demolition of the wall not long after dawn, while two other men dug the trench where the foundation of the new walls would be laid. "We had a warning that couldn't be missed."

"That's precisely why I'm continuing. I don't want them to think they've frightened us."

"Speak for yourself. They've frightened me. What sort of people keep human skulls lying around to use as warnings? And parchment? Why write on parchment? That's what people use for magical books or if they can't get hold of papyrus."

"We keep saying 'they.' What makes us think it's more than one person?"

We moved back as more of the rubble fill in the wall tumbled out, raising a cloud of dust but, to my great relief, revealing nothing else.

"There's no reason it *has* to be more than one, I guess," Tacitus said. "But that skull on the tree and the message makes me think we've stumbled into something big, and I think that kind of secret would involve more than one person."

I shifted to Greek. "You think Romatius knows something, don't you?"

Tacitus shrugged and changed languages as well. "He's a friend of yours, I know—"

"But there were several other people at the *taberna* who could have overheard our conversation. Your blabbermouth servant told the kitchen girl all about it. And who knows how many people heard us at the bath? I couldn't get you to keep your voice down."

Tacitus bowed his head. "For my shortcomings and for those of my servant, I apologize. But something made Romatius nervous. You saw how he reacted as soon as we started talking about missing people. He couldn't get out of there fast enough."

"No faster than you, my friend, if you had a willing partner waiting. Doesn't Julia suspect—"

"It's none of your concern, Gaius Pliny, but I love Julia and will always be faithful to her, after my own fashion. You're hardly one to criticize any man's relationship with his wife, you know." He drew his shoulders back.

"I don't understand the change in your attitude, Cornelius Tacitus."
I shook my head slowly. "When I first met you, you had little good to
say about Julia. You once quoted Semonides' line that a man can't enjoy
a day if he has to spend all of it with his wife."

He cringed. "I said that?"

"Yes, you did."

"In my defense, she was hardly more than a child when I married
her, and a rather immature one at that. In the last couple of years she
has grown up in many ways. Maybe I have, too. Losing the baby made
her a different person and made me appreciate her in ways I hadn't
before. I consider myself lucky to be with her, and I'm sorry you find
yourself trapped in your marriage. I hope you can find some way to
make it tolerable for both of you."

"Are you suggesting that I might come to love Livia?"

"I'm not asking for a miracle, just for an easing of the tension. For
your sake, Gaius. A rope that's stretched too tightly for too long will
snap." He made the motion of pulling on something until it came
apart.

Like a contestant in the *pankration*, I raised a finger to signal my
surrender. I pointed it back at the wall. "This work is going well. I think
I'll go see how Phineas is doing with organizing the library."

"And—with apologies to Semonides—I'm going to spend the rest
of the day with my wife."

Before retreating to the library, I sent Felix back to the quarry. Pompeia caught me off-guard and suggested that Aurora ride with him, to
learn something about the business of the estate and to have time to
get acquainted with her new husband. I couldn't object without raising
my mother-in-law's suspicions.

My mother surprised me when she said, "But Aurora is...needed
here."

"To do what?" Pompeia asked. "Any of the servant girls can pamper
Gaius as well as she can. I've not noticed that she has any particular
skills, but perhaps I'm not fully informed about her...talents." With an
eyebrow raised, she looked from one of us to the other.

———∞∞∞———

"*Aurora, I—*"

Felix started to say something to me, but I stopped him. "You speak Greek, don't you?" I asked in that language.

"Not as well as you, I suspect, but I can manage."

"Let's use it. I'm always wary of talking around strangers. These men don't speak Greek, do they?"

"They're barely more articulate than their oxen," he said with the haughtiness which we servants who work in the house often display toward field hands and laborers.

"You can never be sure. Let's test them. Keep an eye on them over your shoulder." I raised my voice. "On a beautiful day like this, husband, I wish I could take off my gown and ride naked for a while. Just let the sun and the breeze play over my body." I touched my breasts lightly and shook my hair loose.

Felix chuckled. "They didn't even blink until you touched your breasts."

"I suppose it's safe to talk then."

"I know you would rather have stayed at the house with Gaius Pliny, now that you've settled your differences."

He was right, of course, but if I had to be somewhere else, then riding a horse on such a lovely day wasn't a bad place to be. Straddling a horse gave me almost as much pleasure as having my legs wrapped around Gaius. Besides, I really did enjoy Felix's company, and the scenery beggared description. The peninsula on which Gaius' villa sits divides Lake Comum into two long, thin branches. The main roads run on either side, near the lake. We were on a smaller road in the center of the peninsula. The forest around us was thick and green and beyond the trees rose the Alps, still snowcapped in July.

For the rest of the trip Felix had questions about the house in Rome, where he would soon be working. He was uneasy about leaving a place where he had lived and worked for over thirty years to move into a position of authority in a larger house.

"I don't know how people will regard me, coming in as an outsider," he said. "I'd resent me, in their place."

I told him as much as I could about the place and the people. As we talked I began to realize that I didn't know as much about them as I should have. Some of his questions I couldn't answer. Since I was the master's *favorite and my mother had been the elder Pliny's mistress, perhaps others in the household were reluctant to confide in me.*

When we arrived at the quarry in midafternoon it seemed odd to hear myself, for the first time, introduced as Felix's wife. Eustachius, the owner of the place, offered us something to eat and assured us that the stone would be loaded and ready to go in the morning. I tried not to stare at his left arm, or rather the stub of it protruding from the sleeve of his tunic, but he noticed me looking. I wished Felix had warned me.

Eustachius, a swarthy man of about forty, sat with us on a bench outside his house and his diminutive wife, Nicera, set wine, bread, and cheese on a table in front of us. "To answer your question before you have to ask it, lovely lady," he said, "I got it pinched between two big blocks of stone when they shifted on a wagon. It was completely crushed. We had no choice but to cut it off at the elbow like this."

"I'm sorry. I didn't mean to be rude."

"No matter. After ten years, I'm used to it. And my right arm is as strong as two arms for most men." He held the limb in front of my face and flexed the enormous muscles. "So, Gaius Pliny is tearing out the wall my old dad and me built for his dad, eh?"

"You worked on the wall?"

"Sure did. It was a small job, so my father put me in charge of it."

"Could I ask you a few questions about it?"

"By all means, but you'll have to wait until dinner." He got to his feet. "If I don't crack the whip over these louts, they'll not have your load of stone ready by tomorrow."

<hr />

As the sun comes up over the Alps there is a fleeting moment when it turns the snow on the peaks pink and orange. I had not gotten up this early just so I could enjoy that ephemeral sight, but the lovely dawn proved some small compensation for a sleepless night without Aurora. I was coming out of the *latrina* when one of the servant girls, hardly more than a child, ran up to me.

"My lord, come quickly." She turned and ran toward the back gate of the garden without waiting to see if I was following.

When I caught up to her, she was bending over a woman lying

on the ground, with a hood over her head and her hands tied behind her. From the indistinct noises she was making, I guessed she was gagged.

"I found her when I came out to pick some sage," the girl said. "I didn't know what to do."

"Untie her." That much seemed obvious.

Kneeling and removing the hood, I recognized Rhoda, one of Livia's servant women. As soon as I loosened the gag, she cried, "My lord, my lady Livia has been kidnapped!"

VIII

Do not yield to misfortunes, but advance more boldly
to meet them, as your fortune permits you.

—Virgil

RHODA COULD NOT be calmed down. We carried her into the garden and got her something to drink, but she kept scream-ing, "They took her, my lord! It was horrible!" The racket waked those of the household who weren't already up. Tacitus, Julia, Pompeia, and my mother and Naomi soon stood around us. Naomi took the girl in her arms and tried to comfort her. I noticed that Pompeia made no such move, even though Rhoda was one of her servants, not one of ours.

"Settle down," I told Rhoda, patting her knee. "You're safe now. You've got to calm yourself and tell us what happened."

She took several rapid breaths. "Three men stopped us, my lord. On our way back from the lady Tertia's house. It was horrible. Instead of heads they had skulls."

"You mean they were wearing masks that looked like skulls."

She shook her head vigorously. "No, my lord. They had skulls instead of heads, just like I said."

I wasn't going to argue with a delirious woman. "Did they harm Livia and Procne?"

"Not that I saw, my lord. But they killed the driver. He tried to stop them. He hit them with his whip." She let out another long wail. "And they took the other man, Brennus."

The driver was a good man. He did what he was supposed to do,

108

try to defend his mistress. "Do you know what happened to Livia and Procne?"

"One of the men said to be careful with them. He was angry about the driver getting killed. 'Nobody was supposed to get hurt.' That's what he said."

"That's a hopeful sign," Tacitus assured me.

"We were all tied and gagged, my lord, and had bags put over our heads. I was taken off in one direction. It sounded like my lady Livia and Procne and Brennus were being carried off in another direction."

"Where were you before they dumped you here?"

"I was kept in some kind of a building, my lord. He dropped me on a marble floor. I had that bag over my head, so I couldn't see anything. All I know is, the place smelled awful and it had some sort of slimy stuff on the floor." She grabbed at a place on her gown. "This."

"Could you hear anything? Animals? Other people moving around?"

"No, my lord. I'm sorry."

"You have nothing to be sorry about. We're just glad you're safe."

"If she was on a marble floor," Tacitus said, "it could mean she was in a house. I wonder if we could find it."

"You've seen how many houses there are along the shore of this lake. It's like the coast of the Bay of Naples before Vesuvius erupted. Some of them are used only during the warmer months. I don't know how we would ever find a particular place. And what good would it do now?"

"I suppose you're right, but we've got to start somewhere." Tacitus turned to Rhoda. "Someone brought you here on horseback, didn't they?"

"Yes, my lord. I was thrown over the horse, like a big sack, in front of the rider."

"Do you have any idea how long you were on the horse?"

"It didn't seem like very long, my lord. But I was so scared. He couldn't...keep his hands off me, and there was nothing I could do."

Pompeia grabbed my arm. "Why are you sitting here talking, Gaius? My daughter is in the hands of some monsters. They've already killed one person. Why aren't you out looking for her?"

I forced myself to speak calmly. I've always prided myself on my ability to remain calm in a crisis. When Vesuvius erupted, I forced myself to sit in the garden of our house copying some passages of Livy. My hands hardly shook at all, mostly from the tremors of the earth. "First we have to determine where to look," I said, clipping my words, "or we would just be wasting our time."

Pompeia's voice reached a frantic pitch. "Livilla didn't want to marry you, she said, because she was afraid of the danger you're always getting yourself involved in. Now I see she was right to be worried. If anything happens to Livia, I'll—"

"Something already has," I said so sharply that she backed away from me. "I'll do everything I can to make sure nothing *else* happens to her."

"My lord," Rhoda said, pulling away from Naomi, "you need to look at something." She touched a brooch fastened haphazardly on the side of her gown. In the confusion and the dim light we hadn't noticed it.

"That's Livia's!" Pompeia said. "It was her favorite. She wore it all the time."

I recognized the brooch. Anyone who was around Livia for more than a day couldn't help but recognize it.

"There's something pinned to it, my lord," Rhoda said, "inside my gown. It's a note. The man said only you were to see it."

"Unfasten it."

Rhoda loosened the brooch and reached inside her gown to retrieve a note, written on parchment, folded in thirds and sealed by a piece of wax with the image of a skull pressed into it, the same image on the note we'd found on the road. My name was written across the front. Even at first glance I was sure it was the same hand that had written the warning message we received on the road.

I took the brooch and the note and stepped away from the crowd around Rhoda. Before I gave the brooch to Pompeia I examined it to see if it had been damaged. It was large enough and the pin long enough to serve the same purpose as Aurora's hidden knife. Turning the object over, I saw DEL inscribed on the back.

The bastard cousin whom I'd never heard of until this summer was suddenly cropping up all over my life.

When Tacitus started to follow me, I held up a hand. "They said it was for me only."

"Isn't that what the fellow said when he handed Caesar a note on the Ides of March?"

"Yes, and Caesar didn't read it and you know how that turned out. Let me read it before I decide whether to show it to anyone else. Something very odd is going on here, and I prefer to be cautious. I'm told that this note is for me, so I'm going to read it first. Alone."

Entering the library, I found a thin-bladed knife. The seal was so bizarre that I hated to break it. Cutting around the piece of wax, I managed to remove the seal without damaging it. I put it on a shelf and unfolded the note. When I had read it several times, I held it over the flame of a lamp, then drew it back. Refolding it, I dropped two blobs of warm wax on it and pressed my own signet ring into both of them.

"But why won't you show it to me?" Tacitus said one more time, like a persistent child, as we rode with a group of our servants to the place where Livia had been attacked. "Don't you trust me? If you don't trust me, then Julia and I should just pack up and be on our way."

"It's not a matter of trust," I said. "The message was intended for me. I'll show it to you when it makes sense to do so. Right now we've got to find Livia. The body in the wall will have to wait. A few more days won't matter to him."

"But don't you think Livia's kidnapping is directly tied into whatever happened to the man in the wall and to whoever he is? That must be what the note is about. Why won't you tell me?"

"The note said nothing about the body in the wall. It was about Livia's kidnapping."

"And you don't think there's a connection?"

"I didn't say that. I will tell you what the note said after I've had a chance to talk to one other person about it. Please, just be patient."

The twist of Tacitus' mouth reminded me that patience is not one of his virtues.

We were riding down the road that ran along the east branch of Lake Comum. Rhoda had given us the best estimate she could of where they were when they were stopped. I'd been surprised that they were travelling so late in the day, but Rhoda said Livia and Tertia had gotten into an argument and Livia had left in a huff. I didn't have to ask who started the argument.

Regardless of my lack of feelings for Livia, I had to find her. I would have felt the same obligation for anyone who had been seized like this, even if I had never met them. Though I'm no philosopher, I agree with Plato that there are some absolutes in this world, and Justice is one of them.

"There it is, my lord," one of the servants riding ahead of us called out.

We drew to a halt at the spot where the *raeda* had been pushed off the road and partially submerged in the lake. The attackers had taken the horses, presumably to carry Livia and Procne and the guard, Brennus. Our horses pulled the wagon out and we found the driver's body in it, as I feared we would.

I designated two of the servants. "Hitch your horses to this thing and drive it back to the house. My mother will show you what to do with…him." I realized I didn't know the driver's name. He was one of Livia's servants, from her mother's estate at Narnia.

We left them to that task and began to follow hoofprints leading away from the *raeda*. The road was paved, but its coating of dust had been settled enough by yesterday's rain that we could see where the attackers had gone. I wished Aurora was with us. She could probably glean information from the prints that I was missing entirely. Even when I first knew her as a child, she had shown an uncanny ability to read animals' tracks, a technique her father had taught her. When we played together on my family's estates, she had honed her skill. She tried to teach me, but I couldn't master more than the basics.

After a short while the tracks turned off the road and into the woods. "We've lost them," I said.

We dismounted and examined the area as closely as we could, in ever-widening circles, but the layers of leaves on the ground were so dense and wet that we could no longer follow the trail.

"We know which direction they were headed," Tacitus said.

"Once they went into the woods, they could turn in any direction, at any time."

For an hour or more we searched on foot for any sign of horses passing through—a stray print, a broken branch, droppings, anything—but we couldn't get back on their trail.

"We need to report this to the authorities," Tacitus said.

I took him aside and lowered my voice. "That's exactly what we're *not* going to do."

"Did the note you won't share with me warn you not to?"

"That was part of it."

"Are they demanding ransom? How much? I'm sure they know you're rich."

"They're not asking for money."

Awareness spread over Tacitus' face. "This *does* have something to do with that body in the wall, doesn't it?"

"It seems to have everything to do with it. I'll tell you what the note says when I'm sure I understand it. I value your friendship and your help in the past, you know that. There's someone I have to talk to first. Please trust me on this a little longer."

We heard voices and the sound of horses in the woods on our right. If they were bandits, they were going to be disappointed. All we had was wagons loaded with quarried stone. The only thing we had worth stealing was... me. And we were only lightly armed—my knife and a couple of swords.

Felix raised a hand, bringing our caravan to a halt. "Whoever they are, they're not exactly trying to sneak up on us," he said, as if that would offer reassurance.

The first horse emerged from the woods and I couldn't believe my eyes. "Gaius!...Pliny! My lord." I hoped the others in both parties didn't notice my near slip. As the next horse appeared, I cried out, "And Cornelius Tacitus! Sir! What a surprise." I tapped my heels on my horse's sides and rode forward until I was beside Gaius, our horses nuzzling one another. Felix stayed with the wagons.

"What are you doing out here, my lord?"

Gaius' face was dark with worry. "Livia's been kidnapped."

"By the gods! When? Where?"

"It happened yesterday evening." He told me the whole story. "We followed their trail into the woods but lost them. We thought perhaps they had gone through the woods to this road."

"We've seen no sign of them, my lord."

Gaius shook his head. "I don't know what to do."

"Perhaps if I rode over there with you, my lord. I might see something—"

"That's an excellent idea," Gaius said. I could see the relief on his face. He told one of his men to ride along with Felix. The other man turned with us and Tacitus, and we started back through the woods.

"If they did come this way, my lord," I said, "you've probably destroyed any trail they might have left."

"I know, but I had to do something."

"I didn't mean to be critical, my lord. As far as you know, there were three men."

"That's what Rhoda said. One of them took her off in a different direction, so I think there were only two men with Livia and Procne and Brennus."

"And four horses?"

"Yes, but I don't know, of course, whether they had their captives riding the horses or put the women on horses with them."

"Either way, I doubt they could cover their trail completely, my lord, unless they were quite skillful about it. Four horses leave a lot of prints... and other evidence."

When we arrived at the site where the women had been attacked, Gaius and I dismounted. I motioned for him to stay to one side and I walked back down the road, in the direction from which the raeda had been coming.

"One of the horses pulling the raeda was wearing hipposandals, my lord."

"That's not unusual for a horse pulling a load."

"No, it's not. But it could make him easier to track. The hipposandals make a clearer, deeper print than a bare hoof."

Leaving Tacitus and the servant to hold the horses, Gaius and I followed the tracks leaving the raeda.

"Here's where they left the road," he said after we'd gone about twenty paces.

He turned into the woods, taking my hand and pulling me after him. When we were out of sight from the road, he embraced me, not out of passion, I could tell, but out of fear. I held him and felt him tremble until he drew away from me and let out a long breath.

"All I can think about," he said, "is what if they had taken you?"

I took his face in my hands. "My dear Gaius, we've got to focus on finding Livia."

"I know, I know. But how?"

"I think we ought to stay on the road."

"Why? They went into the woods here."

"Just follow me."

We emerged from the woods and walked another thirty paces until I found what I was expecting. I pointed to the tracks. "This is where they came back onto the road. They removed the hipposandals so they could travel faster."

Gaius swore an oath, the strongest I'd ever heard from him. "So Tacitus and I were wasting our time tromping through the woods. How could I be so stupid?"

"You weren't stupid, Gaius. They tricked you." We walked a bit farther up the road. "Here's where they went back into the woods. Do you see that stream over there? I suspect they rode into it and followed it for a while. It's what I would have done. It would make it impossible to track them until they left it."

"Are you saying we won't be able to find them?"

"I'm just saying it will be more difficult. We could get more men, spread out over a wider area. Maybe we should bring some dogs."

"I don't think that's a good idea," Gaius said.

"Why not? You want to find her, don't you?"

"Of course I do. But they left a note, pinned to Rhoda's gown."

"What did it say?"

When he finished telling me about the contents of the note, I could only shake my head. "What are you going to do?"

"I simply don't know."

"Gaius, you have to find your wife. There can't be any uncertainty about that, can there?"

At Aurora's urging we followed the stream back into the woods, looking for a place where a rider might have emerged from it. We left our horses with the servants on the road to avoid spoiling any tracks the kidnappers might have left.

"Something feels odd," I finally said. "The trees along here are younger. It's as though there was once a path or a small road through here."

"I think you're right." Tacitus measured one of the small trees against his own height. "It doesn't look like anyone's been through here in quite a while, though."

"Someone came through here in the last day or so, my lord," Aurora said. She pointed to a broken twig on one of the trees. Then she knelt and sniffed at the leaves. "Someone on horseback."

"How can you tell?" Tacitus asked.

Aurora pointed to the spot where she was kneeling. "A horse's urine has an aroma all its own, my lord. Would you care—"

"You're the expert," Tacitus said, raising a hand. "I'll take your word for it. Mare or stallion?"

"Mare, my lord, and in heat."

Tacitus' jaw dropped.

A dozen paces or so farther on, just before we came over a small rise, we found more evidence of the recent passage of a horse, with the flies buzzing happily around the pile.

"No need to sniff that, I hope," Tacitus said.

"It speaks for itself, my lord," Aurora said.

As we topped the rise, we stopped in amazement. "Is that really a house?" I asked.

What we were looking at was a modest villa, obviously long deserted. Trees grew up through the opening above the atrium. Because it was so deep in the woods, it had been surrounded by a wall to keep out animals. The wall had been breached in several places. We made our way down the rise and stepped through one of the openings. We entered the house itself through a broken place in the back wall of the peristyle garden.

In its shape and arrangement of rooms the house was ordinary, if somewhat small. An *exhedra* dominated the back wall of the garden, and small bedrooms ran along the side walls. The first feature that differentiated this house from anything I'd ever seen was the large pool in the center of the garden.

"That's no *piscina*," I said. Like the soaking pool in a bath, this pool was clearly intended for human occupants, not fish. It was filled now with leaves and debris from the trees and the carcasses of several small animals. The smell of decay permeated the whole place.

"This certainly could have been the place where Rhoda was kept," Tacitus said.

"Gaius, come look at this," Aurora called from where she was looking into one of the rooms.

We joined her and peered into the dimness of the room. It contained a broken-down bed, but what stopped us was the frescoes. Erotic scenes on the bedroom walls of a house are nothing unusual, but erotic scenes featuring men and very young boys were something I'd never seen.

"That's revolting," Tacitus said. "Yes, I said it's revolting. I can find a young man attractive now and then—you both know that—but a child? No, never! Not a child!"

Aurora shuddered. "This is an evil place."

Tacitus went off to check the rooms on the other side of the garden. Aurora and I made a quick survey of the rest of the house. All of the rooms were decorated in a similar fashion. One of them, off the atrium, seemed to show signs that someone had been there recently—especially the remnants of a small fire.

I knelt and looked more closely at the floor, which was covered with same green moldy material that was engulfing the whole house. In this room there was a smear on the floor. I bent lower and sniffed at it. "You don't need Brennus' nose to tell that this is what was on Rhoda's gown. This must be where she was lying on the floor."

"Why don't we take a sample," Aurora said, "and compare it to what's on her gown, just to be sure. I'll use the hem of my gown. There's no point in messing up your tunic."

"And you'll get a new gown in the bargain."

She smiled. "That thought did cross my mind. I don't think this stuff will ever wash out."

Tacitus came back into the room, carrying a small wooden animal and a peculiar mask. "This looks like a child's toy," he said. "The mask is designed to cover the upper part of the face. It would make it difficult to identify the wearer, while leaving the mouth unobstructed for..." He pointed to the paintings on the wall.

"I wouldn't call it a skeleton mask," I said. "Would you?"

"No, there's nothing skeletal about it."

"Well, let's bring those things with us."

We agreed not to talk about what we had seen when we rejoined my servants. None of us really wanted to talk about it. I couldn't help but wonder why an entire house was devoted to such disgusting activity. Where did the boys come from? What happened to them? Had there actually been boys there, or was this just someone's demented fantasy? The toys and the mask that Tacitus had found were certainly real.

I had to get my focus back on Livia's kidnapping. The villa was probably just a convenient hiding place that the kidnappers were aware of. I couldn't see any connection beyond that.

"What I don't understand," I said to Tacitus and Aurora as we rode toward my villa, with my servants a discreet distance ahead of us, "is how someone knew where Livia would be, and when."

"You don't think it was a random attack?" Tacitus asked. He sounded relieved to have something else to talk about.

"I *know* it wasn't random."

"Oh, yes, the note that you won't tell me about. Have you told anyone else? While you were in the woods, perhaps?"

"I think someone knew she was going to be on the road," Aurora said, earning my gratitude for cutting off the argument about the note.

"So it had to be someone in Gaius' house," Tacitus said.

Aurora shook her head. "Not necessarily. They were attacked while returning from visiting Tertia at Pompeius' house. Isn't it more likely that the plan was initiated from there?"

"How would someone know it was the right *raeda*?"

I snorted. "With those garish colors, how could you miss it?"

"But what would anyone in Pompeius' house have to do with this business—whatever this business is?" Tacitus asked.

"He and Livia's father were business partners," I pointed out.

"What kind of business?"

"That's the question I can't answer, and it may be the crucial question."

"Is any of this going to help you locate Livia?" Tacitus said. "Aren't you afraid they'll do something to her?"

"The note did promise no harm would come to her. I can tell you that much."

Tacitus snorted. "And you trust the word of kidnappers?"

"What choice do I have? They did no harm to Rhoda, beyond frightening her."

"Gaius, they killed the driver."

"Rhoda said the leader was angry about that. No one was supposed to get hurt, he said. I'm going to find Livia as quickly as I can, but where would you have me start?" I gestured at the woods around us. "Which direction? Tell me, which direction?"

We returned to the stable around noon, and Barbatus, full of questions as usual, was helping us dismount when Pompeia came rushing out to meet us, with my mother, Naomi, and several other women around her like her *clientela*. I sent Aurora to compare the smear on her gown with whatever was on Rhoda's, though I had no doubt they would match.

"You've come back without her," Pompeia said angrily.

"We couldn't find her," I said.

"You didn't have any trouble finding somebody else, apparently." She glared at Aurora's departing back. "I thought that one was with her husband."

"We ran into them, on their way back from the quarry, while we were looking for Livia. Aurora helped us see where the kidnappers' trail went. Or at least one of the kidnappers' trails."

"Well, then, why aren't you still looking for my daughter?" Her complexion reddened to almost match her gown.

"Because the trail ran out," I said. I would have preferred that it run out rather than leading us to that damnable villa. "We have no idea *where* to look, and we need to think about what we're going to do before we go dashing off in all directions, or in any direction."

I tried to turn away, but Pompeia shifted her bulk to stay in front of me.

"What did that note say?" she demanded. "If they're asking for ransom, you'd better not hesitate to pay it."

"There was no mention of ransom." *At least not ransom money, so, fortunately, I wouldn't be faced with that dilemma. Not that it really would be a dilemma. Regardless of how I felt about Livia, I would do whatever was necessary to get her back. And then I would find the bastards who took her and killed one of our servants and make them—*

"If not ransom, then what do they want?" Pompeia asked.

"All I can tell you is that they promised not to hurt her."

"Oh, and you believe them?" She put her hands on her broad hips and jutted her chins at me defiantly.

"They didn't hurt Rhoda," I countered. "All we can do right now is accept what they say. That gives us time, I think, to formulate a plan. But, before I can do anything, I need to talk to my mother, in private."

Everyone fell quiet and stood away from us as I took my mother's arm and led her from the stable through the rear gate of the house and to my room. Sitting in one of the chairs and folding her hands—looking more drawn and frailer than usual—she didn't say anything until I had lit a couple of lamps and closed the door.

"This is about something in that note, isn't it?" she asked as I took a seat across from her, at the writing desk. "Something you haven't told anyone yet."

I had told Aurora, but I nodded. Unlocking the small box where I keep a bit of money and my most important documents pertaining to this estate, I took out the note and broke the two seals I had put on it. "Let me read it to you."

Mother raised her eyes to me expectantly.

"It says, 'We will give you back your wife in return for a document of your father's written on parchment and sealed with a skull. It must be unopened. In two days you will be told where to deliver the document. You will have one day after that to comply. Your wife and servants will not be harmed. We regret the death of the man who fought against us. We didn't intend for anyone to get hurt. Do not inform the magistrates. Remember, you have three days.'"

Mother's face clouded in confusion. "What document?"

"That's what I'm asking you. I have no idea what they're talking about."

"But how can you—"

"That's exactly the problem, Mother." I snapped the words. "I can't give them what I don't have. But if I don't give it to them, I don't know what they'll do to Livia."

"Who are 'they'?"

I had to work to keep my voice from rising. "I don't know that either, so I can't communicate with them and tell them that I don't have what they're asking for."

"Do you think they'll harm her?"

"They say they won't, if I do as they ask. And they did regret the death of our driver."

"How nice of them to apologize." She took the note from me and looked it over.

"Is anything about it familiar? The style of writing, perhaps?"

She shook her head.

"You're the only person who might know what they mean. What sort of document could they be talking about and where could my father have put it?"

She shook her head. "I don't know, Gaius. By the gods, I wish I did. Your father was a secretive man. He had business dealings he never told me about. Remember, I was only fourteen when I married him. He was forty. He always treated me like a child."

"Can you tell me anything about what he might have been involved in that someone doesn't want me to know about? Whatever this document is, they specify that it has to be unopened. That sounds more than just secretive to me. It sounds sinister."

She shrugged and looked up at me apologetically. "All I know is that he had various business dealings with Livius, Pompeius, and the elder Romatius. The four of them sometimes did things together. At other times I think your father would work with one or the other of them. Livius was his best friend in that group."

"Were they his only business contacts?"

"No, but they were the most frequent."

"Did he ever form a *collegium* with any of them?"

"I heard that term a few times, when they didn't know I could hear them, but they always stopped talking about it as soon as I came into the room."

That might be my first clue about what I was looking for. A *collegium* is always formed for a specific purpose. The partners record how much they're investing and how the profits are to be shared. "Do you know what business they had together? Were they insuring something? Importing something?" I've found that, even when someone says they don't know anything, if I keep asking questions, I can sometimes jar a memory loose.

"All I know is that something your father and Livius were doing had some connection with the village on the other side of the lake, near Old Comum."

"Did they cross the lake often?"

"Livius did, perhaps twice a month. That's why it wasn't anything unusual that last time he made the trip. He would go across, spend a day doing whatever it was he did, and then sail back. That's what Livius had done. He was on his way back when he drowned." She paused, as though she had to force herself to continue. "Your father seemed a very different man after that night. I think he blamed himself for Livius' death."

"Why? You said he wasn't with him."

"He thought he should have persuaded him not to go, or somehow been able to save him."

"Were you aware of any conflict between them?" A disagreement over some business matter could have led to a falling out between the partners of a *collegium*, particularly if there was a great deal of money involved.

"No, dear. As I said, they were quite good friends. From the time you and Livia were babies, they talked of a marriage between you two. And now that's come about, long after both of them died. It's as though Fortune ordained it."

I nodded, but I thought Nemesis—Fortune's evil sister—might be a more appropriate divine power to be invoked in this case.

"Someone other than Livius and my father—someone who's alive now—must have known about this *collegium*," I said, "if that is in fact what's involved here. And they must know it has some connection to the body in our wall. That's why this is happening now. Pompeius and Romatius are still alive, aren't they?"

"Yes. They both must be about sixty or older, and the last I heard Pompeius wasn't in very good health."

I knew the elder Romatius was bedridden and losing his mind in Comum, living with his son. "Where does Pompeius live?"

"With Tertia and her husband, in the house where Livia went to visit. Or I should say, Tertia lives there with Pompeius. It's his house."

The place Livia visited right before she was kidnapped! That couldn't be a coincidence. "What dealings did Pompeius have with Livius or my father?"

"You'd have to ask him."

"I intend to." I picked up a stylus and writing tablet. "Now, one more thing. What can you tell me about a deserted villa deep in the woods a few miles from here?"

"Is there really such a place?"

"Yes, I saw it this morning. So you've heard of it?"

"Only rumors, years ago. What does this have to do with finding Livia?"

"The green slime that was on Rhoda's gown came from that villa. It's where she was taken after the women were kidnapped."

"Livia wasn't there, though?"

"No, but whoever took her knows that place. And they know the story behind the body in the wall and don't want me to learn any more. All of this trouble started when we found that body. There has to be a connection between it and my father's business dealings. But what could he have been involved in—"

"Gaius, I wish your father had been the paragon of virtue you think he was."

IX

*No man ever wetted clay and then left it, as if there
would be bricks by chance and fortune.*

—Plutarch

TACITUS, JULIA, AND AURORA sat in silence as I finished
reading the kidnappers' note to them. The light from the lamps
on each end of the table flickered across their faces. We had gathered
in the library, with the door closed and Phineas on guard against any
interruptions. I sat down on a bench next to Aurora. She moved her
leg so that it was touching mine, sending a surge of comfort and desire
through me. Tacitus and Julia were sitting on the other side of the
table. I passed the piece of parchment around so each of them could
examine it.

Tacitus spoke first. "And you have no idea what this document is
or where it might be?"

"Absolutely none. Nor does my mother. Phineas hasn't found anything with that seal on it in my father's papers." I waved my hand over
the next table, strewn with my father's letters, contracts, and other
personal papers. I had told Phineas to put everything else aside and
concentrate on sorting those out. "It might be some sort of *collegium*
agreement—"

"Sealed with a skull?"

"That's what sounds so bizarre," Julia said.

"So what are you going to do?" Tacitus asked. "Ride down to Pompeius' house and demand he give you back your wife?"

"What makes you think Pompeius is behind this?"

Tacitus raised his hands in a gesture I'd seen him use in court to direct a jury's attention. "Isn't it obvious? Livia visits his house, says something about the body in the wall, and is kidnapped."

"But what about the skull and the warning on our way back from Comum? That must have been prompted by our questions in the *taberna*. Pompeius couldn't have known anything about that. And there were two other men in the *taberna* who showed an unhealthy interest in what we were saying."

"What about the elder Romatius? You talked to his son."

"Whom I've known since we were children." I didn't like Tacitus' accusatory tone. "His father's bedridden. How could he be involved?"

"A man can give orders from his bed and pay people to do things."

"And other people couldn't help but hear us because *you* wouldn't keep your voice down, and then your loose-tongued servant—"

Tacitus tried to glare me into silence, but Julia turned to him. "What is he talking about?"

"Unfortunately," Tacitus said, lowering his head, "Marullus, the servant who accompanied me, told one of the serving girls in the *taberna* about the skeleton. Apparently he thought it would impress her enough to…"

Julia gave her husband a withering glance. "I wonder where he learned to do that. But it means, within hours, the story was being told—and no doubt embroidered—all around Comum."

Aurora put a calming hand on my arm. "If Pompeius or Romatius is behind it, would they have done something so blatant? They might as well step forward and confess."

"She's right," Julia said. "Men of our class don't go around threatening and kidnapping people."

"No," I said. "We do worse. We take them to court."

"So who are we looking for then?" Tacitus asked. "Somebody we've never heard of?"

"Somebody who has some connection to that old villa. We need to find out who owns that place."

"It seems to me," Aurora said, "that the 'who' isn't the most important question right now. It's the 'where,' and I mean where is this document that somebody wants very badly? We need to focus on finding that."

I looked around the library in desperation. "How can I possibly find something like that after so many years?"

"As much as I hate to add to your distress," Tacitus said, "if it was so important, it might not even be in the library. Your father might have hidden it somewhere more secure."

"I've already considered that, but I felt we had to start searching here. You're right, though. He could have dug a hole anywhere and stuck it in the ground. He could have stuck it in another wall. I've got just three days to find it, and I don't even know where to *begin* looking."

I propped my elbows on the table and cradled my head in my hands. Aurora put her arm around my shoulder.

"We'll find it, Gaius," she said softly, "and we'll get Livia back."

"What I don't understand," Julia said, "is why someone is going to such lengths to retrieve this document after so long a time. If it's so important to them, why haven't they done anything in the last twenty years?"

"It has something to do with the body in the wall," I said. "I can't see any other explanation. Somebody other than my father and Livius must have been involved in whatever resulted in that man's death. They thought it was all covered up. After Livius drowned and my father died they weren't worried about anyone finding out about it. Then that body tumbled out of the wall."

"When did your father die, Gaius?" Julia asked.

I had to think for a moment. "A little over a year after the wall was built. My mother and I were at Laurentum at the time."

"What happened to him?"

"I've been told that he went out to the stable to check on a horse that had been ill. Somehow the animal became agitated and trampled him."

"Was he there by himself?"

"I think so. Barbatus found him."

"Perhaps we should talk to Barbatus," Tacitus said.

"Why? What does my father's death have to do with Livia's kidnapping?"

"You just said that someone other than your father and Livius must have been involved with the body in the wall. Maybe somebody wanted to be sure your father couldn't say anything."

"Are you suggesting that my father killed that man?" My mother's comment about my father being less virtuous than I wanted to believe rang in my head. As my voice tensed Aurora took my hand.

"No, not at all." Tacitus shook his head. "But he might have known who did."

"Maybe that's why this missing document is so important," Aurora said. "Important enough to kidnap somebody."

"And to kill a man," Julia added somberly.

"That's why we have to find it," I said. "Until we do, we have no hope of getting Livia back."

"Gaius," Julia said as we got up from the table, "do you realize that you never call her your wife?"

"Probably for the same reason," Tacitus cut in, "that we call the Furies the Eumenides—the kindly-minded ones. Push the evil away by never calling it by its real name."

As unkind as Tacitus' comment was, it wasn't far from the truth. To me the title "wife" implied a connection that I would never feel with Livia.

I called Phineas in and, for the next several hours, all of us searched the library from top to bottom and side to side, checking the walls and floors for hiding places, looking under and behind every bookcase. We unrolled every scroll to make sure nothing had been concealed inside one of them. Because I didn't want to provide grist for the household's gossip mill, I put a finger to my lips to caution the others against any casual talk. Phineas has shown himself capable of keeping my confidences, but this matter was too important to take a chance.

As we worked I tried to reassure myself that whoever was holding my wife—I forced myself to think those words—would not harm her. If they did, they would lose any bargaining power. The note did not contain a threat, just a demand. Whatever was in this document we were searching for, someone wanted it very badly. That made me think it must incriminate somebody in something—such as the murder of the person in my wall. The timing of the discovery of the body and Livia's kidnapping could not be pure coincidence.

—❦—

With five people looking for one document, the library felt crowded, so I decided to pursue a line of inquiry of my own. I told Gaius I would be back in a few minutes. I guess he thought I was going to the latrina *because he didn't ask any questions. But I headed for the stables.*

Barbatus had been on this estate when the body was hidden in the wall, even before then. I knew Gaius didn't particularly like or trust the man and didn't want to have him raise questions by interrogating him, but I thought somebody ought to see if he had any information about what had happened then. Like Gaius, I found him overly inquisitive. Maybe, though, it was time to mine that source. I thought I might have better luck, approaching him as servant to servant, horse-lover to horse-lover.

My step quickened as soon as I heard a horse whinny. I found Barbatus grooming one of the animals, a roan mare.

"Well, missy," he said in his raspy voice, "what brings you back here?"

"When we were riding yesterday, I noticed my horse was favoring his left front leg. I thought we should take a look at it."

His eyes narrowed. "Oh, we should*? Has Gaius Pliny put you in charge of the stables now?"*

I was startled by his antagonism. He was always so officious around Gaius. "No. I love horses and was just concerned about that one. He's a fine animal."

Barbatus stroked his beard, which was much grayer than his brown hair and made it difficult to guess his age. "Which one?"

"The black one with the blaze on his face."

"The gelding?"

"Yes." Not unlike my husband, I thought and then scolded myself for being unkind.

Barbatus went to the corral where the other horses were penned and gave two sharp whistles. The black gelding perked up his ears and trotted over to the fence. Barbatus scratched him between the ears. "Missy here thinks there might be something wrong with you," he said. "I haven't noticed you limping, but I'm sure she knows better. Let's take a look."

"Do you have a different whistle for each horse?" I asked.

"They don't understand names, but they can learn to respond to their

own whistle." He stepped through the rails of the corral and lifted the horse's left front hoof. "I don't see anything lodged in the hoof."

"Maybe he bruised it on a rock. It could be better by now. I know he was favoring it yesterday."

Barbatus let go of the horse's hoof and stepped back through the rails of the fence. "Or it could be that you just made up an excuse to come out here." He stroked his beard slowly, menacingly. "What do you really want?"

There was no point in trying to keep up the pretense. "I was wondering what you might know about the body we found in the wall. You were here when that wall was built. Has anybody asked you what you know?"

"Nothing." He spat, barely missing my feet. "That's what I know about that body. Nothing. Why do you think I would know anything?"

"I'm not saying you had anything to do with his death. Not at all. I was just wondering if you recalled anything unusual that happened about then."

"That was when that scoundrel Delius tried to get my daughter to run off with him."

"Your daughter?" A name popped into my head. "Is Leucippe your daughter?" She was one of the older women servants on the estate. A woman with "horse" as part of her name had to be the daughter of a man who loved horses as much as Barbatus did.

He smiled. "Yes. You're a clever one, missy. She used to go to the market in Comum with my lady Plinia. That's where she met Delius. He was a freedman. He worked for a goldsmith there. He came out here a few times to see her. I hated him the first time I saw him. They thought they had their plans. He was going to buy her freedom, I'm betting with stolen money. But I wasn't about to let her run off with the likes of him."

"How did you stop him?"

"I didn't kill him and stuff him in that wall, if that's what you're thinking. He came to get her one day. My lord Caecilius was here with me and told me to deal with him however I saw fit. I gave him the beating he deserved—even knocked out a couple of his teeth—and sent him running off with his tail between his legs."

"Did somebody see him leave?"

"Yes, just ask Leucippe. She was screaming for me to stop."

"Leucippe is married to—"

"Nereus. He'd always fancied her, so I married her to him. He's a solid, reliable fellow. They've given me two grandchildren."

And I'll bet Leucippe is deliriously happy, I thought.

"May I ask about a couple of other things?"

"You may. That doesn't mean I'll answer."

"You found Caecilius' body, didn't you?"

"After he was trampled by a horse, yes."

"Did he often come into the stable?"

"Not often. One of the horses was ill. My lord Caecilius wanted to see about him." He shook his head slowly. "He never was as good with the animals as he thought he was."

"Did you see anything that might have made you think he had not been killed by the horse?"

"Do you mean, did somebody kill him and leave his body in the stall?" He twisted his mouth before he answered. "I was surprised. That particular horse had always been gentle. But he was standing right over the body."

"Was there any blood on the horse?"

"On one of his hoofs, yes. I remember wiping it off."

"All right. One more thing, if I may. Do you know anything about an old deserted villa a few miles south of here, back in the woods?"

"The Fox's Den? I've heard of it, but not in a long time."

"Why do you call it the Fox's Den?"

"That's what people used to call it. I guess because there's all sorts of animals that have taken it over, mostly a family of foxes. Nobody pays it any mind these days. I haven't heard anybody mention it in years."

"Do you know who owns it?"

Barbatus shook his head. "Like I said, didn't even know it was still standing. Now, missy, unlike you, I have work to do."

When I returned to the library, Julia raised her eyebrows in a question. "Sorry I took so long," I said. "I've been talking to Barbatus."

We stopped looking through my father's papers to listen to Aurora's report of her conversation with Barbatus. When she finished I sent Phineas to talk to the older servants in the house to see if any of them knew anything about the old villa.

"It seems to me," I said, "that there are several points that we need to connect. Livia was kidnapped near her uncle's villa. At least one of the servant women was taken to the old villa, the Fox's Den, if you will, before she was brought here. Tacitus and I were in Comum, and unfortunately, the story of the body in the wall got spread around there. Someone from Comum must have put that skull and the warning in the tree."

"They might even have been watching," Tacitus said, "to make sure we got it and nobody else did."

"That would mean somebody from Comum put it there, don't you think?"

"And not long before we got to the spot."

I slapped my hand on the table. "But because we don't know who heard about it in Lutulla's *taberna* and how far the story spread from there, we have no idea where to start looking. That's what makes me feel like one of those poor wretches who's thrown into the arena with a blindfold over his face and forced to fight enemies he can't see. What hope does he have?"

"But Livia's kidnapping," Aurora put in, "didn't happen anywhere near Comum. It happened when she was returning from Pompeius' villa, and Pompeius is still alive." She turned to me.

I sat back in surprise. "Are you suggesting that Livia's uncle could have kidnapped her?"

"Why not?" Julia said. "Men have been known to sell their children into slavery. What's a little kidnapping, especially if you didn't intend for anyone to get hurt."

"At this point," Aurora said diffidently, "I think we have to ask all sorts of questions, even the ones that make us most uncomfortable. If anyone knew about the true nature of your marriage, Gaius, they might think you were behind it."

"How can you suggest such a thing?" Julia asked.

Aurora leaned forward, as if to insist on her point. "The two girls who went with Livia could have said something. I've seen servants come into a house with a visiting master and try to impress everyone with a story. You have no idea what the conversation in the kitchen is like while you…you people are chatting in the garden."

"So someone in that house could have heard about the discovery within hours after it happened. We'll have to talk to Rhoda." I put my hand on Aurora's. "Would you find her and bring her here, please?"

As Aurora left the library, Tacitus gave a dismissive snort. "Pompeius can't be involved. He's in his sixties, at least. I can't see him riding around in a skull mask. And Rhoda said there were three men. They were strong enough to kill the driver and overpower Brennus and three women."

As much to defend Aurora as to keep the topic open, I said, "You're right. At his age Pompeius isn't likely to take an active part, so I agree that there are others involved—servants or hired thugs. Which just makes it that much more troubling. Not only do we have to ask *whom* we're dealing with but also how many. My father and Livius are dead, and yet someone is threatening us. We have to conclude that someone else is involved."

"But who?"

"We talked to Romatius' son and were met with the skull and a note on our way home. Livia visited her cousin Tertia—in the house of her father, Pompeius—and was kidnapped on her way home."

Tacitus sat up straighter. "Are you suggesting that Romatius and Pompeius have some connection to this business?"

"Not the younger Romatius, but I think his father might."

"Then it seems the next step is to talk to Pompeius," Julia said.

"I plan to do that as soon as I can get there. But first I want to talk to Rhoda."

"I hope she's calmed down enough now to answer your questions," Julia said. "Be gentle with her, Gaius. She was badly shaken by what happened."

While we waited for Aurora to return with Rhoda, we looked at the note again. "This was written by its author, don't you think, not dictated to a scribe."

Julia peered more closely at the parchment, running a finger over the letters. "What makes you say that?"

"To begin with, the ink was not evenly mixed. Notice the little lumps here and there." I picked up a letter off the table where my father's papers were scattered. "By comparison, look at how smooth the ink is on this letter. Scribes know how to make ink and to apply it evenly as they write."

Julia looked from one document to the other. "The letters in this note aren't the same size, and the spacing between them is uneven. Could the difference have something to do with the difference between papyrus and parchment?"

"I don't think so," I said. "The note is written the way I sometimes jot things down myself, if I don't have a scribe at hand."

"It's not exactly the sort of thing one would dictate to a scribe," Tacitus said.

"Unless the scribe was in on the plot."

A knock on the door was followed by Aurora escorting Rhoda into the room. The girl stopped just inside the door, with Aurora standing close to her. She had changed into a fresh gown and washed her face. There was no place for her to sit except for a stool in one corner. Aurora saw it and pulled it out, then stood behind me, since she couldn't sit beside me in the presence of another servant.

"How are you feeling now, Rhoda?" I asked.

"Better, my lord. My lady Pompeia has told me to rest for today."

"Good. This won't take long. I'd just like to ask you a few questions about your visit to Pompeius' house and the lady Tertia."

"Yes, my lord. I'll tell you anything I can, if it will help get my lady back." She rubbed at her eyes with a cloth, making them as red as her name.

"Did you or Procne say anything to anyone at that house about the body that was found in our wall?"

"Oh, no, my lord." Her eyes widened. "You told all of us not to say anything, and we didn't."

"That's good to know." *If it's true.*

"But, my lord…"

"Yes, is there something else?"

"It was my lady Livia, my lord." She wrung her hands. "She couldn't stop talking about it, about how awful it was."

"Who was she talking to?"

"First to her cousin, my lord, the lady Tertia."

"'First'? That implies someone else was second."

"Her uncle, Pompeius, came into the garden while they were talking, my lord. Then my lady Livia told the story all over again."

I tried not to show my surprise and anger. "How did Pompeius react? Did he say anything?"

"No, my lord. He listened for a bit. He seemed troubled, as anyone would, I guess, then he went back into the house."

"Why did my wife cut her visit short? You said there was some kind of argument."

"Yes, my lord. The lady Tertia told her she was tired of hearing about the skeleton, but my lady Livia kept coming back to it, or comparing things to it, especially when she saw the mosaic on the floor of the *triclinium*."

"What was so special about that?"

"It's a skeleton, my lord, a big skeleton."

Julia leaned toward the girl. "Is there anything else we should know?" I realized she was signaling for an end to the questioning.

"No, my lady. That's all I saw or heard." Rhoda drew a deep breath and exhaled with a sniffle, like someone who has been crying.

"Thank you, Rhoda," I said. "This has been helpful. You can go now."

"Do you want someone to go with you?" Julia asked.

"My friend Thais is waiting outside, my lady. She's been sitting with me."

"Good," Julia said. As Rhoda stood, Julia got up and embraced her.

Aurora opened the door and closed it behind Rhoda, then sat down beside me again.

"I can't believe that Pompeius kidnapped his own niece," I said, "but I suspect he knows something about whatever is behind all of this. I'm not quite sure, though, how to go about questioning him without seeming to accuse him."

"You can ask him if he has any idea who might have done it," Tacitus said. "You don't have to suggest that you see any connection between the kidnapping and the body in the wall."

"You could pay him a visit," Aurora said, "to talk about the kidnapping and ask for his help in finding Livia."

I nodded. "I certainly want to see his reaction when I tell him about the kidnapping."

"Pompeia has a good reason to visit her elderly brother under these circumstances," Aurora said, "with us to accompany her." She pointed to herself and Julia.

"No," I said quickly. "You women are not to get involved in this. These people are not playing a game. Do I need to remind you that they've killed a man already?"

Aurora touched the nick in her earlobe, a habit she has acquired when thinking. "It would be helpful to see with our own eyes how they react when they're told and not just have a disinterested servant's description."

"She's right," Julia said. "I think it's an excellent idea. You men never suspect that we women are capable of observing. Look at what Aurora learned from Barbatus. We can sense if there's anything odd in the air at Pompeius' house. Now, if your mother went with us—"

I stood up in alarm. "No! Absolutely not! Pompeia certainly has a legitimate reason for going over there, but I will not let you drag my mother into this mess."

Even on a nice day, a closed raeda gets very warm. I opened the small window over my head, but it didn't help. Julia said she would have let me ride with her, Plinia, and Pompeia in the other raeda—Pompeia's open one—but she knew Pompeia wouldn't stand for it. Only a servant like Naomi, who's practically a sister to her mistress, gets that privilege. And I can't ride a horse out in the fresh air, like Gaius and Tacitus and the men accompanying us. I'm crammed into this rickety old wagon with splinters in my bottom and six women—servants of Pompeia and Julia— whose names I barely know and who are only slightly less annoying than the splinters.

Maybe if I could get this hair off my neck...

As soon as I pulled my hair back, the girl sitting closest to me noticed the missing piece of my ear. Somebody always does. At least she didn't reach up and touch it, as some people do without even asking if I mind.

"What happened to your ear?" she asked.

"A man tried to attack me," I lied. Every time someone asks, I try to devise a new story. I've always loved Odysseus, that "man of many turns."

He had the scar on his leg. I wonder how many different ways he explained that.

"What happened to him?"

I leaned toward her, as if taking her into my confidence. "Let's just say he lost something a man would consider more valuable than a piece of his ear."

The girl's jaw dropped. "You're joking...aren't you?"

She edged away from me and all the chatter in the wagon trailed off. I knew I wasn't winning any friends, but I've never felt accepted among the other servants because of my mother's relationship with Gaius' uncle and now because others are aware of my friendship with Gaius. No one would hurt me or say anything to my face. Reprisal would come from Gaius, not me, but—

The wagon drew to a halt, jolting us into more intimate contact than any of us wanted.

"This is where Livia was kidnapped," I heard Gaius say. He was showing the spot to Pompeia and Plinia. So we were about half an hour from Tertia's house. It was actually Pompeius' house, I had gathered from the conversation as we were preparing to leave. Tertia's husband was serving on the staff of the governor of Baetica but she had stayed behind to take care of her ailing father. Although the third daughter, she was the only one who had lived to adulthood and survived childbirth, twice.

I rested a hand on my belly. How would I find the courage to tell Gaius that I was carrying his child? How would he react? I'm sure he would want to emancipate me and acknowledge the child. I could hardly imagine Livia's reaction. On the other hand, she's made it clear she's not going to give him a child....

"If any of you need to relieve yourselves," Gaius said, putting his head in the door at the back of the raeda, "this is your chance. We'll get underway again shortly."

The other women piled out of the wagon and headed into the woods on either side of the road. I got out, but just to stand and stretch. I've heard pregnant women talk about how often they have to pee, but I hadn't been affected in that way yet. Gaius looked down at me from his horse and mouthed, "I'm sorry." I patted his horse and managed to rub his leg.

The rest of the trip went by quickly enough. When we arrived and sorted ourselves out, I attached myself to Gaius, with the two men he had brought with him. I knew everybody wondered why I was here, since I wasn't a servant of any of the women.

Tertia's steward looked dismayed when twenty people landed on his doorstep. The baskets of food we brought with us seemed to ease the worry lines on his face. We hadn't brought any extra rooms or beds, though. I could have offered to share a bed with Gaius, just to save space, but I knew I would be crammed into a small room with two or three other women. Sitting right on the lake, the house was large by comparison with its neighbors, but nothing like our house in Rome, or even the villa at Laurentum.

The atrium was decorated with the types of frescoes one sees in any well-to-do Roman house. At regular intervals around the wall, though, were niches holding busts of members of the family, including several women. As we passed through into the garden, I noticed one, in an inconspicuous corner, of a woman identified as POMP PAUL.

"Why, Aunt Pompeia!" Tertia said as our company entered the garden where she was sitting, watching her two young boys toss a ball. "What a delightful surprise." She stood and scanned our faces. "Did cousin Livia come back with you?"

"That's why we're here, dear," Pompeia said dolefully.

"What do you mean?"

"I'm afraid Livia was kidnapped yesterday as she was leaving here."

"Kidnapped? By the gods!" Tertia clutched her sons closely to her. "Who—"

"That's what we're trying to find out," Gaius said.

"This is my son-in-law, Gaius Pliny," Pompeia said. "This is his friend, Cornelius Tacitus and his wife, Julia. And you know my cousin, Plinia."

"Of course," Tertia said, "although it has been a long time."

Plinia nodded and offered Tertia a quick embrace. "It's nice to see you again, my dear. And your handsome sons."

Tertia had the boys step forward. They were sturdy children, with the black hair that seemed to characterize this family. "This is Marcus. He's six. And this is Lucius. He's four."

"Pompeius is blessed to have lived to see his grandchildren," Plinia said, rubbing each boy on the shoulder. "Blessed indeed."

"We've come to tell Pompeius this difficult news about Livia," Pompeia said, "and to see if he can tell us anything that might help us find her."

"Well, I'm delighted to see you," Tertia said, "but my father isn't here."

"We need to talk to him." Gaius' voice took on a new urgency. "Where is he? When will he be back?"

"I'm afraid I can't answer either question, Gaius Pliny. He left sometime during the night while cousin Livia was here. One of our horses is gone. I don't know where he went or when he'll be back."

"He didn't say anything to anyone?"

"No. That's what's so odd. He didn't take anyone with him either. No one knew he was gone until the next morning."

"Weren't you worried?" I asked.

"It's not the first time he's done something like this. I suspect he's seeing some woman."

"I thought he was getting old and feeble," Pompeia said.

"Apparently not as feeble as he seemed to be," Tertia said. "He harnessed the horse and left without anyone hearing him."

X

Fortune is like glass—the brighter its glitter,
the more easily broken.

—Publilius Syrus

THERE'S NO WAY I can track him," Aurora said as she studied the whirlwind of hoofprints around the stable. "If we had
known he'd taken a horse, we could have kept ours out of here until
we examined the area. This is hopeless." In a soft voice she added, "I'm
sorry, Gaius."

"You don't have anything to apologize for. You can't do the impossible." I looked down the lane leading from the house to the main road.
Our arrival had obliterated any trace of hoofprints that might have
been left before Pompeius reached the paved main road. "Let's go back
to the house. I imagine dinner will be ready soon. We'll spend the night
and leave first thing in the morning."

"When we go back in," Aurora said, "take a look at the busts in the
atrium. I guess they're all members of the family."

"I would assume so."

"One of them is inscribed 'Pompeia Paulina.' Why would your
mother-in-law not want to talk about her?"

"As she said the other evening, there are people that you just don't
want to be related to. If you are, you'd like for everyone to forget it,
especially certain highly placed people."

"Her brother obviously didn't feel that way."

"I'll look into it. It could even be another woman by the same name
and not Seneca's wife."

139

I simply didn't know what to do. Staying here wasn't going to get me any closer to finding the document I needed to rescue Livia. Because Pompeius had bolted the way he did and when he did, I suspected that he knew something about the kidnapping or knew who did. Tertia claimed to have no idea where he might have gone. This was not her home. She had been here only a few months, since her husband left for his province, so she was not aware of her father's habits or his current associates. But I found it hard to imagine a man of his age carrying on with a woman.

We got back to the house as the women were finishing a quick bath. By the time Tacitus and I had walked around the atrium and then bathed, dinner—consisting mostly of the provisions we had brought—was ready. With only six of us reclining, the dining room offered plenty of space. Tertia, a very subdued Pompeia, and my mother occupied the high couch. I was given the guest of honor's position on the middle couch, with Tacitus and Julia reclining above me. I noticed the other servant women glancing oddly at Aurora as she took her place behind me and resolved to ask her what that was about.

Conversation around the *triclinium* was desultory. I didn't want to bring up the subject of Pompeia Paulina again in front of my mother-in-law. Tertia had told us everything she could about Pompeius' business dealings, which was nothing. Their scribe was supposed to be looking through Pompeius' records to see if he could find any reference to a *collegium* involving my father or a sealed document that my father might have left with Pompeius. I held out little hope that he would. We had all expressed our dismay over Livia's kidnapping, so there was nothing new to be said about that.

As a rule I don't drink heavily at dinner, but tonight so many things were wrong that I wanted to plunge into a bowl of wine and just forget all the unsolvable problems and unanswerable questions facing me. It didn't help that the wine was a very good Chian.

The only topic of conversation left seemed to be the décor in the *triclinium*. That would have been unexceptional—garden scenes on the walls and a mosaic on the floor—had it not been for the subject of the mosaic. As Rhoda had told us, it was a human skeleton, but she had not known what she was looking at. The skeleton was decked out in a regal robe and wore the crown of the goddess Tyche/Fortuna. A meander pattern ran around the edge. Over the skeleton's head was a quotation from Horace: "Fortune makes fools of those she favors too much."

"Who designed the floor?" I asked Tertia.

"My father."

"Blame my bluntness on this excellent wine, but I've never seen Fortuna portrayed in so gruesome a fashion. And the quotation from Horace isn't the sort of uplifting apothegm people usually put in a decoration like this."

"My father is very fatalistic," Tertia said, "about daily life and about life in general."

"He's always been that way," Pompeia said, "since we were children. He used to say, 'Fortune has us by the balls, and can give us a squeeze when we least expect it.' Of course, he is thinking of just you men."

"That's still his favorite expression," Tertia said ruefully. "He wanted to have it worked into this mosaic floor, but Mother persuaded him to use that quotation from Horace instead."

"Your mother always did have better sense than your father," Pompeia said. "And I can say that because he is my own dear brother."

My mother crooked her head over her shoulder to hear something that Naomi had to say, then turned back to the rest of us. "Naomi tells me there's a phrase in one of the Jewish holy books, by a man named Isaiah, that says, 'Let us eat and drink, for tomorrow we die.'"

"Was this Isaiah a gladiator?" Tacitus asked. "I've heard gladiators say pretty much the same words at their feasts the night before a bout. And Petronius has Trimalchio display a silver skeleton to the guests at his dinner in the *Satyricon*. The thing is strung together so he can flop it around like a child's doll. He recites a little ditty about it.... Oh, how does it go?"

From behind me Aurora said, "Forgive me, my lord, but I can quote it."

"Please do."

Aurora stood like a student reciting before a class. "He says,
  'What a pitiful little wretch is man.
  We'll all be thus under death's hand.
  So let's live well, while live we can.'"

"Yes, exactly," Tacitus said, applauding. "I knew it was something cheerful and uplifting like that." He raised his cup in a toast. "I guess it's a universal sentiment."

"And a universal fate," I muttered to myself. But I wasn't ready to surrender Livia to it. I drained my cup, sat up, and handed it to Aurora to refill.

She gave it back to me half-full with a disapproving look and, as she bowed her head to me, whispered, "Getting drunk isn't going to solve anything, my lord."

I drained the cup in a gulp and pushed it back into her hands.

The next morning I was awakened by a pounding on my door, which was in rhythm with the pounding in my head.

"Gaius," Tacitus said through the thick wood, "we need to get going. We're waiting for you in the stable."

It took me a moment to recall that we had decided after dinner the previous evening that Tacitus, Aurora, and I would ride back to my villa. The key to saving Livia was a document of my father's, and we weren't going to find that at Pompeius' house. Since Pompeius himself wasn't around, there was no point in spending any more time here. My mother, Pompeia, Julia, and the servants would stay on here for a couple of more days to visit. It would be a relief to me to have them out of the way for that time.

I used a chamber pot, decided yesterday's tunic was clean enough, and stumbled out to the stable.

"You look awful," Tacitus said. "Are you going to be able to stay on a horse?"

I blinked a couple of times and looked in Aurora's direction. "I just might need some assistance." To me my voice seemed to slur.

Julia gave Tacitus a lingering kiss before a servant helped him mount.

I moved close to Julia and lowered my voice. "You agreed that you would try to find out anything you can about Pompeius' activities. Do it when my mother-in-law isn't around."

She pulled away from me and looked up at her husband. I realized the wine must still be noticeable on my breath.

"Sometimes," I reminded Julia without getting any closer to her, "people reveal more in a casual conversation than under direct questioning. Just keep your ears open." I stepped on the mounting stone and got a boost from the servant.

"See if he has a personal favorite among the servant women," Tacitus said without looking at Aurora or me.

"Well yes, that, too," I said, settling on my horse and extending my hand to pull Aurora up behind me, to the surprise of the stable boy who was helping us. "If Pompeius returns or you learn where he might be, send a servant to notify me at once. And tell him not to spare the horse."

My mother and Pompeia appeared at the edge of the stable yard. Pompeia's mouth fell open at the sight of Aurora on my horse, with her arms clasped tightly around me.

"We'll see you ladies in a few days," I said with a wave of my hand.

My mood was no less morose than it had been at dinner last night—how could it be, if we were no closer to finding Livia?—but having Aurora's arms around me and her body pressed against mine did make the day seem more bearable.

"You know," Aurora said in my ear, "after seeing us like this, Pompeia probably suspects that you had Livia kidnapped."

I grunted. "I won't deny that the idea has crossed my mind. I will deny that I would ever do it. We shouldn't be punished for what we think."

I hate to see Gaius so troubled that he resorts to wine. I held him tightly and put my head on his shoulder. "I haven't had a chance to tell you what Eustachius, the quarry owner, told me about building the wall in your house."

"What does he know about it?"

"He was in charge of the work. He said your father stood over his crew during the last two days, almost like he was one of the workers. They missed a day's work because of a storm."

"The storm that drowned Livius."

"I'm sure it was. But your father insisted they finish the work right away."

"Because he didn't want anyone to discover what was in the wall."

"That doesn't mean he killed the man."

Gaius still wasn't convinced. *"But, if he didn't, he must have known who the man was and who did kill him. And he must have consented to having the body hidden in the wall. He is complicit, if not actually guilty of murder. That must be what my mother meant."*

When we rode into the stable yard of my house, I was surprised to see my largest *raeda* from the house in Rome sitting to one side. Barbatus was brushing down the horses that must have pulled it, speaking softly to them, almost crooning. One horse was munching a carrot.

"When did this arrive?" I asked him.

"Less than an hour ago, my lord."

"Who came in it?"

"A girl named Xenobia, my lord. Your man Phineas seemed awfully glad to see her."

"That was quick," Tacitus said. "Like winged steeds."

"Yes, my lord. But they don't have wings, so it was very hard on the horses." He turned to me. "So is riding two on a horse, if I may say so, my lord."

"You may not," I snapped, my head still throbbing. Aurora slid off the horse and held the reins while I dismounted, rather clumsily. "I wonder why she used this."

"Full of boxes it was, my lord," Barbatus said. "Don't know where they expect me to put it now."

"Boxes? Of what?" Tacitus said, dismounting in one fluid motion. "Your mother wouldn't need a wagon this large to move, Gaius. How many dresses can a servant have?"

"Not dresses, my lord. Books. Boxes and boxes full of books. Heavy boxes." He patted one of the horses on the neck.

"What? I didn't tell her to bring any books," I said. "Is she in the house now?"

"I believe so, my lord. They was taking the boxes to the library."

We headed straight for the library, with Aurora trailing respectfully behind us, and heard the excited chatter of a man and a woman. Phineas and Xenobia. I expected to find them unpacking scrolls from a box, but they were going over my father's personal papers. They stepped back from the table when we entered.

"Good day, my lord," Phineas said.

"Good day, my lord." Xenobia bowed. "Thank you for bringing me here. I will do my best to justify your confidence."

I didn't tell her that decision was based more on sympathy for Phineas than on an estimate of her abilities. Xenobia was of average height for a woman but, looking at her now from a different perspective, I thought a little plumper than I would find attractive. Her face was full, her makeup a bit too heavy. But perhaps my judgment has been clouded by comparing every woman I meet to Aurora. I hoped I wasn't as giddy around Aurora as Phineas was now. She clearly returned his affection.

"I need some explanation," I said.

"I just did what your letter said, my lord." Xenobia's smile faded.

"Let me explain, my lord," Phineas said.

"Oh, I fully expect you to explain."

When Phineas gets nervous he speaks rapidly and begins to stutter. "You see, m-my lord, I g-gave Xenobia a list of b-books to bring to improve the library here, including all of your uncle's w-works. It was in the letter that you sealed, along with instructions to b-bring the large *raeda*."

"I gave instructions for that?"

He took deep breaths, gulping the air to calm himself, a technique I've seen him use before. "Yes, my lord. You said for her to bring...whatever b-books I thought necessary to improve the library here. I didn't want to...bother you with details. It was all in the letter. I thought you w-would read it, but you didn't. You just sealed it."

"What else was in there? Did I emancipate her? Name you as my heir?" I gestured as though I was really angry. In fact I was having trouble not laughing at myself and the situation, if I could find humor in anything right now.

Phineas' face turned as red as his hair. "No, my lord, of course not."

No harm had been done, and I didn't want to embarrass him any further in front of his beloved. In future, though, I would have to be more cautious about what I put my seal on, even if it was presented to me by someone I trusted.

"Are you still looking through my father's papers? We went over them quite thoroughly yesterday. Don't waste your time."

"I thought it might be helpful, my lord, to have a fresh set of eyes look at things," Phineas said. "Xenobia has noticed something curious."

I turned my attention to the girl, who could not conceal her eagerness to atone for Phineas' overreaching. "What have you found?"

"I'm not sure, my lord." She picked up a piece of papyrus from the pile in front of her and handed it to me. "It was rolled up inside a scroll. It seems to be some sort of agreement about a loan and interest."

"Interest?"

"Yes, my lord. It's signed by Caecilius—your father, I assume—with his seal at the bottom and by a Pompeius and a Romatius, who also put their seals on it. Do you know them?"

I nodded as I read over the agreement, which took up only a single sheet of papyrus. "It says they agree to pay a tidy sum in interest to Caecilius and his heirs in perpetuity."

Tacitus took the document from me and read it. "But it doesn't mention the amount of the loan or its purpose."

"And I wonder why Livius wasn't part of the deal," I said. "They were partners in other ventures."

"Yes, my lord," Phineas said. "We've found some other contracts, and they were always signed by the four of them."

"The date on this one is after the time Livius died," Tacitus noted.

"Get Decimus and bring him in here," I told Phineas. As he left, I turned to Xenobia. "Since you'll be working here, you should know that my steward also handles the accounts for this estate. Decimus, and his father before him, have had that position for almost thirty years now." On my other, larger, estates, I have a servant whose primary responsibility is to keep the accounts, but this estate isn't large enough to warrant that division of duties.

"Yes, my lord."

When Decimus entered the library, I told him who Xenobia was and what her duties would be.

"A woman as our scribe, my lord? That will be...unusual." He might as well have said "unthinkable."

"Phineas will be coming up here at regular intervals to oversee her work."

"Very well, my lord."

"She's had good training." I don't know why I felt like I had to argue a case. I was the master. All I had to do was to give the order and it was done. "And she's already brought something to my attention." I showed him the document Xenobia had found. "Do you know anything about a loan that my father made to Pompeius and Romatius?"

"Not much, my lord. My father told me that your father had told him to expect this sum from these men every year. He understood that there was some kind of written agreement, but he never saw it. Nor have I. I've sometimes wondered what I would do if they didn't pay, but they always do. They're honorable men."

Or frightened men, I thought. I dropped the piece of papyrus back on the table. "That money is what makes the difference between profit and loss for this estate, isn't it?"

"Yes, my lord. I'm sorry to say that the production from the estate is marginal at best. It's been that way for years."

I could almost hear him thinking, *If you paid more attention to the place, you would know that.*

"Once we get Livia back," I said, "I intend to make some changes. The people I've brought in from Tuscany should have some ideas about how to improve the crops, especially the vines. I'm going to talk to Pompeius and Romatius about this loan. If they're legally obligated— and this document says they are—I'll expect them to continue to pay, but I don't want the estate's profit to depend on something like this."

"No, my lord, of course not. Is there anything else I can help you with?"

I dismissed him and turned back to Xenobia and Phineas. "Have you found anything that might be the document I'm supposed to find? It's written on a piece of parchment and sealed with the sign of a skull." I picked up the seal I had removed in one piece from the first warning we received and showed it to them. "Like this, I believe."

Xenobia shuddered. "That's someone's seal, my lord? It's hideous."

"I think it was used only to make an impression on particular occasions. I'm not certain that what I'm looking for will even be here."

"We'll look through everything again, my lord," Xenobia said.

"If you find any sealed documents, don't open them," I said. "Let me do that."

"Certainly, my lord," Phineas said.

"At some point I'll talk to Pompeius about this," I said, "but now I'm focused only on getting Livia back."

"We would expect nothing else, my lord," Xenobia said. "It's obvious to all of us how much you love her."

So young and already a mistress of sarcasm and double meaning. Or perhaps she really couldn't divine my true feelings. Yet, Aurora assures me that I'm not very good at hiding them.

"What are we going to do?" I asked Tacitus. "I feel like one of the daughters of Danaus, ordered to carry water in a sieve. I can't do it. How can I do it? We must talk to Pompeius, but no one knows where he is. What if he's gone for three or four days? We don't have that much time. The only thing that could save us would be for Pompeius to show up at my door just now."

Tacitus chuckled. "That only happens in a badly contrived play, when the author has written himself into a corner that he can't get out of."

We were standing outside, near the spot where the wall in my garden—the place where all the trouble had started—was being torn down. Half of it was gone, and the trench that outlined the new wall had been dug. Some of the blocks removed from the wall were already in place in the trench. The workmen had finished for the day.

"At least you haven't found any more surprises in this wall," Tacitus said.

I pointed to the two men coming toward us across the garden—my steward Decimus and Livia's uncle. "That's Pompeius," I told Tacitus.

Tacitus laughed out loud. "By the gods!"

Decimus and Pompeius stopped with the wall between us. I couldn't have been more surprised if Livia herself had appeared at the door. Because of his height Pompeius had no trouble talking to us over the wall.

"Have you learned anything?" Pompeius asked without any more formal greeting than a nod. "Do you know where Livia is?"

"I might ask you the same thing," I said.

"Me? How would I know? I just got back to my own house an hour ago and was told about the kidnapping. I got a fresh horse and came here immediately."

His unshaven face, shaggy gray hair, and dirty tunic lent truth to his story. He was certainly elderly, but I wouldn't have described him as feeble. "Where have you been?" I asked.

He hung his head, then looked back up. "I went to see a woman."

"What woman?"

"A woman with whom I've had a…long-standing…connection."

"Why did you leave when you did, so late at night?"

"I didn't want to appear rude to my niece and my sister, but they annoyed me so much I had to get away from them for a while. They are two of the most disagreeable women I've ever known. I still can't believe Pompeia found not one, but two, men who were willing to marry her. I waited until they were in bed so they couldn't say anything."

"Didn't your daughter think there was anything unusual about you leaving?"

"She knows that I sometimes go off for a couple of days, and she knows not to ask any questions. Now, is there anything I can do to help you find Livia?"

Which meant, I was sure, that he wasn't going to answer any more of my questions. But why was he here? Was he brazen enough to kidnap his niece, then appear at my house full of concern for her? Was he trying to keep tabs on our inquiries, to learn what we knew? Or was he making a genuine offer of assistance?

"Your mother said there was a note. It gives you only a couple of days to turn something over to the kidnappers. May I see it?"

I had either to play along with whatever dramatic scene he was staging or accuse him of the crime to his face. "Come with me," I said.

I hoisted myself over the wall, led Pompeius to my room, and unlocked the box in which I was keeping the note. The bones from the wall, along with the skull we had encountered on our way back from Comum, were in the larger box Aurora and Julia had brought out. I decided not to mention them, or the note we had found with the skull, or the items we had picked up at the old villa—all of which were also in my locked box. If Pompeius knew about those items, he might say something that would give him away. If he didn't know about them, he didn't need to at the moment.

He took the kidnappers' note and stepped out into the garden, where the light was better. Looking up from the note, he said, "And you have no idea what they want or where it is?"

"None whatsoever. If I did, I would hand it over and be done with this whole business."

Pompeius nodded. "I would expect nothing less from you."

I couldn't tell if he was reassuring himself or considering a threat. "In looking through my father's papers, I have found a note with your seal and Romatius' on it, promising to pay interest on a loan. Are you still paying that interest?"

"Yes."

"But my father has been dead for years."

"He loaned Romatius and me a great deal of money to make an investment. The interest was to be paid to his estate after he died."

"What was the investment for?"

"For us to buy some property. Your father didn't want to own the property, but he was generous enough to help us buy it."

"Where is—"

"On the other side of the lake. Gaius Pliny, as long as the interest is paid, none of the other details concern you. And the interest is being paid. Now I need to get back to my family. As you can well imagine, they are deeply distressed. I'm going to take some of my men and see if I can find Livia. We know this area better than you do."

As he walked away, I called after him, "What do you know about a deserted villa a few miles from here, deep in the woods?"

He stopped and seemed to gather himself before he turned around. "Just that there is a deserted villa in the woods. Why do you ask?"

"We found evidence that at least one of the women who was kidnapped was taken there."

"Not Livia?"

"Apparently not. Do you know who owns that place?"

"No, I don't." He turned toward the front of the house before I could ask anything else.

"I told you we'd never get Gaius into a boat," Tacitus said as we shoved off to cross Lake Comum. "I'm none too fond of the idea myself, but if you think it will let us learn something, I'll go."

I settled myself into the front of the small craft as Tacitus unfurled the sail. "The only thing we learned from Pompeius that we didn't already know," I said, "was that he and Romatius bought property on the other side of the lake. It may have something to do with the body in the wall. We don't have much time, so we need to explore as many possibilities as we can. Gaius can examine the bones while we do this."

"How do you expect to identify a piece of property after all these years?"

"I don't think it was property as in land. That's why I asked you to bring those things you found at the old villa."

The breeze was light but brisk enough to keep us moving and make the boat bob in the water. I've never had any problem about getting sick in a boat, so I was surprised when I began to feel my stomach fluttering. I tried to ignore it until the feeling got so strong I had to lean over the side and vomit.

"Is there anything I can do for you?" Tacitus asked from behind me.

"No, thank you. I've been feeling nauseous the last few days." I put a hand on my belly, a gesture I find myself making more and more often. It's so incredible to me that I'm carrying Gaius' child.

Tacitus gave me a paternal smile. "When are you going to tell Gaius?"

"What? Did Julia—"

"No. She was sick a lot when she was carrying our child."

"I just don't know how he'll take it. I know how Livia will take it, but I don't know what Gaius will say or do."

"Do you know how long—"

"I've missed two monthlies."

"It won't be long before he, and everyone else, will be able to see what's happening, you know."

I took a deep gulp of the crisp air. "I know. It will have to be soon. Have you ever fathered a child that lived?" For some reason, the solitude or the bright sun, something made me bolder.

"None that I know of. Admittedly, I could have planted a seed here and there. I do hope Julia and I will be able to have a child who survives. People of our class seem to lose so many children these days."

"And then some bastards take young ones to that villa." I placed a protective hand on my belly.

"Do you think what was going on there has anything to do with the body we found in the wall?"

"The children had to come from somewhere. Livius made frequent trips across the lake, for some purpose that no one seems to understand. What if he was buying young boys?"

"Then I hope it took him a long time to drown. But you're suggesting that Gaius' father provided funds for Pompeius and Romatius and Livius to bring boys to the villa."

I nodded.

"But the agreement we saw was signed after Livius' death."

"True, but Livius was the one making trips back and forth across the lake. Something over there is tied into the villa, I'm sure. And one of the kidnappers took Rhoda to that villa. However tenuous it may be, I think that's a connection worth investigating."

The old town of Comum, now reduced to a village, had no dock, so we pulled the boat up on the shore and walked a short distance to the main street of the little town. Tacitus, with his height and his equestrian stripe, drew people to the doors of the few shops along the street. I took the mask from the villa out of the bag I was carrying and asked if anyone knew what it was. All I got was heads shaking.

We had passed one shop when somebody jumped Tacitus and knocked him down. "You can't take me back! I won't let you!" he shouted.

"We're not going to hurt you!" I cried. "We just want to talk."

Tacitus managed to subdue him. "Come on," I said, "let's sit down. Nobody's going to hurt you."

When we were settled in what proved to be his parents' shop and home, I took a closer look at him. He was about my age, with hair almost Germanic-blond and a face that could have been copied from a statue of

Adonis. His hands shook as his mother handed him and us some wine to drink.

"You're one of the boys who was taken to the villa, aren't you?" I said.

"Yes. My name is Gaius Fulvius. This is my mother, Porcia. My parents had nothing. They sold me to a man named Catulus. At least that's what he said his name was."

"I cried over him every night," his mother said. "But we had no choice. Please understand that."

"I know parents sometimes find themselves in that position," I said. "We want to find out as much as we can about that villa and who was there."

When her son didn't respond, Porcia said, "He won't talk about it. He showed up here one day, after he'd been gone for two years, but he won't tell us anything."

"We know what happened there," I said.

"You don't know what happened there," Fulvius said, rising halfway out of his seat. "You can't know unless you were there."

"We know what you were forced to do," Tacitus put in. "We've seen the frescoes."

That seemed to reassure Fulvius, I wanted his mother to leave us alone, but the living quarters behind the shop consisted of one room.

"We just want to know who was there," I said, "not any details about who did anything to you."

"I don't know who was there. They all wore masks like the one you have. The only person I knew by name was Lucius."

"Who was he?" I doubted that was his real name, considering that Livius had called himself Catulus.

"He lived at the villa and looked after the boys there. He wasn't what you'd call kind, but he kept the men from doing some of the worst things they wanted to do to us. When no men were there, he fed us and tried to get us to play like normal boys, but we had little interest in doing so. He carved toys for us."

"Like this?" I took the wooden ox out of the bag.

"Yes, that's one of his. He was quite good. He carved the masks."

"How did you get out of there?" Tacitus asked. I could sense that Fulvius wasn't comfortable talking to a man, but I couldn't tell Tacitus to stop interfering.

Fulvius sighed deeply. "One night another man came to the villa and told Lucius that Nero had been killed. We weren't sure who Nero was or what that meant. The man said armies were marching toward Rome. He was frightened. What if they found the villa? Lucius told the man he would take care of things and sent him away. Then he told us to get our clothes and come with him."

"How many of you were there?" I asked.

"There were six of us in the villa then. He led us through the woods to the lake and found a boat. He got us across and pointed us in the direction of our homes. 'That's all I can do,' he said. 'I'm sorry it can't be more.' Then he sailed back across the lake."

"Are any of the other boys still around here?" I asked.

He shook his head. "A couple of them didn't even come home when we got off the boat. I can't say I blame them, since their parents had sold them. A couple of the others have died recently. As far as I know, I'm the only one left."

"Were any other boys ever brought back over here?"

"No. While I was there, some of the boys got too old, and that man Catulus came and said he was going to take them back home, I've never found anybody over here who knows of a boy who came back. Do you know what happened to them?"

I knew from Tacitus' glower that he was suspecting the same thing I was. Livius was killing the older boys and dumping their bodies in the lake. Maybe one of them fought back and caused his boat to capsize. That would make the boy a hero in my eyes. "No, I'm sorry, Fulvius. We don't know," I said.

XI

Nothing is more dangerous to men than
a sudden change of fortune.

—Quintilian

I WAS AWAKENED BY A tumult of noise—someone pounding, on a door perhaps, others shouting. People seemed to be running. Aurora sat up beside me, her hand and her chin on my shoulder, as a heavy knock sounded on the door of my room.

"My lord," Felix said through the door, "there's something you need to see."

Slipping on a tunic, I opened the door slightly and put my head out. It was still pitch dark. Lamps flickered here and there in the garden. "What is it?"

"It's Brennus, my lord. He's at the back gate."

"Brennus? Is he all right?"

"Bruised and scratched, my lord, but otherwise unharmed. Decimus was going to come get you, but I volunteered because I thought..."

"Yes, of course. I'll be right there." I closed the door. "Wait a few moments," I told Aurora, kissing her quickly. "Once everybody is away from here, you can slip out. Just don't let anyone see you." She nodded and I joined Felix in the garden. "What's going on? How did he get here?" The image of Rhoda trussed up and dumped at my door hadn't faded yet.

"He managed to escape, my lord, and make his way back here. I'll let him tell you the story."

Brennus was sitting on the ground just inside the back gate. I was

155

glad to see everyone moving in that direction, many of them carrying lamps. Aurora would be able to get out of my room without anyone noticing where she had been. Decimus and Barbatus stood over Brennus, who was wearing a slave's manacles. His hands were fastened behind his back and a chain ran down to leg irons which gave him only limited movement. From the bruises and scrapes on his face, I could tell he had fallen during his escape or been maltreated by his captors.

Barbatus had a hammer and a chisel. As I approached, he popped the manacles off Brennus' wrists and began to work on the irons on his ankles. When he saw me, Brennus tried to stand.

"Steady, man," Barbatus said. "If you keep moving around, I'm likely to slip and take your foot off."

"It's all right," I assured Brennus. "Stay where you are. What happened? How did you get here? Is Livia all right?"

"Yes, my lord, she is. And so is Procne, but they're in chains, just like these. The fellow who was supposed to take his turn guarding us tonight fell asleep. I knew I couldn't get the women out without waking the guard, so I decided to make my break and get help."

"You were fortunate that you were awake."

"I kept myself awake by pressing on the manacles until it hurt, my lord. I thought there might be a chance the man would fall asleep."

"Is there only one?"

"There are two, my lord, but they were taking turns guarding us. The other one had gone to get some supplies."

Tacitus had now joined the circle around Brennus. Out of the corner of my eye I saw Aurora hanging back on the fringe of the group.

"I thought you were attacked by three men," Tacitus said.

The leg irons fell off and Brennus got to his feet, stretching his stiff limbs. "We were, my lord, but we've not seen the third man since we were taken off. It's just been the two. The third man rode off with Rhoda."

"Where are they?" I asked.

"In a shepherd's hut, my lord."

"Can you find it again?"

"I'm sure I can, my lord."

"How did you find your way here in the dark?"

"As you know, my lord, I have a very keen nose. I've been called a son of a bitch for that reason, as well as others. When we were carried off, they were short one horse. I was tied up and forced to walk behind them. I paid attention to any plants we passed. This time of year, at the height of summer, there are many scents in the air. When I escaped, I followed what I could see and what I could smell back to the road and then up to here."

"Didn't your captors blindfold you?" Tacitus asked.

"No, my lord. They wore masks, hideous skull-like things, so they didn't bother to blindfold us."

"You've acted very bravely," I said. "I'll see to it that you're rewarded."

"Thank you, my lord. Let's just get my lady back. I'm ashamed that I wasn't able to protect her in the first place."

"I'm sure you did all you could."

"It'll be light in an hour or so," Tacitus said. "Let's get some men and horses ready to go after these bastards."

"My lord," Brennus said, "I think a large force might frighten them into doing something drastic. They're acting on someone else's orders. I'm sure of that. They don't seem to be vicious men."

"They killed the driver," Tacitus pointed out.

"He lashed one of them with his whip, my lord. Until then I don't think they meant to hurt anyone. They haven't harmed my lady Livia or Procne, but I'm not sure how they'll react if they're attacked."

I took Brennus' advice to heart. As soon as it was light, Tacitus, Aurora and I got ready to set off with him to find the kidnappers. I felt Aurora's tracking skills might be as useful as Brennus' nose. We also took Grillus, the freedman who serves as the estate's doctor, because I was afraid someone might get hurt if it came to a confrontation. As Brennus had said, these men would strike if provoked.

Just before we mounted, Aurora took me aside. "Do you think this is wise, Gaius, to go with so small a number? You're letting Brennus determine how we proceed. How do you know he's not leading you into some kind of trap?"

"Brennus has been in my household since he was a child, just like you. He came here a few days ago. He doesn't know anyone here. How could he be involved?"

"I don't know. It just seems his escape is…convenient."

I knew better than to disregard Aurora's instincts and suspicions. "We'll be extremely cautious. Are you armed?"

"Always, my lord." Aurora patted her thigh at the spot where she carries the knife I gave her, strapped under her gown.

"What's your plan, Gaius?" Tacitus asked.

"It will depend on what we find when we get to the hut. I suspect the kidnappers will move somewhere else when they find Brennus gone."

"I'd bet on it. They'll know that he'll lead a rescue party back to the place."

As we rode, Brennus pointed out places where he had fallen the night before. With his ankles chained and his hands fastened behind him, I was amazed he had been able to move at all. We passed the spot where Livia and her party had been seized. About a quarter mile farther down the road Brennus signaled for us to stop.

"We turned into the woods here, my lord." It was the spot where Aurora had said the kidnappers rode into a stream. "If I may, I'll lead on foot so I can pick up the scents I need to follow. The horses will mask the smells of the plants." We held the reins of his horse as Brennus advanced ahead of us, raising his head and turning it from side to side.

"It's like following a two-legged dog," Tacitus whispered to me as we rode behind him.

Half an hour later Brennus raised his hand to stop us. We dismounted and walked quietly to where he was standing on the edge of the woods. In front of us was a pasture, overgrown because no one had kept sheep in it for some time. A few small trees had sprouted here and there. About twenty paces off to our right stood a small windowless hut, made of mud wattle with a thatched roof. Near the door was a spot where a fire, presumably for cooking, was still smoldering.

"That's it," Brennus said, "but I think they're gone. I don't see any horses."

With swords drawn, Tacitus and I crept up to the hut, but Brennus was right. The door was open, showing how empty the place was. We stood in the doorway and surveyed the room. On one side of it sat a small table and a rickety chair.

"What's that?" Tacitus said, raising his sword to point at something on the table.

In the dim interior I couldn't make out what the object was until I stood right over it. Then I gasped. "By the gods, it's a finger! Somebody's little finger."

"Whose do you think it is?" Tacitus asked.

I regarded the finger with horror, trying not to think about the agony a woman had endured here, but I could almost hear the screams still echoing around the hut. "It's long and slender, so it must have come from Procne." Although Livia and I had rarely touched one another, I knew how short and pudgy her fingers were. "The blood isn't completely dry, so the injury was quite recent, probably only an hour or two ago."

"You were prescient to bring Grillus along," Tacitus said. "Procne will need some care when we find her."

The finger wasn't the only thing on the table. Someone had taken soot from the fireplace and written on the table, in barely literate Latin: IF YOU FOLLOW US WE CUT OFF MORE.

"The writing is different from the note that was pinned to Rhoda's dress," I said. "Whoever wrote that was an educated person. This, I think, was written by the underlings who are actually holding Livia."

"They've panicked and fled," Tacitus said. "Now how do we find them? Brennus' nose isn't going to do us any good."

"They headed south, my lord," Aurora said from the doorway behind us, "across the pasture, and not long ago."

When I turned to her, I took in a breath and had to collect myself. The sun behind her gave her an aura like a goddess. "Can you...can you track them?" I asked.

She stepped into the hut and broke the spell. "It should be easy enough. People in a hurry leave plenty of traces. And I've seen bloodstains." She saw the finger for the first time and gasped. "Oh, dear gods, so that's why. Somebody was bleeding pretty badly, I'm afraid. They didn't take time to wrap the wound. I don't think they're too far ahead of us."

As we mounted our horses Brennus said, "One of the men kept saying he wished they had hidden in the cave instead of this place. He always said it like it was a place they knew, 'the cave.'"

"Eustachius' quarry is in that direction, my lord," Aurora said, pointing southeast. "That seems a likely place to find a cave."

The high grass in the meadow made tracking the kidnappers' horses so easy even I could see where they had been. It became more difficult when we entered the woods on the other side of the opening, but Aurora did not seem to be deterred. In a short time she led us to the far edge of the woods.

Putting a finger to her lips, she said, "There's a bloodstain over there. They dismounted here and went off in that direction, leading their horses. We're at the edge of an abandoned part of the quarry, to judge from the way it's overgrown. Eustachius told Felix and me that they have stopped working some of it. There must be a trail down over the ledge."

Leaving our horses with Brennus, we followed Aurora to a trail that, as she had predicted, led over a cut in the ledge and down into the quarry. It was narrow; leading a horse down it must have been difficult. Trees and bushes grew up in the cracks left where stone had been cut.

"Watch the droppings," Aurora said as we started down, single-file. "They're fresh. So is that bloodstain." She pointed to a smear on the rocks beside us. "I suspect someone was trying to leave a trail."

The neighing of a horse brought us to a stop.

"That sounds close," I said.

"The animal is in a cave." Aurora dropped to one knee. "I think they're just around that outcropping."

"What's our plan of attack?" Tacitus asked.

"I wish we could get somebody behind them," I said, "but even if there is another entrance to the cave, who knows how long it would take us to find it. We'll just have to rely on surprise and superior numbers."

"But they have hostages," Tacitus said.

"That's why we have to act quickly."

Drawing my sword, I took the lead now, with Tacitus right behind me. The trail broadened into a ledge and we could hear several horses snuffling. Ahead of us a cave opened. Motioning Tacitus to a halt, I crept forward until I could look around the rocks and into the cave, which was about the size of the atrium in a typical house, but with a low enough ceiling that a man could barely stand in it. Two men, wearing skull masks with open mouths like the masks worn by tragic actors, sat next to a fire, the only source of light in the cave. The horses were tied up behind them.

On the other side of the fire Livia and Procne huddled together, still in chains and gagged. Procne, moaning and sobbing softly, clutched her hand against the bosom of her gown, which was now a splotchy red. The flickering light playing on Livia's face showed her fear. She was close to tears but tried to comfort Procne, clanking the chains on her wrists. I didn't know she was capable of such tenderness.

"Be quiet over there," one of the men growled, picking up a small rock and throwing it at Livia, as though she were a bothersome dog. It struck her in the face.

That's one more thing you'll pay for, I thought.

At my signal Tacitus advanced and crouched beside me. Aurora and Grillus stayed behind us. Grillus did not look comfortable with a sword in his hand. Brennus might have been a better choice for a fight, but, knowing someone was injured, I had to bring Grillus down here.

I stood up and stepped into the opening of the cave, with Tacitus on my left and Aurora and Grillus behind us but in view. "Drop your weapons!" I ordered the kidnappers.

Both men jumped. One of them raised his hands, but the one who had thrown the rock grabbed Livia by the hair. She let out a muffled yelp.

"I think it's you that'll be dropping your weapons," the man said, brandishing his sword over Livia's head. The mask gave his voice an eerie quality. I could almost believe I was talking to a skull in a cave.

Livia's eyes bulged as she tried to plead with me. I had no choice but to drop my sword and signal for Tacitus and Grillus to do the same.

"That's better," the man said. "Now, we've got us a standoff here." He clearly had not considered what he might do if his plan went awry. I hoped to take advantage of his uncertainty.

"We can settle this," I said, "as long as no one else gets hurt."

"I didn't hurt nobody," the other man said plaintively. "It was all him. The man in the wagon, her finger—all of it—it was him."

"Shut up, you fool!" his partner barked.

To my surprise, Aurora pushed past me, her hands out to show that she held no weapon. "We need to take care of Procne's wound," she said. "She'll die from the bleeding if you don't let us help her. This man is our doctor. If you'll let her come over here, I'll trade places with her, so you'll still have two hostages. You've already killed one person. Don't make it worse."

"I didn't kill nobody," the second man snapped. "I told you, that warn't my doin'."

"Then, please let us take care of her before she dies. She's losing a lot of blood."

"All right," the more timorous man said. "You come over here, behind us."

"You fool!" the man who held Livia said. "What do you think you're doing?"

"Tryin' to get us out of this alive."

"Wait! No!" I reached out for Aurora but she was already beyond my grasp.

The man holding Livia looked at me. "Oh, she means something to you, does she? All right, girl, get over here."

As Aurora walked toward him, the kidnapper shoved Procne in our direction. Grillus put an arm around her and took her to the entrance of the cave, where the light would let him see what he could do for her.

The men took one appreciative look at Aurora as she walked past them, then turned their attention back to us. They did not see Aurora, taking up a position behind them like a sentinel, nod slightly at me and place her hand on her thigh, where her knife was strapped. She had managed to do what I wanted to do—get someone in the enemy's rear.

"I know you don't want to hurt anybody else," I said, trying to keep their focus on me. I didn't know exactly what Aurora was planning, but I knew it was important to keep them looking forward. "You don't have to. Whatever you're being paid to do this, I'll give you twice that amount if you'll just release my wife and my servant."

The kidnapper shook his skull head. "You know what we want."

"*You* don't want it. Whoever is behind this wants it. I swear, whatever they're paying you, I'll double it. No, I'll triple it."

The two men looked at each other. The second man, who seemed to be the weaker, less resolute of the two, might have agreed, but the stronger, bigger man shook his head. "We got orders. There's not enough money to take care of us if we don't do what we're told. You know what you have to do to get *her* back." He gave Livia's hair a sharp tug. "And this other one here." He jerked his head toward Aurora. "She is right pretty. You've got a good eye, sir."

I'd have given anything if a nonexistent god could have struck the man dumb. Livia's face turned malevolent, her eyes burning into me. That was the look Medea must have given Jason when he announced he was leaving her to marry someone else.

"But I don't know where the document is." I had to rein in the genuine frustration in my voice and keep talking calmly. "How can I give you something I don't have and can't find?"

"That's your problem. And hers, too, I guess." He lifted Livia by her hair until she was standing and slowly raised his sword toward her throat. "Maybe seeing her bleed a little will convince you that we're serious."

Livia's eyes bulged in terror. She stretched her manacled hands out to me in supplication, trying to say something, but could only moan through her gag.

In one swift, fluid motion Aurora reached under her gown, pulled out her knife, and stabbed the man in the back. His body arched forward into a bow, his sword hand flailing backwards and punching Aurora in her stomach. She held on to her knife as the man's sword clattered to the floor of the cave. Livia collapsed as he let go of her. Aurora pulled her knife out and reached around the man to plunge the weapon into his chest. Blood spurted and she pushed him away from her. As he fell to the ground he tumbled over Livia and his hand flopped into the fire, but he didn't notice. The acrid smell of burning flesh filled the cave.

Tacitus and I lunged at the other man, who was frozen in shock. Before he could raise his sword we had him on the ground and disarmed. "Please don't kill me!" he screamed. "Please don't kill me!"

"Do you have him?" I asked Tacitus, who nodded and sat on the man, pinning his arms behind him and snatching off his skull mask. I turned my attention to Livia.

The dead man's blood was in Livia's hair and starting to run down her face. She was trembling, as though about to have a seizure. I removed the gag, although I knew her screaming would be ghastly, and it was, heightened by the echoes in the cave. I held her close and her terror dissolved into wrenching sobs and incoherent babbling.

"It's all right," I said softly, rocking her like a baby. "You're safe now. It's all right."

I looked over her head at Aurora, who was searching the body of the man she had killed. She would not meet my eyes so I could mouth my thanks. From under the dead man's tunic she extracted a small leather pouch and tossed it to me. I opened it to find gold coins and keys. I used the keys to free Livia and took her in my arms again. Tacitus placed the manacles on the other kidnapper, with his hands behind his back, then unshackled Procne.

"How is she?" he asked Grillus.

"I need to cauterize her wound," the freedman said. He handed his sword to Tacitus. "Could you put that in the fire, sir?"

Tacitus shoved the dead man aside with his foot, knocking off his mask, and laid the tip of the sword in the fire. The man's hand was black where it had fallen against the hot stones.

"This will hurt," Grillus told Procne, "but we must do it to stop the bleeding."

Procne pulled back from him, and Grillus tightened his grip.

"We don't have any choice, girl," he said. "That fellow did a brutal job of cutting off your finger. I don't have any other way to stop the bleeding. Hold on to me, as tightly as you need to. It'll be over in just a moment."

I saw Grillus wince when Procne grabbed hold of his arm and began to squeeze. Her eyes had the wild look of one of Dionysus' Maenads, but inspired by terror instead of by wine.

"Now, sir," he said to Tacitus, "can you take her injured hand and hold it out as straight and steady as possible?"

Tacitus knelt beside Procne and did as Grillus asked him. The freedman lifted the sword out of the fire and touched the glowing tip to Procne's injury, in spite of her efforts to pull away. Her skin sizzled and Procne screamed and fainted. Livia vomited in my lap.

"We need to get back home as soon as possible," I said, smoothing Livia's hair.

Aurora wiped her knife clean on the dead man's tunic and put it back in its sheath. "Why don't we go to Eustachius' house?" she said. "It's only a short distance from here. I'm sure he and his wife can help us take care of Procne and clean everybody up."

"That sounds like an excellent plan," Tacitus said, untying the horses' reins. "Let's get everyone loaded up. We could make our work easier if we just threw this bastard over the ledge into the quarry." He kicked the dead man.

"No," I said. "I want to know if anyone in Comum knows him or knows who his friends are. That could lead us to the man behind all this."

We hoisted the kidnappers over two horses like bags of wheat. The three of us men would lead the animals in our little caravan. Grillus had the horse carrying the dead kidnapper. I led the horse Livia was riding—uncomfortably. Tacitus led the horse with the second kidnapper, who was chained and gagged, draped over it. Aurora rode a horse with Procne sitting in front of her.

When we had made our way up the narrow trail and were on level ground, Brennus joined us with our own horses. As we mounted and spread out a little, I gave the reins of Livia's horse to Brennus and dropped back to ride alongside Grillus. Placing a hand on the dead man's back, I leaned over to Grillus and said softly, "Just to be sure you understand, I killed this man. Tacitus will swear to it, and I'd better not hear you telling anyone otherwise."

"Why would I, sir? That's exactly what happened."

Then I grabbed the second kidnapper's head and turned it up so he could see my face. "If you try to say anything to the contrary," I snarled, "it will be the last words you ever utter, and no one would believe you."

Our arrival at Eustachius' house set off a flurry of activity. The quarry owner and his wife seemed undaunted by the sight of a missing finger. When I noticed Eustachius' missing arm, I realized they must treat the loss of fingers and limbs on a regular basis. They cleaned Procne's wound, put an ointment on it, then made Livia and Procne drink something to calm them, and put them to bed. With everyone tended to, they sat us down to some bread and wine and listened to our story of the kidnapping and rescue with open mouths.

"Well then, let's take a look at this lot," Eustachius said. "Who's this you've got trussed over the horse with the wound in his back?" He pulled the dead man off the horse and took in a quick breath when he saw the gaping hole in his chest.

"He was threatening my wife."

"That I can understand, sir," Eustachius said. "But vicious blows, front and back?"

I now realized how improbable a story I was trying to concoct. "There was a scuffle. The fellow was quite strong."

"Then we'll just leave it at that, sir." He pointed to the blood on the front of Aurora's gown. "Was she injured? Do we need to tend to her?"

"No. That's just from Procne's hand and the general confusion. We've all got some blood on us." Aurora had said hardly a word on our short ride to Eustachius' house. I could see that she was shaken by what had happened. She almost seemed to be in pain, and I wanted to hold her in my arms and comfort her—and be comforted by her—but...

"Well," Eustachius said, "however it happened, sir, you've done the world a favor by taking this scoundrel out of it."

"You know him?"

"He used to work for me. Name's Publius Aurelius. He's a freedman from Comum."

"Used to work for you?"

"Yes, sir. He was an all-around troublemaker. I sent him away about five years ago."

"So that's how he knew about the cave."

"The one on the north side of the quarry?"

I nodded.

"He and some other rascals used to hide out there, I believe."

"Is this one of them?" Tacitus asked from where he was standing guard. "Before we gagged him, he said his name is Doricles."

Eustachius stood over the second kidnapper, who lay shackled hand and foot. "Can't say that I've had the misfortune to know this one. Shall we hear his story?"

Tacitus removed the man's gag. "I suspect he'll say anything to save his skin, but we'll try to sort the wheat from the chaff."

I met the fellow's eyes and rested my hand on the hilt of my sword to remind him of my threat. As he took a deep breath I asked, "Who hired you to kidnap my wife and my servants?"

"I don't know, sir, and that's as true a word as I've ever spoken."

"How can you not know who hired you? Somebody gave you a lot of money." I was carrying the pouch of gold coins Aurora had taken from the dead man under my tunic.

"Lutulla give us the job."

"Lutulla? The owner of the *taberna* in Comum?" Tacitus and I exchanged a glance. The *taberna* where we had lunch with Romatius? What could she have to do with this business?

"Yes, sir, that very one."

"Why would she want to kidnap my wife?"

"She didn't, sir." The man squirmed against his chains.

"But you just said—"

"She told us to go to a certain place and meet a man who had a job for us. He had left half the money with her, and we would get the other half when the job was done."

"Where did you meet him?" Tacitus asked. When we question someone, we often alternate between us, to keep the person off balance, to make him look back and forth, uncertain where the next question is coming from. And different questions occur to each of us. Sometimes Tacitus pretends to be more friendly while I press hard; at other times we reverse the roles.

"Out at a temple, on the east side of town. It's been tore down, maybe never finished."

My father's temple!

"Who was he?"

"I'm telling you, sir, I don't know. He had on a skull mask, like the ones Publius and me was wearing. We never saw his face. He told us what to do. We rode with him and kidnapped the people in the *raeda*. He took one of the women off with him and we took the others to the hut."

"Who killed the driver?" Tacitus demanded.

"That were Publius, sir. I swear it, by all the gods. The man in the mask was furious when it happened. I think he'da killed Publius on the spot if he didn't need him. He told us we wasn't to lay a hand on any of the others, just wait to hear from him."

I took my turn. "Did you lay a hand on any of the others?" Even if I didn't love Livia, I would kill this bastard on the spot if he had done anything to her.

"No, sir! By all the gods! Publius wanted to have some fun with your servant girl, but I wouldn't let him. She can tell you that. And so can your fella, the one that escaped. I wouldn't let Publius touch any of 'em."

Tacitus landed a solid kick in Doricles' back. "Because you're such a nice fella."

"No, sir," Doricles said, grimacing. "I was just afraid of what the man in the mask would do to us. And I needed the money."

"You've lost the money," I said, "and the only thing you have to be afraid of now is what we're going to do to you."

"Yes, sir, I know." He began to cry. "Please have mercy, sir."

With his one arm Eustachius grabbed Doricles by the shackles and lifted him like a child. "I've got a place where I can lock him up until we can get him to the magistrates."

"Is it hot and stinking?" I said.

"Like the lower levels of Tartarus, sir." Eustachius smiled grimly.

"Well, if you don't have anything worse, that will have to do."

Eustachius' wife managed to find clean clothing that fit most of us reasonably well, for which I paid her. She and Aurora did a hasty job of removing the equestrian stripes from my tunic and Tacitus' and stitching them onto our new garments. There was no sense trying to clean the clothes we'd been wearing when we arrived.

I was sitting beside Livia's bed a couple of hours later when she awoke. She looked around the small, dimly lit room in confusion, then sat up in fear, breathing rapidly, her eyes wide.

"It's over," I said, putting a hand on her arm. "You're safe now."

She clutched my hand tightly. "Where am I?"

"We're at Eustachius' quarry."

She looked down at herself. "What is this rag I'm wearing?"

"We had to find some clean garments. These were the best we could do under the circumstances." I touched her hair. "We cleaned you up as best we could. We'll go home whenever you feel like you can travel and you can get a proper bath then."

"I don't think I'll ever feel clean again."

I wondered if Doricles had been telling the truth. "Did they—"

"No, the little one stood up to the bigger man. But they touched me when they chained me and gagged me. That's enough." She shivered and drew the bed covering around her. "Where is Procne?"

"She's asleep in the next room."

"And those awful men?"

"One's dead, and the other is locked up. They're not going to hurt you."

"What about the third man? There were three."

"We'll find him. He can't get to you now."

Knowing where everyone was seemed to settle her. She took a deep breath. "Oh, Gaius, it was horrible. They held poor Procne down and cut off her finger. He sawed at it with his knife." She raised her hand and made a sawing motion, back and forth. "She kept screaming. I don't think I'll ever be able to forget that scream."

"I promise you, it's all right," I said. "Procne's been tended to. No one can harm you."

Livia sat quietly for a moment, then scowled at me. "Where's Aurora?"

"She's resting outside."

"Bring her in here."

For a moment I thought Livia might want to thank Aurora for saving her life, but I wanted to keep up the pretense that she hadn't been involved in what happened. I needed to convince Livia that she hadn't actually seen a servant woman plunge a knife into a man's heart.

"Why don't we just try to forget what happened in that cave—"

"Bring her in here, Gaius. Right now." The accustomed edge returned to her voice.

Aurora responded to my summons and stood before Livia with her head down and her hands, still shaking slightly, clasped in front of her, an appropriate servile posture, but she also seemed to be grasping her belly. I stood off to one side and slightly behind her.

"Where is your knife?" Livia demanded, sitting up in her bed.

"My knife, my lady? What—"

"Don't try to put me off. Show me that damn knife."

"But, my lady—"

"Take off your gown!"

I stepped up beside Aurora. "You're going too far, Livia. Why would I let a servant of mine carry a knife? She could be severely punished for doing that."

"I know, and I intend to see that she is." She glared at Aurora again. "I said, take off your gown."

I started to protest this humiliation again, but Aurora said, "Yes, my lady." She unpinned her gown at the shoulders and let it drop to the floor, grimacing and putting a hand on her belly as she did so. I never thought I would turn away from the sight of Aurora nude, but at that moment I couldn't bring myself to look at her. Before I lowered my head I did notice a bruise at her waist, from Aurelius' elbow I was sure.

"Where is it?" Livia said. "Where have you hidden it? Did you stick it up your ass? I'm sure Gaius wouldn't do something like that to you. Some men, though, turn you over and mount you like a filthy catamite. No woman should have to endure that. Why are you making those faces? Turn around!"

Aurora groaned. "My lady—"

"Livia, dear," I said, "you were panic-stricken. The only light in the cave was from the fire. Perhaps you've gotten things mixed up. Now just lie back and rest a bit longer." I nodded to Aurora, who picked up her gown, fastened the pins, and left the room without looking at me.

"I will not have her under the same roof with me, Gaius. Not ever again," Livia snarled. "I know what I saw, and I know that you…you love her." She half sobbed. "You've always loved her."

"Livia—"

"It's so obvious even that damn villain in the cave could see it. I want you to send her away. No, as your wife I *demand* that you send her away."

I couldn't shout at her, the way I wanted to, for fear that someone outside would hear me, as I was sure they could hear her, so I stood over her bed and shook my fist at her. "No. I'm sick and tired of your demands. I have married her to someone, as you demanded. That's as far as I will go. She has been a member of my household since we were children. I will never admit it to anyone outside this room, but she saved your life, by putting her own life in danger. It was her plan, not mine. She could have let him kill you, you know."

Livia drew back, as though afraid I actually would hit her. Her lip curled. "Wouldn't that have worked just fine for the two of you?"

I turned to leave and said over my shoulder, "I won't even dignify that with a response. She saved your life, Livia. Don't you ever forget it."

"Oh, I'm sure you'll never *let* me forget it."

XII

The less we deserve good fortune,
the more we hope for it.

—Seneca

I WAS SITTING ON *the ground beside a small pond behind Eusta-chius' house. The water was warm because of a hot spring that flowed into it, his wife, Nicera, had told me. I had my feet in the water when Gaius found me. He sat down, but not as close as I wished he would. I knew he couldn't, even though no one could see us back here. Because the ground around the quarry was so rocky, few trees grew, but a row of bushes ran along this side of the pond.*

"Are you sure you want to do this?" I asked him. "With Livia on a rampage, you're taking a big risk even speaking to me."

Tossing a pebble into the water, he said, without looking at me, "I'm sorry. She shouldn't have humiliated you like that."

"It's not the worst thing that ever happened to a slave."

Gaius cringed, the way I see him do every time he hears that word in connection with me. "Please don't think of yourself that way."

I studied the ripples the pebble made and reminded myself that, after any disturbance, calm does return. "How else can I think of myself? It's what I am, what I have been almost all my life."

"I've told you I would free you, any time you say you want me to."

"And I've told you that's not necessary. I want to belong to you. This is the only way I can."

He sat silently for a moment, then asked, "What did you do with your knife?"

"I gave it to Tacitus. He'll give it back to me when Livia's not around."

"It would be safer if he kept it or gave it to me for a while."

"All right, if that's what you want."

"You'll get it back," he added quickly. "I promise that." He finally looked at me. "What made you think to give it to Tacitus?"

"I knew you would have to deny that I killed that man, so I thought it would be better if I wasn't carrying a weapon. Someone might think to search me."

"Thank you for...what you did."

"You can't even say 'for saving her life,' can you?"

"Apparently not. Why did you do it?" He tossed another pebble, a bigger one that hit the water with an audible plop.

"What else could I do?" I ached to call him by his name, but I couldn't risk being heard, and I didn't want to call him my lord. "Surely you wouldn't want me to let her die."

"No...of course not." He didn't say it quickly enough. "It was a brilliant plan."

I shrugged. "It worked at the battle of Cannae, so I thought it was worth a try."

"Cannae? Hannibal?"

Even when we were children, doing our lessons together, Gaius was more interested in oratory and poetry than in history. He even wrote a Greek tragedy. Suppressing my laughter as we read it together was one of the hardest things I've ever done. I, on the other hand, cherished every word I could read about Hannibal and even imagined him to be one of my ancestors. "Yes. Hannibal had his Numidian auxiliaries pretend to surrender. You Romans foolishly accepted them and put them behind your lines."

"Oh, right. And at a crucial moment they fell on the legions and slaughtered them."

"The worst defeat in Roman history." I tried to suppress the tinge of pride that I felt. "Obviously Publius Aurelius never heard about it."

"A serious deficiency in his education, but lucky for us."

We sat quietly for a moment and the last of the fear I had felt in the cave seemed to drain out of me, to be replaced by a new worry. "Are you going to send me away, like she wants?"

"You heard her?"

I managed a little smile. "I think everyone between here and the Alps heard her. You were much quieter, like you are when we make love. So, are you going to do what she ordered you to?"

"'Ordered' isn't the term I would use. She gave me a choice."

I drew my knees up and wrapped my arms around them, trying to ignore the cramping in my belly. "You're playing word games with me. That frightens me. Does it mean you're going to send me away?"

"No. I would never do that."

"But she said she wouldn't stay in the same house with me." I felt myself close to tears.

Gaius took a deep breath. I wasn't sure what he was going to say, and I could hardly believe the words when I heard them. "Then obviously she'll have to find somewhere else to live, won't she? She has several estates to choose from."

"Will she have to live with her mother? The woman can't stand to be around her mother." I wiped my eyes as memories of my own mother welled up.

"She once said that Pompeia had told her she wished Livia had never been born. How can a mother talk to her own child like that?"

"Giving birth doesn't make a woman a good mother. What do you think Livia will do?"

"Liburnius left her a nice place in Umbria. Her mother has no control over that one." Gaius flipped another pebble into the pond and turned to face me. "But don't worry about her. Are you all right? You keep grimacing and holding your belly."

"Still shaken, but all right, I think. I've never experienced a feeling like that—a wave of such…anger and fear." I straightened my legs as the pain in my belly eased. I didn't want him to know how much I hurt.

Gaius took out the money pouch I had found on the dead man. It jingled as he hefted it.

"You look like the commander who's taken loot in a battle," I said.

"Plucked off the dead body of a vanquished enemy. I haven't counted it yet, but there's quite a bit in here, all gold. I think I'll split half of it among you, Brennus, and Grillus—good commanders should divide the loot among their loyal troops—and give the other half to Procne. That might begin to compensate her for losing her finger."

"Won't people wonder why you gave some to me, if I didn't kill that man?"

"You led us to the cave. We couldn't have found it and rescued Livia without you. I can truthfully tell people that much."

It took some doing, but I persuaded Livia to stay overnight, mostly for Procne's sake. That gave me a chance to send a messenger to my villa, letting my mother and Pompeia know that Livia was safe. I assumed they had returned from Pompeius' house by now. Because I was concerned about Aurora, I asked Julia to come down and bring Felix. I said she had been injured in the struggle to rescue Livia. I knew I couldn't ask my mother to come down here, but I felt another woman should be here. Nicera gave Livia and Procne something to drink which, she said, would let them sleep through the night.

Tacitus and I were given a room with two beds to share for the night. Brennus was put in with Eustachius' slaves, and Aurora was given a room by herself, since, Nicera said, there was no space in the quarters their two female slaves shared. I could see in her eye that she knew where I would actually be spending the night, and she did not object. I suspected she had made certain Livia got a good dose of the sleeping potion.

Our hostess left us some scented oil and enough water in a basin in our room for us to clean up minimally. While we waited for everyone to get to sleep, Tacitus and I talked about what had proved to be an eventful day.

"So you'll pay a heavy price either way," he summed up as he settled back on one of the beds. "If you don't divorce Livia, you'll have her as your wife for who knows how long."

"I'm sure she'll outlive me, just for spite."

"On the other hand, if you divorce her, it'll cost you dearly."

"It's more than just the money." I stretched out on the other bed, with my hands behind my head. "She would make a scandal—spread gossip—that would leave my mother unable to face anyone. And I'm afraid of what she might do to Aurora."

Tacitus sat up. "Do you think she would harm her?"

"I'm afraid she might try to do something, even if we stay married. She does not tolerate rivals. Remember what she did to her first husband's...catamite." I wondered if knowing that she was not loved by her mother had made Livia incapable of loving anyone else.

"That's right. Sold him to work in the mines, didn't she?"

"And was proud of what she'd done. I'll bet the poor bastard's dead by now."

"Or wishes he was," Tacitus said. "But surely she wouldn't attack Aurora directly. She must know what your reaction would be."

"She could arrange for an 'accident,' though, like the fall in the bath that killed Liburnius."

Tacitus trimmed the wick of one of the oil lamps on the table between the two beds. "I hate to even ask this, Gaius, but do you think she might try to harm *you*?"

"That's entirely possible, Even if she lives somewhere else, I feel like I'm going to have to constantly be on guard. She could suborn one of my slaves.... Oh, that's enough. Let's talk about something else."

"Right. I assume we're going to Comum tomorrow to talk with Lutulla about her involvement in this whole scheme."

"Somebody at her *taberna* heard us talking," I said, "when we had lunch with Romatius. It all goes back to that. She must be involved, though I don't think she's behind it all. We do have to see what she knows."

"But you have other plans for tonight, don't you?" Tacitus smiled broadly. "And you're eager to put them in action."

"I think it's about time." I opened the door and peeked out. Eustachius' house was one of several buildings surrounding a well, almost like a small town built around a forum. Everything—including the stable—was made of stone, with thatched roofs. Moonlight, in a clear sky, reflected off the walls and made it so easy to see that it felt almost like daytime, especially for me, since my eyes are more comfortable in dim light. The neigh of a restless horse came through the open stable door, but no one was stirring.

"Don't forget this," Tacitus said, handing me Aurora's knife in its sheath. There were still traces of blood on it. "I tried to clean it up some more, but blood is damned hard to get rid of. She may have to soak it when we get home."

"Should I give it back to her?"

Tacitus nodded. "Definitely. Her having it was what saved us today. I don't think I'll ever get that scene in the cave out of my mind. She didn't hesitate, did she?" He made two thrusts, imitating what Aurora had done. "I tell you, my friend, once you've seen a woman kill a man, it's hard to look at her in quite the same way again."

Staying close to the wall of the house, I came to Aurora's door and knocked—two quick knocks, a pause, and a third knock, our signal. She opened the door and I slipped inside. I took her in my arms and kissed her, but then she pulled away.

"I don't mean to dampen your enthusiasm," she said, "but I've got some cramps in my belly. It might help me if I could soak in the warm water in that pool behind the house."

"Cramps? Are you ill?"

"No, I feel all right except for the discomfort in my belly. I just want to soak in some warm water and see if that helps. Nicera gave me some extra oil so we can bathe." She kissed me on the cheek.

I laid her knife on the bed.

"Thank you, Gaius," she said. "Thank you for trusting me."

We crept around the edge of the main building and made our way to the pond. With the cooler night air settling in from the mountains around us, a slight mist rose from the water's surface. Aurora didn't hesitate. She took off her gown and waded into the water, bending over to splash some on herself.

"Come on," she said quietly. "It feels wonderful."

I laid my tunic beside her gown and entered the water. It quickly came up to our waists, and we knelt down, as we would in a public bath, to immerse ourselves. She ran her hands over my chest and I couldn't erase the image of those hands killing a man.

"Are you feeling better?" I asked her.

"Not really." She groaned. "Something's...wrong. Hold me, Gaius!"

As I put my arms around her, she bent double and blood began to flow from between her legs.

The next morning Livia said she and Procne felt well enough to travel, so Eustachius hitched a pair of horses to one of his smaller wagons. I couldn't help but marvel at how deftly he did the job with only one hand. Grillus and two of Eustachius' men would ride along as guards. I sent a note with Grillus telling my steward, Decimus, to put Eustachius and his men up overnight and to feed them well.

I didn't even try to suggest that they take Aurora with them. She was in no condition to travel and, if Livia didn't want her under the same roof with her, she certainly wouldn't have her riding in the same wagon. I just wanted Livia out of sight so I could check on Aurora, who was being tended to by Nicera.

"I'll see you when we get back tomorrow," I said, standing beside the wagon. Livia sat on the seat with Eustachius—but as far away from him as possible—while Procne lay on some blankets in the back.

"I doubt that you will," Livia replied.

"What do you mean?"

"I've decided I'm going to Tertia's house as soon as I can get my things packed. From there I'm not sure where I'll go, probably to Umbria. I'll let you know."

"Livia, it doesn't have to be this way." I looked up at her and tried to take her hand, but she pulled away.

"I don't see how it can be any other way, Gaius, if you won't…"

Jerking her head back in the direction of the house where Aurora was, she paused to give me one more chance to accede to a demand which I could not, and would not ever, meet.

"Once you've gotten over this shock," I said, "we can talk more calmly."

"I doubt I'll ever get over it, and I don't think we have anything to talk about." She drew her cloak more tightly around her, as though protecting herself from me. "I will not divorce you or consent to you divorcing me, but I've told you what has to happen if you expect me to live with you as your wife. Is your answer any different than it was yesterday?"

"No."

I wondered what price I would pay for uttering that simple but powerful word. The divorce itself wouldn't be hard to obtain, even if Livia objected. Money was the issue. Livia's dowry had been large and, as any man of foresight in my class does, I was keeping it in a separate account so it would be readily available in case of a divorce. The courts are adamant about an ex-wife getting her dowry back. But, if I initiated the divorce, there would also be a substantial penalty based on the size of the dowry. I would have to sell at least one of my estates to pay that penalty.

"No," I repeated more decisively, stepping away from the wagon. "My answer is no different. And it never will be."

Dry-eyed, Livia turned to Eustachius. "Let's go. We want to get there before dark."

Tacitus and I had planned to leave at dawn to ride to Comum and see Lutulla, but I wasn't going anywhere until I knew Aurora was out of danger. Nicera had explained to me what happened.

"There was a nasty bruise on her belly," she said. "She must've been hit harder than anybody realized during that scuffle in the cave."

It was the third hour when she finally gave me permission to see Aurora. I sat on the edge of her bed and took her hand. She looked drained, her hair loose and uncombed. She gripped my hand tightly. "How are you feeling?" I asked.

"I'm all right." She fought back tears.

"Why didn't you tell me you were carrying my child?"

"Why didn't you tell me you were going to make me get married?" She couldn't stop the tears any longer. She let go of my hand and put both of her hands over her face. "Oh, Gaius, I'm sorry. I'm so sorry."

I put a hand on her shaking shoulder. "Sorry for what? You have nothing to be sorry for."

"I couldn't figure out…how to tell you. I knew Livia…would hate me even more, and it would make things…so complicated for you, for us."

"But we would work it out. And, if I'd known you were pregnant, I would never have brought you along."

"And you would never have found Livia without my tracking skills."

She had me there. "Well, I know you're not going any farther with us. Nicera says you need to rest for a couple of days. When Eustachius returns with the wagon, he'll take you to our house."

"Could you send a note to Julia and ask her to come with him? I think she would be a great comfort to me because of what she's gone through."

"I've already done that. Does she know...everything?"

Aurora nodded. "I didn't tell her. She suspected and asked me. We were in the *latrina* and she was having her monthly. She asked me when my last one was."

I wrinkled my nose. "You women actually talk about that sort of thing?"

"Would you prefer that we compare our lovers' faults? When I hesitated to answer, she knew immediately. I needed to tell somebody. I didn't know how to. She swore she wouldn't tell anybody, not even Tacitus."

"Of course. I'll have to tell him. I sent the messenger before this happened. I just told Julia that you were injured in the struggle to save Livia, and I told her to bring Felix."

"Oh, yes, my husband. I'd forgotten about him. It would look better to have him by my side, wouldn't it?"

"But let's not spread the news any further." I leaned over to hug her. "Now you rest. And listen to Nicera."

Aurora pulled the blanket up to her chin. "It's very sad. She's lost two babies like this herself."

While Tacitus and I packed a couple of spare tunics which we had purchased from Nicera, I told him what had happened. His reaction wasn't what I expected.

"It's a tragedy, yes, Gaius, but you should also be relieved. Think what a huge problem it would be if Aurora did have your child. Of course, if she has another, you can remind everyone that she's married now."

I sat down on the bed. "I know. Livia would bring the house down

on my head. But I'm never going to have a child by her. If Aurora bore
me a child, I could emancipate her and adopt the boy, make him my
son legally."

"Some children are girls, you know. May the gods be thanked."

"Well, of course—"

Tacitus clapped me on my shoulder. "Aurora's in good hands. Right
now you can't do anything about that situation, and we need to talk to
Lutulla, so let's get on with it."

We put manacles on Doricles—Nicera said they had more use
for them than she liked—hoisted him onto a horse and set out for
Comum. By the time we rode into town the sun was setting. We managed to find a magistrate who would lock Doricles up for the time
being. Then we turned to finding a room. The crowd in Lutulla's *taberna* was so large and noisy we knew we would never get a chance to
talk with her or find rooms there.

"I guess it will have to wait until morning," I said as we found lodging at an inn a block away from her establishment.

I cursed when the racket from the street below awakened me. My
house on the Esquiline has no windows, so I never have to put up with
this. People were shouting and seemed to be running in one direction.
Then I smelled smoke.

"Tacitus, wake up!" I reached over to the other bed and shook my
friend.

"What? What?" He is a sound sleeper.

"Something's on fire. We've got to get out."

There was no sign of a fire as we ran down the stairs and into the
street. We looked in the direction the people were moving and I realized that flames were rising from Lutulla's *taberna*.

"Come on!" I yelled. "We've got to help her."

"She's probably not the only person in there," Tacitus said. "I'm sure
people are trying to help all of them."

"I hope so. Then we can concentrate on Lutulla."

The *vigiles* were organizing lines for people to fill buckets at the
fountain on the corner and pass the water along, but the building was

large and the fire already had a good start. I approached the man giving orders and said, "There's a fountain in the courtyard. Why aren't people getting water there, too?"

He studied my equestrian stripe and decided he had to answer me. "Because the only entrance to the courtyard is through the *taberna*, sir. I wish we could get to it, but I can't send people into a burning building."

I made certain others could see my equestrian stripe and began shouting, "Where's Lutulla? Has anyone seen Lutulla?"

No one could answer my questions. I went into one of the neighboring buildings which overlooked Lutulla's courtyard and ran up the stairs. Barging into someone's apartment, I looked out the window until I saw her. Lutulla was at a window on the upper floor of her building, but she was motionless, leaning on the window as though she had passed out, with one arm draped over the sill.

I ran back downstairs. "I see her," I told the captain of the *vigiles*. "She's at a window. We need to get her out."

He was a sturdy man, with scars on his face and arms that testified to his devotion to his work. "Sir, my first responsibility is to keep the fire from spreading. It's too risky to send somebody in there."

I had no authority here to order anyone to go into the building.

"Gaius, there's nothing we can do," Tacitus said.

I pulled him far enough away so that others couldn't overhear us. "We have to save her," I snapped. "She knows something about this skull business, something that somebody doesn't want us to know."

"But how—"

I turned away from him and ran to the fountain on the corner. One of the people filling buckets was a woman who had wrapped a cloak over her *stola*.

"I need this," I said. "I'll buy you a new one." Before she could agree I pulled the cloak off her and submerged it in the fountain. Then I threw myself into the water, making sure my tunic and my hair were thoroughly soaked.

With the cloak wrapped around me and pulled up over my mouth and nose, I ran back to the door of Lutulla's *taberna*. As I entered the building I heard Tacitus shouting, "Gaius, no!"

Smoke was heavy and acrid in the dining room, but I could make out two sets of stone stairs on the far side, one directly at the back of the building, the other several yards to the right. Which one led to the part of the upper floor where Lutulla was, I could only guess. Through the thickening smoke I could see that each set of stairs led to a landing, but I couldn't be sure which way they turned after that. My wet clothes weren't going to protect me against the smoke and heat for long. I could hear the roar of the fire in the kitchen.

I took the set of stairs on the left and choked out a sigh of relief when I got to the landing and saw that it turned to the left. That should take me toward the exterior wall of the building, which was where I thought I would find Lutulla. I hoped I could find her soon. The floorboards were already warm enough for me to feel them through my sandals, like walking on the floor of the *caldarium* in a bath. From somewhere I thought I heard voices, but it could just have been the creaking and whistling of the fire.

I had to keep wiping my face with the wet cloak to reduce the sting of the smoke in my eyes. The set of stairs I had chosen led to three rooms opening off a landing on the upper floor. Unless I had completely lost my sense of direction in the smoke, the middle door, straight ahead of me, should open into a room with a window overlooking the courtyard of the *taberna*. That was where I would find Lutulla.

The door stuck at first and I was afraid it was locked. One more good shove, though, forced it open and I saw Lutulla hunched over by the window. I called her name, but she did not respond. *What if she was already dead?* I thought. *I might be risking my life for nothing.* The way the smoke was filling the room, I knew I had to get her—and myself—out of there at once.

When I got to her and put my hand on her shoulder, she stirred slightly. A wave of relief passed over me. At least she was alive, but her face was bruised and battered. Someone had beaten her badly. She wasn't conscious enough to stand up and walk with me. All I could do was wrap the wet cloak around her and hoist her over my shoulder.

I reached the foot of the stairs and stopped to shift Lutulla's weight before I made a dash for the door. I had just taken a step toward the front of the *taberna* when part of the wooden floor of the upper story collapsed in flames in front of me. All I could see was the burning furniture from a bedroom. One body, in flames, rolled out of what had been the bed, and writhed on the floor, screaming. Another burning body lay still. The stench of burning flesh filled the dining room. If I couldn't get out of there in a moment or two, Lutulla and I would suffer the same fate.

But there was another door, the one that led out to the courtyard where Tacitus and I had eaten lunch with Romatius. Where was it? The smoke was so thick by now that my eyes were burning and I could hardly draw a breath. Lutulla seemed to be getting heavier. With that burden over my shoulder I needed to breathe or I was going to pass out.

Turning in the opposite direction from the collapsed and burning floor, I staggered a few steps and came to a wall. Feeling my way along it, I found the door.

It was locked, not just with a bar but with a key. And the only person who knew where that key was hidden was unconscious and draped over my shoulder.

XIII

*Fortune…can bring about great changes in
a situation through very slight forces.*

—Julius Caesar

IN DESPERATION—and futility, I feared—I pounded my fist
against the door. Damn it! I had survived the eruption of Vesuvius,
escaped being buried in ash with my mother. Was it my fate now to
die in this flaming hovel? I clutched the Tyche ring and the image of
Aurora's face flashed into my mind.

As I was forced to my knees by the smoke and Lutulla's weight,
I pounded the door again and called out as loudly as I could. Surely
someone—

A deep *thud* sounded against the door. Then another and several
more in rapid succession. I blinked, trying to clear my eyes enough to
see what was happening. The blade of an axe split the door near the
lock. With another blow I could see light flickering through the growing crack. Someone on the other side must be holding a torch.

"Gaius Pliny!" It was Tacitus!

"I'm here! How did—"

"Climbed the wall. Get away from the door!"

With another blow the door caved in enough for me to see my friend
and several other men with axes and large hammers. Others behind
them were holding torches to light their work. Two more resounding
blows brought the door crashing down. I lunged toward the opening
and fell at Tacitus' feet. He and the other men lifted Lutulla off me.

"Be careful," I said. "She's alive, but she's been beaten."

"Get them away from here!" Tacitus ordered. "This place isn't going to last much longer."

A light, steady rain set in just before dawn. It doused the fire from Lutulla's *taberna* and prevented it from spreading to the surrounding buildings, but it also kept the smoke from dissipating. When a building that large burns and collapses, the smoldering ashes can cast a pall that lingers for several days.

By the fourth hour, when the rain had let up, Tacitus and I were standing on the balcony of the room in an inn where we had taken Lutulla. Being on the third floor, we could see over the intervening buildings and had a clear view of the ruins of Lutulla's place.

At dawn I had sent a messenger to my friend Romatius at his villa outside of town, asking for any help he might give us, especially in the care of Lutulla. He had responded by sending the freedman who served as a doctor for his household—a Greek trained at the temple of Asclepius on the island of Kos—who assured us that Romatius himself would be in town later. The doctor was treating her now in the room behind us.

"There were two other men in one of the rooms on the upper floor," Tacitus said. "They didn't get out."

"I know." I suppressed a shudder at the memory.

"They could have been us, if we had gotten rooms there."

I groaned and shook my head. "I wish I could have—"

"By the gods, Gaius! You can't save the whole world. You risked your life and saved one woman. You couldn't have done any more."

"Do you agree now that Lutulla knows something important about this mystery?"

Tacitus nodded vigorously. "Something crucial, I think."

I motioned for the doctor to come out where we could talk to him. "How is she?" Tacitus asked the doctor.

"She's not doing very well, sir," the man said. He had the worst teeth I've ever seen in a doctor—two missing and several discolored. "She's in pain from some broken ribs and a broken arm. I've patched those up. I believe she has some injuries inside. That's why she's coughing up blood. She needs to sleep." He held up a small vial. "I wanted to give her syrup from the poppy to make her do that, but she insists that she has to talk to you first."

"Let's hear what she has to say." I entered the room and Tacitus followed me. I gave the doctor money to get something to eat and hoped he would not have his ear pressed to the door while we talked. Hippocrates' oath says doctors should never disclose anything they hear their patients say, but I preferred to put this fellow where he couldn't hear anything to begin with.

When the door was closed Tacitus stood against it, to block any unexpected visitors. I sat in the chair beside Lutulla's bed that the doctor had used. Lutulla grabbed my hand and kissed it.

"They tell me you saved my miserable hide, kind sir."

"I couldn't let the secret of your chicken recipe perish," I said.

She chuckled, and the pain in her ribs made her regret it.

"The doctor said you wanted to talk to me. I also have some questions for you."

"Well, sir, you have the right to ask me anything. Go ahead, and then I have some things to tell you."

I took a moment to organize my thoughts, as I would if I were presenting a case in court. From the brief contact I'd had with her, Lutulla seemed wary, so I decided to throw her off balance from the beginning. "We captured two men who kidnapped my wife. The survivor says you gave them the job."

Lutulla's eyes widened in fear. "No, sir. I did no such thing."

"You didn't hire them?" I don't know why I had expected to get the truth out of a villain like Doricles. He would say anything to save his life.

"No, sir. I didn't hire them myself. You see, once in a while I get a message offering jobs to men who…aren't too particular about how they earn their money."

"Who offers such jobs?"

"I don't know, sir. By the gods, I don't know. A message will be left outside the door of my room, along with a small bag of gold coins. The message tells me how many men are wanted and where they are to go to receive further instructions. I'm to keep some of the money and give them the rest. They'll be paid the full sum when the job is done."

"What kind of job?" Tacitus asked.

"Jobs no honest man would do, I'm sure, sir. There's just jobs that have to be done, though."

"Like kidnapping someone's wife," I said.

Lutulla tried to sit up but collapsed back on the bed from the pain in her ribs and arm. "Please, sir, you've got to believe me—"

"And they killed the driver of our *raeda*."

"Oh, sir! By the gods, I knew nothing about that." She held up her good arm as if to swear. Her tears began to flow. "It had to be that bastard Publius Aurelius."

"That's what we've been told. You don't think Doricles would do it?"

"No, sir. Doricles is a bit simple. He needed the money and Publius Aurelius vouched for him."

"Have you ever asked the men what they do?" Tacitus put in.

"That I have, sir, but they won't tell me. They've had such a fear put into them."

"Do you always recruit the same men?"

"Mostly, sir. But some of the men refuse the second time. Aurelius, though, he never refused."

"How long has this been going on?"

"Oh, ten, maybe twelve years, sir."

"How often do these messages appear?" I asked.

"Sometimes twice in a month. Other times, it'll be some months between them. I never know."

"What do the messages look like?"

"They're written on parchment and they have a seal on them, a seal of a skull."

Tacitus and I exchanged a glance. "If you think these men are being recruited for criminal activity, why do you participate?"

"I don't know exactly what they're being asked to do, sir, and I'm not a rich woman."

"But you owned the *taberna*."

"No, sir. Your father built it and owned it. He left it to you when he died, on the condition that I would continue to live there and run the place."

I jumped up from the chair. "What? I know nothing about this!"

"I'll explain it to you in a bit, when you're finished with your questions. I am not rich, by any means, and the men I pick for the work are even poorer than I am."

With my mind still reeling from the revelation that I owned a piece of property in Comum which was now a pile of ashes, I paused before I asked my next question. "Do you think the attack on you last night and the burning of your...our *taberna* had any connection to these messages?"

"Oh, I know it did, sir."

"How do you know that?"

She touched her face. "The man that beat me, sir, he wore a skull mask."

I felt like I had turned a corner and found not one but two pathways before me. How many unexpected twists would I encounter in this maze? "But why would he attack you like this—try to kill you, in fact? You've never had any threats before, have you?"

Her eyes laid an accusation on me. "No, sir. I'm sure it has to do with the questions you've been asking, about something that happened twenty years ago." She yawned and grimaced from the effort.

"Do you want me to get the doctor? He can give you something to help you sleep."

She shook her head. "I just need to close my eyes. We can talk some more later."

I walked out on the balcony, almost reeling, and leaned against the wall of the building. Tacitus took my arm, led me through the room and closed the door.

"I know you're shocked," he said. "We need to talk where she can't hear us."

"Could anything she's said be true?" I held my head in my hands because it seemed to be spinning. "From what I've learned in the last few days, I wonder if I know anything about my father. Was he involved in something that led to the murder of the person buried in the wall of his house?"

"No, I'm sure he wasn't."

Tacitus was saying what a friend should say, but I wasn't sure I believed him. "Then why is she making these outlandish claims? How could my father have kept his ownership of that *taberna* a secret from my mother and everyone else in his household? There's no record of it in his accounts."

"She's just trying to get you on her side, Gaius. She faces serious charges of being involved in a kidnapping and a murder. And who knows what other 'jobs' she's recruited men for over the past ten years. I wonder if we could compile a list of serious crimes committed in the past, say five years, and compare it to the times when Lutulla got these messages."

Tacitus' face brightened as he had another idea. "You know, she could be the one behind it. This outrageous story about bags of money and anonymous notes and men in masks could be nothing but an attempt to cover her tracks."

I shook my head. "Livia and others have seen the men in masks, and we found a bag of gold coins on Publius Aurelius."

"But they don't know who was giving them orders." He poked me in the chest. "I'll bet it was Lutulla herself. She could have set the fire and hit herself."

"You saw her face. Nobody could inflict such bad wounds on herself."

"Soldiers have injured themselves to get out of service."

"Broken ribs? A broken arm? Coughing up blood?"

"Maybe she went farther than she intended. One of my father-in-law's men once became so frightened that he drove a spear through his foot and left himself lame. Agricola had him flogged and assigned him to cleaning up stables."

"But Lutulla was unconscious when I found her."

Tacitus gave a derisive snort. "Pretending to be unconscious is one of the easiest acts in the world. I've done it many a time to avoid having to say anything when a…partner is leaving the next morning."

"You're being absurd. She could have died in that fire."

"Rot! I'll bet, if somebody hadn't gotten to her pretty soon, she would have miraculously recovered and scrambled out that window. That's why she was lying there and not somewhere farther inside the building."

I leaned against the wall. "She must have some proof of what she's said."

"She'll probably just say it was all destroyed in the fire." The corner of Tacitus' mouth turned up. "Another possibility has just occurred to me. Maybe men are being recruited to do things that don't get reported to the authorities."

"What—"

"Lutulla said some of the men wouldn't accept a second job. I can think of some things no man would do a second time. By the gods, I've done some of them."

"You mean—"

"Yes, my dear Gaius, playing the catamite, Ganymede to some wealthy man's Zeus—some man who cannot risk having his identity revealed."

"Such…activities aren't against the law."

"But if a man cares about his position in society—or perhaps in his own household—he will want to keep his predilections as secret as possible. She said he sometimes hires more than one man at a time." Tacitus shrugged, as if to say that nothing more needed to be said.

"No, you must be wrong. We know that Aurelius and Doricles and another man were hired to kidnap Livia."

"We have no idea what other men have been anonymously hired to do over the years."

"Well, we have to go back in there and see what Lutulla has to tell us." I reached for the door.

The owner of the inn appeared on the stairs. "Is everything all right, sirs?" he asked.

"We're about to go back in. Do you need something?"

"I'm concerned, sir, that my man you sent with the message hasn't returned."

"Oh, the doctor said your man would come back later with Romatius. The doctor traveled by himself on Romatius' fastest horse."

"I see." He still looked dubious. "Thank you, sir."

Lutulla had propped herself up in the bed and washed her face. With the soot removed, I could see how badly she had been beaten. Both eyes were turning purple. Tacitus' theory about hitting herself was patently ridiculous. The left eye was almost closed. She was holding a wet cloth up to it. Her left cheek had a couple of long gashes on it, most likely made by the ring of the person who beat her—a right-handed person.

"You said you had some things to tell me," I began.

"Yes, sir. And to show you."

"All right. I'm listening."

"You'd better sit down, sir. You'll probably not believe what you're about to hear."

"I know I won't," Tacitus said.

I awoke from an uneasy sleep to find Julia sitting by my bed. She took my hand and smoothed my hair, like a mother comforting her child.

"I'm so sorry, Aurora," she said. "As soon as I heard that you'd been injured, I was afraid it meant exactly this." That was enough to start my tears.

"What if…what if I can't ever have a baby?"

"Oh, losing a baby doesn't mean you can't have another. This happened only because you were hit. How are you feeling?"

I showed her the bruise, which was quite large by now.

"How did it happen that you were close enough to that villain for him to hit you like this?"

"What did Gaius tell you?"

"His note said he had killed one of the kidnappers and captured another."

"That's the story he's going to put out, but I did it." Her eyes opened wider and wider as I told her the story.

"And you hadn't told Gaius about the child?"

"No. I just couldn't find the words, and he's been so worried about Livia, as he should be. But I can't have Gaius' baby. I mean, I mustn't. What would Livia do?"

"You're right. She'd probably demand that Gaius sell you to someone

who would take you to Armenia or Lusitania. But you do have a husband now. If you get pregnant again, everyone can assume the child is his."

"Livia would never believe it." I bit my tongue to keep from telling Julia that Felix was a eunuch. I had promised him that much. "So how can I keep from getting pregnant?"

"Well, the most obvious answer to that question is not to couple with Gaius. Failing that, there are, shall we say, various ways of coupling."

I could feel myself blushing.

"It looks like you've tried at least some of them. There's no substitute for the real thing, though, is there?"

I knew I was turning as deep a red as the stripe on Gaius' tunic.

"One of my servant women swears by a method that she claims a doctor recommended. Immediately after the completion of the act, she squats down and sneezes three times."

I laughed out loud. "That would certainly kill the mood."

"All I can say is, she's never been with child."

"I can't imagine myself doing that."

Julia turned serious. "There is something that could help. The sap from a plant called silphium has been used by women for ages. You take a sip of it up to two days after coupling and you will not get with child."

"Where can I get some of that?"

"It has become increasingly difficult to find in the past few years."

"So it's expensive."

"I believe it is, but I know a place where we can probably get you some."

"But—"

"Don't worry. I'll pay for it. Right now, though, I need to let Felix come in and see you. He's been very solicitous the whole way down here."

I had completely forgotten about my husband. "Must you?"

"He needs to know the truth if he's to help you propagate a lie."

"Of course." I turned my head to the wall.

Lutulla beckoned me to sit down again beside her bed. Tacitus leaned in the doorway leading out to the little balcony, from where he could see the ruins of the *taberna*.

"What do you have to say?" I asked Lutulla.

"I need to start with the worst of it," she replied, "because it will explain all the rest." She sighed deeply and winced at the pain in her ribs. "You see, I was your father's lover."

"I don't believe you," I said without emotion, although by now I was ready to believe almost anything someone told me about my father. Tacitus shook his head.

"I'll tell you the story," Lutulla said, "then I'll show you the proof, from your father's own hand. Believe it or not, I was once a young, pretty girl. I met your father when I was working in a *taberna* on the other side of town. He wasn't married then."

"You say that as though it exonerates both of you."

"Love needs no defense, sir. It will happen where it must happen. I had no expectations of your father. I knew he loved me, but a man of his class can't burden himself with a woman of my class."

I was finding it difficult to breathe. She might as well be talking about Aurora and me. Did she know about Aurora? How could she?

"He married your mother," Lutulla went on, "as he should have, but he continued to love me. We had a child, a daughter. She was such a darling"—her voice broke—"but she died of a fever before her fourth birthday. Your father doted on her, even called her Caecilia."

I gasped. For a man of my father's class to give his family name to a child who was not born to his wife was a bold declaration. "Did my mother know about this child?"

"I imagine she did, sir. I've never met her—never had reason to— but I'm terrible sorry for any pain I've caused her."

"She lost a daughter as well," I said, "shortly after her birth."

Lutulla coughed up some blood. "I didn't know that. Her name was Caecilia as well, I assume."

"Yes, of course."

"Your father made plans to build a temple on the edge of town, dedicated to Rome and Augustus in Caecilia's name."

"But he never finished it."

"No, sir, he died before he could. I always thought it was my daughter he would be honoring. Now I don't know."

But now I knew why my mother had reacted the way she did when I suggested that we ought to finish the temple. She must have known about Lutulla's daughter. If I decided to finish the building, I would certainly wait until after she died.

"Temples cost money," I said. "And it takes money to build and operate a *taberna*. The expenses for the temple are in my father's accounts, though there's no mention of dedicating it in anyone's name."

"No, sir. It was just to be a temple to Rome and Augustus. He planned to put Caecilia's name on it right at the end of the construction."

Whichever Caecilia he had in mind. "There's nothing in any of his records to show that he ever spent a *denarius* on the *taberna*, either to build it or to maintain it."

"Sir, all I know is that he paid for the building eighteen years ago. After that, twice a year I received enough money to keep the place going. I asked your father once where he got that kind of money. He said it was interest on an investment he had made."

"Did my father bring the money to you?"

"No, sir. That's the odd thing. He told me to go out to Caecilia's temple—and I'm sorry, but that's how I've always thought of it—and I would find three bags of money hidden under the main floor. I was to go out there on the evenings before the spring equinox and the autumn equinox. Not at any other time. I did as he told me, and the money was always there, in bags sealed with that skull seal."

"Even after he died?"

"Yes, sir. He told me that, if anything happened to him, one of the documents he gave me would guarantee that the money would always be there."

Tacitus straightened up. "Didn't you ever try to find out who was leaving the money?"

Lutulla turned her head with an effort. "No, sir. Gaius Pliny's father said it would cost me my life if I did."

I sat back, trying to make sense of what I was hearing. What sort of investment could my father have been involved in that was so secretive someone would kill to prevent anyone knowing about it?

"You mentioned a document. What is it and where is it?"

"Buried, along with some others that you need to see." Lutulla lay back on the bed and sighed with the exertion. "Go to the courtyard behind the *taberna*. There's a fountain in the center."

"Yes, I saw it when we had lunch there. It has that lovely statue of a little girl with a pail—" I stopped and Lutulla read the question on my face.

"Yes, sir. She's the very image of my daughter. Your sister, if I may be so bold."

When I could speak again, I said, "Once I've gone to the fountain, what do I do?"

"Count four paving stones due north from the fountain. Raise the fourth stone on the right and you'll find a leather pouch. It should answer your questions. Your father told me to give the things in it to you, if the need arose. I asked him how I was supposed to know if the need had arose. He just said I would know." She patted my hand. "Now, sir, if you don't mind, the doctor said he has something that will make me sleep. I'd like that very much."

Tacitus called Romatius' freedman into the room. Before he administered his potion, I told Lutulla, "Once I have a better understanding of what's involved here, we'll think about rebuilding the *taberna*."

Tacitus and I picked our way through the smoldering rubble and into the courtyard of my ruined *taberna*. Even after the rain, I could feel the warmth through my sandals. The courtyard was paved with straight rows of squared limestone, not the cheaper tufa stone I probably would have used. My father, it seemed, had spared no expense in providing for his mistress. We stopped beside the fountain.

"Which side is north?" Tacitus asked. "When I can't see the sun like this, I always have trouble figuring that out."

I pointed in the right direction but didn't move. "Let me think about this for a moment, please."

"What is there to think about?" Tacitus said. "Four paving stones..." Then he followed my gaze. "Oh. Sure, take as much time as you need." He stepped away from me.

The fountain was a rectangle, three feet across and six feet long, built of limestone blocks, coming up to my waist. On the south end of it, on top of the wall, sat a large block with a face carved in it. Water came out through a pipe protruding from the mouth. On the west side at the south end was placed a life-sized bronze statue of a little girl, in a sitting position with her feet in the water, reaching toward the stream of water with her bucket. When I ate lunch here I had barely noticed the statue. Now I couldn't take my eyes off it.

I studied the statue from across the fountain, then walked around and stood beside it. It was a fine piece of work, from the delicate strands of hair to the glee on the child's face, down to her graceful limbs. I put a hand on her arm and could imagine her playing in this very spot. Why had my father commemorated this child in such lavish fashion but done nothing for the daughter that my mother lost shortly after her birth when I was four years old?

When my father died I was too young to deliver his eulogy. Now I wondered what I might have said. I couldn't praise him for being involved in some shadowy business which might have led to a murder. Nor could I spell out the details of his intimate relationship with a serving girl which led to the birth of a child. Would I reveal how he hid money from his family so he could build a business for that woman? In sum, could I say anything I would want to engrave on his tombstone?

In the past few days I had learned that both my father and my uncle—my adoptive father—had children by women other than their wives. My father's daughter died, and I had not been able to locate my uncle's son. Yesterday my servant Aurora lost the child I would have had by her, while saving the life of my wife, who had sworn she would never give me a child. Fortune seemed to be having a grand laugh at my expense as some sort of vicious cycle took another turn.

I kissed my sister on the top of her head and turned north, hoping to find something that would help me make sense of all this.

Tacitus had already stepped off the four paving stones. "There's a problem, though," he said. "There are two rows of stones. Depending on which way you're facing, either one of these could be the fourth stone on the right. Why didn't she tell us which one?"

"She's old, probably addled from the beating she took. She knew what she meant. It just means a little more digging for us. That looks like a tool shed over there."

The shed was far enough away from the main building that it had escaped the blaze. We found tools that Lutulla used to cultivate the herb garden growing on the west side of the courtyard and the vines that climbed the wall there.

"You take that one, and I'll work here," I said as I plunged a spade into the joint between one of the fourth stones and the one beyond it. Tacitus went at the other with a pick. I pried up my stone and had removed several shovels of dirt but found nothing. I dropped to my knees, scraping at the dirt with my hands. "Are you finding anything?" I asked Tacitus.

"Nothing. And the scratches on this stone make me think somebody was digging here recently."

"May I ask who you gentlemen are," a voice said from behind us, "and why you're digging in my mother's courtyard?"

I turned to see a young man stepping out from behind the shed. I tightened my grip on the shovel and Tacitus stepped away from me. We've learned that two are more effective against one when the two are spread out.

"I am Gaius Pliny, and this is my friend Cornelius Tacitus. Who are you?"

"I am Gnaeus Lutullus, son of Lutulla."

"I didn't know she had a son," I said. "How old are you?"

"I'm sixteen, sir, so, to set your mind at rest, your father was not my father."

From his name—the masculine form of his mother's name—I could deduce that he had no father, in the legal sense. He was too young, by several years, to be my father's child. With dark wavy hair and an aristocratic nose, he was a respectable-looking boy, almost my height. His father was probably a man of some status here in town who could not acknowledge a bastard child, or perhaps someone passing through Comum who never knew what he had left behind.

"Why would you say such a thing?" I asked, though I knew his reason.

"My mother told me about your father, sir, and the daughter she had by him." He nodded toward the fountain. "And she told me that, if anything ever happened to her, I was to dig something up and give it to you. My only concern is whether you really are Pliny."

I held out my hand so he could read my signet ring.

"Thank you, sir. Just a moment." He stepped behind the shed and came back carrying a leather pouch.

The pouch was tied at the top but bore no seal. When I opened it I found another pouch bearing my father's seal on the wax over the knotted string. For a moment it was difficult for me to speak.

"Were you in the *taberna* last night?" Tacitus asked.

"No, sir. I was across town, with…a friend. I came over here just before dawn when I heard about a fire on this side of town. When I saw what had happened, I retrieved that pouch, as my mother had instructed me to." He was putting on a brave face and having difficulty keeping it up. "Then I hid back here. I didn't know what to do next."

"Didn't you know that Gaius Pliny here rescued your mother from the fire?"

Lutullus' face brightened and he clasped Tacitus' hand. "By the gods, no! I heard people saying different things. I figured she was dead."

"She was badly injured," I said. "Right now she's in a room in Macer's inn. I assume you know it."

"Yes, sir. May I see her?"

"The doctor tending her has given her something to help her sleep. Perhaps you can stop by later in the day." But he was already off.

Tacitus and I brushed off one of the tables and sat down. "This is my father's seal," I said as I examined the pouch.

"I'm very relieved not to see a skull," Tacitus said. "Lutulla certainly thought ahead. Something could have happened to her at any time and you would never have known about this pouch."

I broke the seal, untied the knot and shook the pouch to dump the contents onto the table. They consisted of three documents, one of which was an all-too-familiar-looking piece of parchment, folded and sealed with the skull ring. DO NOT OPEN was written below the seal.

The other two documents were papyrus sheets, rolled up but not fastened or sealed on the outside. I opened one to find a deed to the *taberna* and the instructions that it was to be left to me upon my father's death, with Lutulla remaining as the occupant of the building as long as she wished. My father had signed his name and pressed his seal at the end of the document. It had also been signed and sealed by someone—presumably a town official—whose name I did not recognize.

When I laid it down, Tacitus picked it up and ran his eyes over it. "You'll need to keep this one. It answers a lot of questions."

"Almost as many as it raises," I said.

The next document I picked up was made of two sheets of papyrus glued together.

"Looks like it was cut from the end of a scroll," Tacitus said.

I smoothed it out. "It's a letter, from my father."

"Do you want me to step away while you read it?" Tacitus started to stand up.

"No. I don't know what other shocks he may have in store for me. I would appreciate your support." I began to read:

Lucius Caecilius to his dear son Gaius, greetings, love, and regret.

I am writing this when you are five years old, Gaius. If you are reading it, I hope you are old enough to understand and to forgive. If you never read it, then I suppose something has happened to Lutulla and all of my planning has been in vain. All I can do is hope for the best.

The deed to the taberna in Comum is self-explanatory, I suppose. The man who witnessed it—and the copy which Lutulla has—was an elderly friend of my father's. I paid him for his seal and for his silence, expecting that he would die soon after, and he did. The taberna will belong to you after I die. As far as I know, no one except Lutulla knows about the deed, but it is entirely legal. Have no fear on that score. I told her to keep the two copies in separate places.

What you don't understand, I'm sure, is why I built the taberna and set Lutulla up as the proprietor. The answer to that puzzle is quite simple: I love her and want to make sure she is taken care of, no matter what happens to me. If you're reading this, I must assume that you have met her. I beg you to take good care of her.

I hope you will never have to live as I do, in love with one woman but married to another. I wish I could love your mother. "Love conquers all," Virgil claimed. If only that were true. We don't expect love in our marriages, of course. That's not their purpose. Your mother is a fine woman. I'm sure some man could love her. The best I can do is to keep my feelings hidden and insure her happiness. I owe her that much for giving me you.

The plan is that you will eventually marry the daughter of my friend Livius and his wife Pompeia, who is your mother's cousin. I imagine you've at least met Livia. Sad to say, I don't find much charm in the little girl, but she may blossom, just as, from its stalks and thorns, one would never suspect how lovely a rose can be.

As for the sealed document you found in this pouch, all I can tell you is that it must not be opened, except under circumstances I will explain below. It contains information which would ruin several families and involve you in a deadly scandal as well. Having the document protects you, but only as long as it remains sealed. The others involved know that you have the document and that I have promised that it will not be opened and that no harm must come to my family or to Lutulla. She will tell you about the money she receives because of this document. As long as she receives it, the document must remain unopened. If the money stops coming or if someone harms her or your mother, open the document and do what you think is best. I'm sorry I cannot say any more.

I hope you are living well, as the philosophers always urge us to do. Your uncle, Gaius Plinius, has promised me that he will look after you and your mother, if something happens to me, as I fear it might. He is a good man.

Hail and farewell, my beloved son.

"He dated it and put his seal on it," I said as Tacitus took the letter from me and looked over it.

"I'm sorry, Gaius," he said. "I know this was painful to hear."

I leaned back in my chair and looked over at the smoldering pile which testified to my father's love for Lutulla and back at the statue of the child their love had brought into the world. "You love Julia, don't you?"

"Yes, I do now, but I didn't when I married her. How could I? I hardly knew her when we were married." He looked over my father's letter again. "You sound like some addled poet, Gaius. We don't marry for love—"

"I know, I know. We marry for political advantage, or to keep property within a family. Livia's mother and mine are cousins. Do you know how much property we have between us? If we had a son, he'd inherit half of Tuscany. And we should be reasonably happy with that." I sighed like a man about to be led into the arena. "Unless one of us has the misfortune to fall in love."

"You want to go home, don't you, and see Aurora?" Tacitus stood up.

"I need to be sure she's all right, but first I want to talk to Lutulla again."

"What are you going to do about this?" He picked up the sealed document.

"I'm going to have to think about it."

"You aren't seriously considering opening it, are you? In spite of a warning of doom that sounds like it came out of the Sibylline books? Lutulla says she's getting the money. Your father said not to open this as long as she's getting the money."

"I believe it has something to do with this business that's plaguing us."

"Why do you think that?"

"This letter of my father's is dated less than a year after the body was sealed up in the wall. We found the body and suddenly we're getting messages with this skull seal on them and my wife is kidnapped by men wearing skull masks, and Lutulla is attacked by a man wearing a skull mask. There has to be a connection."

"If you open that document, Gaius, it could be like opening Pandora's box. You'd never be able to get all the evils back in."

"It looks to me like the evils have already been loosed. But remember the one thing that was left clinging to the inside of Pandora's box—hope. I hope this document will enable us to learn who was put into the wall and who put him there and who is attacking us."

Tacitus leaned over the table. "What if your father was involved?"

"That's why I have to think about how I'm going to manage this." I gathered up the three documents and slipped them back into the pouch, drawing the string tight. "But first I have to see Lutulla again."

When we got back to Macer's inn the door to Lutulla's room was closed. Her son was sitting outside it.

"Have you seen her?" I asked him.

"There's no response when I knock," Lutullus said. "I guess she's asleep. I didn't want to disturb her."

I knocked, waited, then opened the door partway. "Lutulla?" I said.

Hearing nothing, I opened the door the rest of the way and stepped into the room. Lutulla was lying in the bed, on her back, with her head turned to one side. Someone had pulled a blanket up to her chin. Blood had dried where it had run out of her mouth.

"The doctor must have given her that potion," Tacitus said over my shoulder. "She's quite asleep."

But something about her face didn't look right. I stood by the bed and bent over her, listening for a breath. "No, she's quite dead."

XIV

Fortune and love favor the brave.

—Ovid

I FINISHED THE BOWL of stew Nicera had brought me. "I want
to go home," I told Julia.

"Do you think you can travel?" she asked.

"If I lie down in a wagon, with enough padding, and we travel slowly,
I believe I'll be all right. Gaius is going to go home as soon as he finishes
whatever he's doing in Comum. I know he'll want to see me, and I want to
be there. I want to see him."

"But if you come in a wagon, everyone will want to know what's the
matter. They're already curious that Gaius sent and asked for me."

"Then we'll say I was injured in the struggle to save Livia."

"Oh, is that what we'll say?"

"I'm sorry. I shouldn't assume—"

She patted my hand and smiled. "Don't worry, dear. That's what Gaius
said in his note. Of course I'll back you up. That bruise on your stomach
will testify to how seriously you were hurt. We won't have to share any
details."

I put the empty bowl on the table beside the bed and lay back down. "I
really was surprised at how hard he hit me. I'm not sure if it was with the
hilt of the sword or just his elbow. He jerked so violently when I stabbed
him."

Julia squeezed my hand. "What does it feel like to…to kill a man? You
know, we watch gladiators fight, and we go into a frenzy when one falls, but
what did it feel like to plunge that knife into him?"

*This wasn't something I wanted to talk about with anyone but Gaius.
"I didn't have time to feel anything. I had to strike quickly enough and
hard enough that he wouldn't be able to harm Livia. I saw Gaius' eyes
bulge and his hand go to his mouth. It was all a blur after that—everybody
scurrying around."*

*"I find it quite remarkable that you risked your life to save a woman
who hates you."*

"And lost the life of my child in doing it."

Lutullus stayed by his mother, weeping while Tacitus and I rushed
down the stairs and found the owner of the inn. "Where's the man who
was with Lutulla, that so-called doctor?"

"He left while you were out, sir. He said not to disturb her so she
could sleep for a while and he would check in on her later."

"Have you ever seen him before?"

"Why, no, sir. Is something the matter?"

"Lutulla's dead. That man poisoned her, I'm sure of it."

"Where did he come from?" Tacitus asked.

"He came in not long after you gentlemen sent my man to Romatius' house. He showed me your note, with that dolphin seal on it, said
he was the one you asked for. He was carrying a bag, like I thought a
doctor would."

"Has your servant returned yet?"

"No, sir. I figure he'll come back with Romatius and his people."

I suspected he was going to be disappointed. His servant was almost
certainly lying dead somewhere between here and Romatius' house.

"We need a magistrate," I said, and Tacitus followed me out the
door.

When we reached the corner, we saw a crowd gathered in front
of the ruins of Lutulla's *taberna*. Because he is rather tall, I spotted
my friend Romatius near the front. I hailed him and walked quickly
toward him. His toga was bleached white, to indicate that he was running for an office. It bore no stripe. I was surprised to be reminded that
his family was not of equestrian status. Surely they had the money to
qualify.

"Friend Pliny, what a pleasant surprise," he said. "I didn't know you were in Comum."

I stopped in my tracks. "Surprise? Didn't you receive a note from me earlier this morning?"

He shook his head.

"So you didn't send your freedman doctor to assist Lutulla, as I asked?"

"What on earth are you talking about? I heard there was a fire in town last night, so I came in to see what had happened." As any candidate for an office should do, to show his concern for the city.

"Lutulla's been killed, that's what happened."

"What? How—"

"She was beaten and the *taberna* was set on fire. I rescued her, but someone posing as your doctor came in this morning and poisoned her. I'm sure it was the same man who tried to kill her last night."

"What did he look like?"

"Medium height, dark hair, fair skin, with a scar on his right hand and very bad teeth."

"Don't know that fellow," Romatius said. "My doctor is short, rather stout, with darker skin from his Egyptian mother. I am truly sorry to hear about this." He raised his voice, so the people around him couldn't miss what he said. "Lutulla was much loved. I'll take care of the funeral arrangements for her." Murmurs of approval ran through the crowd. Romatius could count the votes.

"She had a son, I've learned."

"Yes, but he's just a boy. He doesn't have the means to provide even a modest funeral. I'll talk to him and see if he wants to give her eulogy."

"I'm sure he'll appreciate that."

"She will be missed by a lot of people. I am going to miss that chicken of hers, if I'm not being too crass." Romatius turned to face the pile of ashes. "This is a rather desirable property. I wonder what's to become of it."

"I haven't decided."

He looked at me over his shoulder. "You? What do you have to do with it?"

"It turns out my father built the place."

"For Lutulla?" He turned to face me.

"Yes. She was his mistress. I learned just today that I've owned the building since I was six. That's when my father died. I've got the will and the deed."

"By the gods! That's amazing. Are you going to rebuild?"

"I'd rather sell it, but I don't want to throw her son out on the street."

Romatius nodded. "He is a reliable lad, from what I know of him. If you rebuilt, he could probably run the place. He worked here with his mother all his life."

"I don't have anything to hold me here. Would you be interested in buying the property and rebuilding?"

"Let's talk about it under better circumstances, shall we? That will give me a chance to go over my accounts and see how much I might pull together. It's certainly a desirable piece of property."

"Do you have any idea who the boy's father was?"

"Let's just say that, from what I know, the field of candidates would be rather crowded. I wouldn't be surprised to find my own father's name on the list."

"The 'doctor' must have been the third kidnapper," Tacitus said. "Once he knew we had rescued Livia, he had to kill Lutulla to keep her from exposing him."

"I'm sure you're right," I said. "The bastard is certainly bold. He managed to poison her right under our noses."

"We need to talk to Doricles and see what he can tell us."

"I agree. After we do that, we should get back to my house."

Tacitus put a hand on my shoulder. "Julia's been through this herself, Gaius. I'm sure she's taking good care of Aurora. That sort of thing is best left to the women."

"But I *need* to see her."

We returned to the magistrate's office where Doricles was being held. The place had no cells. Doricles was chained to the wall at the rear of the building, along with two other men. They could walk far enough to reach a slop jar to their left and a bucket of water to their right. The magistrate's freedman who was on duty unchained Doricles and, satisfied with the coins I gave him, led us to a small room where we could talk with some degree of privacy.

Doricles was a broken man. He began begging before we were able to say anything. "My lords, if you have any pity—and you seem like very kind gentlemen—please drop me a few crumbs. I did not hurt those women or kill that man. What's going to happen to me?"

"You participated in several heinous crimes," Tacitus said, "even if you only stood by. I have no doubt that you'll be sent to Rome and thrown into the arena, perhaps to fight animals."

Doricles' face went blank at the word "heinous," but he began to rock back and forth and to wail loudly. "Oh, my lords, I don't deserve that."

"On the other hand," Tacitus continued, "you may not live that long. Someone—and we think it was the third man in your party—killed Lutulla. You're the only other person who can identify him."

The wailing grew even louder. "Oh, my lords, I ain't no model citizen, that's for sure, but I never hurt nobody. Please, can you do anything to help me?"

"My wife says you protected her and her servants from the other man, Publius Aurelius, even at some risk to yourself."

"That I did, my lord." Doricles calmed down a bit, wiping his eyes with the back of his hands. "That I did. I'm sorry I couldn't stop him from cutting off that poor girl's finger, but I didn't let him have his way with either of them. I told the women, if Aurelius tried to do anything to them while I was asleep or not with them, to make as much noise as they could and I would come running."

"Because of that I will do what I can to save you from the arena. What other punishment you might suffer, I cannot say."

Doricles grabbed my hand and, much to my dismay, began slobbering kisses on it. "Oh, may the gods bless you, my lord!"

I pulled my hand away from him, put it under the table, and wiped it on my tunic. "In return for my help I expect you to tell us everything you can about the kidnapping."

"Whatever you want to know, my lords. I'll tell you everything. But could I have a drink of water first? One of them other fellas out there don't know the difference between them two pots of water. I'm terrible thirsty."

I stuck my head out the door and asked the guard to bring me a cup of water. I had to watch to make certain he didn't dip it out of the prisoners' supplies. Doricles took the cup and drank greedily.

Tacitus, who is larger and more imposing than I am, drew himself up. "Lutulla said she was given money by some unknown person to recruit two men for a job. But there were three men involved. We know you and Aurelius. Who was the third man? Where did he come from?"

"I don't know what his name was, my lord, but he called himself Vulpes."

"The fox? Why the fox?"

"He was all too proud of how clever he was, my lord. And I have to admit he could come up on a person right unexpectedly, just like a fox."

I looked at Tacitus. The man had been clever enough to pass himself off as a doctor and had killed Lutulla practically in front of us. And he must have been within earshot when I sent the messenger to Romatius asking for a doctor, but I'd never noticed him.

"Did he have bad teeth?" I asked. "Yellow? A couple of broken ones?"

"Yes, my lord. That he did. His was even worse than mine." Doricles grimaced to show us his discolored teeth.

"But he wasn't recruited by Lutulla?" I said.

"I don't think so, my lord. He was with the fella that hired us. He seemed to be one of his men."

"Help me understand this," Tacitus said, leaning over the table like a friend. "As a rule, Lutulla offered you and Aurelius jobs, and you went somewhere to meet a man who would actually give you the job and pay you the rest of the money."

"Yes, my lord. That's it exactly."

"Where did you meet him?"

"At a temple outside of town that somebody started years ago but never finished. There's rooms under the floor of the temple. That's where he was waiting for us, with Vulpes."

"Had you ever been to this temple before?"

"No, my lord, but Aurelius had, so he knowed the way."

"And you went with him, even though you had no idea what you were going to be asked to do?"

"Yes, my lord."

"Why would you do that? Did you know Aurelius well enough to trust him that far?"

"I've knowed him a couple of years, my lord. He's got a bit of a temper, but he's always been a good friend to me. I don't have many of those. He said we could make a lot of money."

"But he gave you no idea what you would have to do."

"Well, my lord, he said it might be something different every time. The one thing he warned me about was that, just by going out to the temple, I was agreeing to take the job, no matter what it was. I remember his exact words. 'Understand that good and clear,' he said. 'If you walk into that temple, you've made the decision to accept the job. Try to refuse and you won't walk out.'"

"Why would you accept those conditions?"

"The money was going to be *so* good, sir." His eyes grew wider. "More money than I'd ever dreamed of. When I found out we'd be kidnapping some women, though, I tried to back out. Vulpes grabbed me and held me, and the man who was hiring us pulled out a sword. He was going to kill me on the spot, so I said I would do it. They promised me the women wouldn't be harmed, just held for a few days until a ransom was paid."

"But then Aurelius lost control when the driver lashed him with his whip and killed the man."

"Yes, my lord. And everything kind of veered off course after that." He made a swerving motion to his left. "But I haven't done nothing to deserve to be put into the arena. Please help me."

I ignored his plea and asked, "What did the man who hired you look like?"

"I never saw him without his mask, my lord. Never saw Vulpes without his either. Aurelius and me kept ours on, like we was told to do, any time we was around the women. It was supposed to be that way so they wouldn't be able to identify us when they was released."

"But you said Vulpes had bad teeth," Tacitus pointed out.

"I could see that much through the mouth hole, my lord. You've seen the masks. And Vulpes complained about his teeth hurting when he ate, like mine do."

"So you and Aurelius stayed with my wife and her servant in that hut."

"Yes, my lord. Vulpes took the other girl somewhere right after we kidnapped them. I hope she wasn't hurt."

"No, she wasn't, aside from some rough handling. She was returned to my villa with a note attached to her gown."

"Good. I'm glad to hear that, my lord. I hope what I've told you has been helpful." He was asking me what I was going to do for him now.

"I need for you to help me a bit more," I said. "We're going to ride out to the temple and I want you to show me exactly where you met the man who hired you and describe what happened there."

Doricles lifted his manacled hands. "That might be difficult, my lord."

"I'm going to make arrangements with the magistrate's man to have you released—"

"Oh, may the gods bless you, my lord!" He grabbed my hand before I could pull it back.

"You will be released into my custody. That doesn't mean you're going out of here a free man. You were involved in the kidnapping of my wife, the death of one of our servants, and the mutilation of another, even if you only stood by and watched. You're not going to escape punishment, but, if you help me find the man who's behind this, the punishment can be lighter."

"I'll do anything, my lord."

"All you need to do is tell me the truth."

The man watching the jail wanted to contact the magistrate before he released Doricles, but I didn't want to waste any more time. I offered him more than I had intended, and that seemed to obviate the need to get any approval.

"The magistrate didn't see him come in last night, my lord," the man—a hunchback—said with a broad grin as he removed Doricles' chains. "So I guess he won't miss him when you take him out."

The ride out to my father's unfinished temple was brief. I wondered now what his purpose had been in undertaking the project but not completing it. He could have left funds in his will for the work. In its present condition, though, it might serve a function other than glorifying Rome. It was far enough away from town that people would not casually pass by it. After a year or two it would be all but forgotten. Bushes had grown up around it, offering some concealment. That would make it a convenient place for people to leave and pick up things, or to hold meetings that were best held out of public view. When I stopped there a few days ago, I had not noticed any evidence that anyone was living in it. The rumors about it being haunted could have been deliberately created to discourage people from doing so.

"It ain't so spooky in daylight, my lord," Doricles said as we dismounted and tied up our horses. "Just broken-down-lookin'."

"You came out here at night?" Tacitus asked.

Doricles nodded. "Aurelius said the man always had people meet him out here after dark, my lord, with just a couple of torches lit."

We went into the door that led to the storage rooms under the temple. The sunlight barely penetrated more than a few feet. I brushed a spider's web out of my way. Three torches were mounted in sconces but there was no way to light them. "I can see how unsettling it would be to come in here at night."

"And imagine how you'd feel, my lord, when a big fella comes out of that door yonder wearing a skull mask. And he's got on a white robe—not a tunic but a long robe—that covers him from his chin to the ground. You'd swear he was floatin' more than walkin'."

"A big man?" I asked. "Do you mean tall, or big like a gladiator is big?"

"Tall, my lord. At least taller than me by about a head."

"We need some light," Tacitus said. "Not everybody can see in the dark, like you, Gaius Pliny. These torches are useless without a flint and some oil."

"May I wait out here, my lord?" Doricles asked, his voice choking. "This is as far as I went. I can't tell you nothin' about the rest of it."

"Keep an eye on the horses for us," I said, waving him out.

"Thank you, my lord." Doricles scampered out the door.

My eyes are better than most people's in dim light. Now that they'd had a few moments to adjust, I stepped through the door that Doricles had indicated. As much by feel as by sight, I was able to locate a small table just inside the door of the room which had an oil lamp, a vial of oil, and a flint on it. I struck the flint and in a moment we had enough light to look around.

"Homey place," Tacitus said. "What are you expecting to find?"

"It seems to me that, if someone is using this room on any kind of regular basis, he must leave some minimal equipment here, like the lamp, rather than bring it along with him every time."

"But then he might run the risk of having it found."

"The rumors that it's haunted would keep a lot of people away. I don't think he would leave a skull mask here. That's something that could be identified and possibly traced to the owner. But a long white robe could belong to anyone."

"Where would he hide even a short white robe?" Tacitus waved an arm around the empty room.

"I suspect one of the stones in the wall can be moved. Bring one of those torches in and we'll get some more light."

"Why don't I drag Doricles in here as well? I don't care how scared he is, we can do the job faster with another pair of hands."

"We won't get them from him."

"What do you mean?"

"See for yourself."

Tacitus stepped out into the passageway and returned with a torch. "Doricles is gone," he said. "And so is one of the horses, the one you hired. Ungrateful little bastard!"

I applied some oil to the torch and used the lamp to light it. "Are you surprised?"

"Yes, but you don't seem to be. Are we going after him?"

"What for? Livia said he kept Aurelius from hurting her. That should earn him a pardon. Lutulla said he's harmless unless he falls under the sway of someone like Aurelius. He's told us all he can. He'll just shrink back into the shadows of some large city."

"I don't imagine he's going to stop until the horse drops under him," Tacitus said.

"He'll have to sell it or eat it to survive. I'll pay for the horse, and I'm not concerned with Doricles. Let's see if we can find a hiding place in here."

We made the trip back to Gaius' villa as slowly as I have ever ridden in a wagon, but I still felt every jolt. Julia and Felix took turns holding my hand. I felt I could squeeze Felix's hand harder than I could Julia's. When we arrived, Julia shooed everyone away and they got me settled in the room that Felix and I were supposed to share. Felix went to get me something to eat, although I hadn't asked for it and didn't really want it.

When Gaius' mother came in to see me, Julia stepped outside.

"That must have been some excitement," Plinia said.

I nodded, hoping to appear weaker than I actually felt. I wasn't ready to face people yet. A day or two of solitude appealed to me. "What did Livia tell you, my lady?" I asked in a soft voice.

"Not much. Just that Pliny and Tacitus killed one of the kidnappers and captured another one. I gather the third one escaped."

"He wasn't there, my lady." I was relieved to hear that Livia had not revealed what really did happen. "Is the lady Livia all right? I know she was badly frightened."

"She left for her estate in Umbria early this morning."

"But I saw the lady Pompeia when we were coming in, my lady." Livia's mother had stood on the other side of the garden and glared at me as Felix and Julia helped me to my room.

"Livia wouldn't let her mother go with her. She said she needed some time to herself. I suppose that means time away from Gaius as well."

"She did have an awful shock, my lady. I hope everyone can just give her time to recover." I wished they could give me time as well, but I knew I wasn't likely to get it, since no one knew—or ever could know—what was really wrong with me.

Plinia sat on the edge of the bed. "Aurora dear, let's talk honestly with one another."

I didn't like the sound of that at all. Honest talk between slave and master, like water coming down a hill, can run only one way.

"We both know," Plinia began, "that your...relationship with Gaius *will only lead to more trouble between him and Livia. I want my son to be happy, just as I wanted my husband and my brother to be happy."*

"My lady, I—" *Plinia held up her hand to silence me. So much for honest talk.*

She sighed heavily and went on. "I don't understand why men can't be content unless they're, shall we say, sowing their seed someplace where they shouldn't. I just know there is no greater sorrow in a marriage than realizing that, when your husband comes to your bed, he is thinking of another woman, that he remembers making love to her. And, when you know who that woman is, the pain is unbearable."

The downhill flow of this "honesty" was about to drown me.

"I am deeply torn," *Plinia went on.* "I know Gaius loves you and that makes him happy. But I am dying." *She paused.* "You're not surprised, so I suppose Gaius has told you."

"Yes, my lady, he has."

"He hasn't told his wife." *She clipped her words.*

"My lady, I'm so sorry—"

"It's not your fault. I wanted to see my son married. I've accomplished that. Now I want to hold my grandchild before my last day comes. You can make Gaius happy, but you cannot give me a grandchild, at least not one I can claim."

Because I'm a slave, just a piece of property. What if I "honestly" told her that this piece of property had been carrying her grandchild? "My lady, I'm afraid I can only make...your son unhappy. In a way I wish we could be ten years old again. Back then we could play together and no one thought anything of the time we spent with one another. Now, if we even exchange a glance across the room, I feel like everyone is wondering what it means."

Plinia cocked her head. "And what does it mean?"

Before I had to answer, the door swung open and Pompeia's ample frame filled it. "Plinia, could I speak with you, please?"

Gaius' mother stepped out of the room, closing the door behind her. I got up and stood next to the door, with my ear pressed against it. Pompeia made no effort to keep her voice down—I'm not sure she can—and Plinia's voice seemed to rise in response.

"Why are you pampering that girl?" *Pompeia demanded.*

"She is a valued member of our household," Plinia replied, calmly but not softly.

"No. She is the major impediment between Gaius and Livia in their marriage. That's what she is."

"I need to remind you that Aurora was involved in rescuing Livia. Gaius himself told Julia that they would not have been able to save your daughter without Aurora's aid."

"But without Aurora, Gaius and Livia could be happily married. Instead, because of her, my daughter has been humiliated and has gone off to her estate. She won't even let me come with her. Marriage is about loyalty and respect, Plinia. Gaius is not showing either of those qualities to my daughter."

"Livia has done nothing to inspire them in Gaius."

"And I suppose that slave girl has?"

Plinia sighed heavily. "You don't understand. Gaius and Aurora have known one another since they were seven. The poor girl was so frightened when she came into our house. She spoke no Latin and only a smattering of Greek. When Gaius befriended her, she attached herself to him like a lost puppy. We even found them sleeping together once—in all innocence, of course."

The memory of that night flooded over me. I was eight years old. My mother and I had been slaves in the elder Pliny's house for about a year. We were at Laurentum when a tremendous storm broke out during the night. Growing up on the edge of the African desert, I had never seen or heard anything like it. I was terrified, but I couldn't go to my mother because she was with Gaius' uncle. I had been told never to disturb them. In spite of that, I tried the handle on their door and found it locked. So I ran to Gaius' room. I just wanted to lie down on the floor beside his bed, but he woke up and took me into the bed with him. When he put his arms around me, for the first time since my father sold me, I felt safe.

Plinia's voice caught my attention again. "Whatever feelings they have for one another are natural and deep."

"You sound like you approve." Pompeia's voice crackled with anger.

"I want my son to be happy."

"Don't you want him to give you a grandson? Would you accept some little bastard slave child?"

I didn't have to be able to see her to visualize the sneer on her lips.

"That's putting it harshly—"

"My dear cousin, if you don't get her out of here, that's exactly what Gaius is going to present you with."

"I think Gaius and Aurora could produce a beautiful baby, but, you're right, it could never be my grandchild."

I lay back down and gave in to the tears I had been fighting.

"This might be what we're looking for," Tacitus said, pulling a stone out of its place in the wall. He held up the oil lamp to peer inside the hole behind it. "There's a bag of some sort in there."

He stepped aside and I reached in to retrieve a large leather bag. Alongside it lay a pair of sandals.

"Those are odd," Tacitus said as I pulled them out.

The sandals had soles as thick as my fingers were long. "They're actor's sandals," I said. "They give the actor height to make him seem more in proportion to his mask and costume."

"They would make a man of average height seem tall, especially if he was wearing a long robe that covered him down to the floor."

"I suspect that's what we'll find in here." I opened the leather bag and withdrew a white robe, shaking it out to hang straight. I held it up to myself.

"It's too long," Tacitus said, "but with the sandals it would fit you just about right."

"And, in dim light, this costume could make you appear to float rather than walk, as Doricles said. So we're looking for someone about my height, rather than a tall man." I put the robe back in the bag and turned toward the door.

"Aren't you going to put those things back?" Tacitus asked.

"I think it's time to go on the offensive. If we take these things, the person who's behind all this will be thrown off balance."

"But he's lost Lutulla and his ability to hire men anonymously. Won't he have to stop?"

"I don't want him to stop, not until I can make him pay for what he's done."

XV

*I never admire another man's fortune so much that I
become dissatisfied with my own.*

—Cicero

AS SOON AS we got back to my villa, I went to see how Aurora
was doing. Tacitus pulled up a stool and sat in front of the door
like a guard. Julia was keeping Aurora company. She gave me a peck on
the cheek and left us alone. Aurora and I embraced and said nothing
for a moment.

"How are you feeling?" I finally asked.

"I'm much better. Julia is being so cautious about me, but I'm ready
to get up and move around. I just hope I can stay out of Pompeia's
sight."

"It probably wouldn't hurt for you to stay in bed another day. I can
say that I've ordered you to do so."

"Yes, my lord." She smiled playfully and took my hand. "Anything
you say, my lord. Can you at least tell me what you've done the last
couple of days?"

Her eyes widened in horror as I told her about pulling Lutulla out
of the fire and then losing her to a killer under our very noses. She
clutched me to her again.

"I could have lost you, Gaius."

"And I could have lost you. But we can't dwell on it. We're both here,
and we're both safe. That's all that matters."

"But what does Lutulla have to do with the body in the wall? Why
kidnap Livia? It doesn't make any sense, Gaius."

"You're right. I thought Pompeius might be involved, as odd as that sounds. But the costume we found in the temple fits someone my size, and Pompeius is taller. This Lucius who was the steward, I guess we'd say, at the old villa, could be involved. But who is he? Where is he? And the man who calls himself Vulpes. He seems—"

"The Fox?" Aurora sat up. "People call that old villa the Fox's Den."

"I thought that was because of the wild animals who've taken over the place, but perhaps not. Did Fulvius tell you anything else about this Lucius?"

"He carved things," Aurora reminded me. "Toys, and probably the masks that the men used in the villa. And he had a couple of broken teeth."

"By the gods! Doricles said that Vulpes had several broken teeth."

"But who is he?"

"Our problem is that we've been looking in so many directions. We haven't put things together. What's connecting all of this information?"

"The connection is the skull mask," Aurora said.

"Exactly. And that takes us back to that old villa and the boys like Fulvius. But I just don't see how it all fits together." I kissed her on the forehead. "Now, you get some rest. I'm going to bathe and ponder. I'll have dinner brought in here for us in a while."

When I emerged from Aurora's room I found Pompeia waiting outside. Tacitus had apparently kept her from simply opening the door and barging right in.

"I knew I would find you here," she said.

"A servant of mine was injured. I wanted to see how she was feeling. Wouldn't you do the same for one of your servants?"

Instead of answering the question, she said, "I want to leave this place, immediately."

You have expressed my fondest wish, I thought. "Where will you go?"

"To my estate at Narnia."

"I don't think you should do that. I can't protect you in Narnia."

She drew her cloak around her. "You haven't been able to protect me or my family here. My daughter's been kidnapped and frightened out of her wits. One of my servants is dead and another has been mutilated."

I hung my head. "I can't deny any of that, and I'm sorry."

"If you'll pardon my intrusion," Tacitus said, "for the lady Pompeia to go to Narnia might be a good idea. As I recall the layout of the estate from my one visit there, it could be more easily fortified."

"Your father-in-law has some of his retired veterans living near there, doesn't he?" I asked.

"Yes."

"Do you think he could ask a few of them to stand guard around the estate until we get to the bottom of this business?"

"I'm sure he'll be glad to. It'll keep them sharp. Should your mother go, too?"

"That would be an excellent idea. She'd be lonely here without any women for company."

"We'll need transportation," Pompeia said. "Livia took all of our wagons."

Of course she did, I thought. "Don't worry. I can provide transportation." *I would carry you on my back if it would get you out of here.*

"When can we leave?" Pompeia asked.

"Let's send a messenger to Agricola right now and ask for his soldiers," I said. "That will give them time to get in position. Then you can leave tomorrow morning. May I have your promise that you will stay at Narnia until I can assure you that the danger has passed?"

"Gaius, I think my daughters are right. No one around you will ever be entirely out of danger."

The next morning I went out to the stable to see Pompeia, my mother and Naomi, and the other women servants off on their trip to Narnia. Aurora stayed out of sight, but Phineas came to say good-bye to his mother and brought Xenobia along. The girl was convivial, but Naomi's displeasure at her son's attachment to a non-Jew was obvious. She and my mother would probably have a lot to talk about during their journey.

As Barbatus was harnessing the horses, I said over his shoulder, "You told me about the beating you gave Marcus Delius years ago. Do you remember if you knocked out any of his teeth?"

"Why, yes, my lord," he said proudly. "Two of 'em."

Teeth! That had to be the link! Vulpes was missing teeth. The unknown Lucius from the old villa was missing teeth. And Marcus Delius was missing teeth. Even the skull in my wall was missing a tooth. I hurried back to my room and got a bag. When I looked into Aurora's room, she was barely awake. I kissed her on the cheek and she opened her eyes wider.

"I'll be gone for a while," I said.

"Where are you going?"

"I want to pay one more visit to that deserted villa. That place is as important in understanding what's going on as the body in the wall itself."

Aurora sat up. "Do you want me to go with you?"

"No. I don't think you're ready to ride yet. Just rest. I'll be back later today."

I rushed back to the stable and told Barbatus, "I need a horse, too."

"Certainly, my lord. May I ask where you'll be going?"

"I'm going to ride along with the women as far as Pompeius' estate. I want to ask him a few more questions."

"Will Cornelius Tacitus or…anyone else be going with you, my lord?"

"Not today. Tacitus and his wife were going to sail on the lake, I believe. I'll have some of Pompeius' servants ride back with me." As we pulled out of the stable yard I added, "Let Tacitus and…anyone else know where I'm going."

"I will, my lord."

I had to keep my pace down to that of the wagons. The whole caravan made a brief stop at Pompeius' house. Tertia informed me that her father wasn't there.

"We haven't seen him since yesterday afternoon," she said. "He left the house then."

Somehow I didn't believe this was going to be an assignation with some woman. "Did he take anyone with him?"

"No, and he wouldn't say where he was going, just that he had to meet someone, 'to settle this business once and for all, like I should have done years ago.'"

"Were those his exact words?"

Tertia nodded. "I've never seen him look so angry and so determined. Could you find him, Gaius? He's not strong, and I'm afraid—"

I touched her arm to reassure her. "I believe I know where he's going. If anyone comes looking for me, just tell them the Fox's Den. They'll know what you mean."

I said a hasty good-bye to the women, mounted my horse, and set off down the road to the turn-off that would take me to the deserted villa.

When I came to the rise that overlooked the villa, I saw two horses tied up there. One I recognized from the decorations on its bridle as Pompeius'. I left my horse tied to a tree on the rise and crept up to the villa, carrying my bag. When I passed the wall surrounding the villa, I heard someone yelling.

"Where is it, old man? What have you done with it?"

I walked through the atrium and stopped at the opening leading into the garden. A man was standing over Pompeius, who was tied up, hands and feet. His captor had a sword at the older man's throat.

"I don't know where it is," Pompeius said, on the verge of tears. "Why does it matter? It's all over with now."

"That was the last mask. It has my mark on it. Somebody can figure out that I made it."

I stepped into view, holding up the skull mask. "Is this what you're looking for, Marcus Delius?"

Delius whirled at the sound of my voice. "By the gods! You!"

"Yes, cousin Delius, it's me."

"Cousin?" Delius lowered his sword and took a step toward me. "It's true, then. Old Gaius Plinius was my father."

"Yes. His sister is my mother. And he adopted me, so in one sense we're not only cousins but brothers, Vulpes."

Delius smirked. "So you know everything. Well, that's just fine. Maybe we should postpone the family gathering until a later time, though, and a less revolting place." He looked around the atrium.

"You spent time here as Lucius, didn't you? You took care of the boys."

Delius raised his sword and shook it at me. "Yes, I took care of them. I never...did what he and the rest of them did." He pointed the sword toward Pompeius and pushed him closer to the pool in the center of the garden.

"I think I understand most of what happened," I said. "What I don't know is how much my father was involved." I took a step toward Pompeius, but Delius held out his sword to block my progress. "What was my father's part, Pompeius?"

The old man squirmed himself around so he could see me. The slimy substance that had grown all over the villa had coated his tunic and his hair. "He supplied money. Livius, Romatius, and I were the ones actively involved."

"Did he know what you were doing with the money?"

Pompeius shook his head. "We needed capital to get started. That's where your father came in."

"I cannot believe my father would ever have consented to be a part of such a vile scheme."

"He didn't know exactly what we were doing. We told him we were selling slaves. Your father said he preferred not to know. And he was so involved with Lutulla and building that *taberna* that he had little interest in anything else. As long as he got his share of the profits, he was content."

"Whatever gave you the idea of setting up a place like this?"

"Livius owned this villa. He and Romatius and I would sometimes bring a few boys here. We realized that other men might enjoy having a secluded spot such as this."

"Wait, are you telling me you set up some sort of *lupinar* for pederasts?"

"I suppose you could describe it in such crass terms. There are a lot of men these days who appreciate the beauty of a young boy. Some men always have. The emperor Tiberius had children at his villa on Capri. The story goes that he called them his 'little fishes.' They would join him in the bath and swim between his legs, nibbling on what they found there. And, of course, I can cite Socrates and Plato to

testify to their love for boys. But keeping a young boy in your household is inconvenient and expensive. It causes tension with your wife.
And young boys have the unfortunate habit of growing up. So the
four of us formed what we called the *collegium calvariae*, the company of the skull. We thought we were rather clever to come up with
that."

"Why the skull?"

"That was your father's idea. His daughter by Lutulla—oh, dear,
do you know about her?"

"Yes."

Pompeius struggled against the ropes. "Well, his daughter by
Lutulla had recently died, and I think he was in a macabre mood."

"Do you swear that the money was his only contribution?"

"He also had property on this side of the lake where Livius could
land his boat and move the boys to this villa. That was his only contribution. On my honor, Gaius, although I guess that isn't worth much,
is it?"

I shook my head. "You bought boys from the other side of the lake,
didn't you?"

"Yes. Livius suggested that we could supply the boys cheaply by
buying them from people over there. Many of those children die at
such a young age. We would actually be doing them a favor by taking
them out of their wretched conditions, providing good food and better
living quarters than they could ever dream of." He sounded as though
he had convinced himself that he was speaking the truth.

"But they grow up, don't they? What happened to them then?"

"Well, then Livius would take them back across the lake and set
them free."

I snorted. "Free to tell everyone where they had been? What they'd
been doing?"

I could see that, until this moment, Pompeius had never let himself
doubt what Livius told him. "Are you suggesting that the boys—"

"I'm reminding you that the lake is very deep."

"Oh, dear gods!"

"How many boys did Livius 'return'?"

"Only eight or ten."

Delius kicked Pompeius. "Only eight or ten? Do you think that excuses you?"

"I didn't think we were hurting anyone. The operation ran for only a few years. Not enough time for many of the boys to mature."

"My friend Cornelius Tacitus has talked to a man who was here as a boy. He said no one on the other side of the lake knows of any boys who actually returned, except in that one case."

Pompeius began to cry. Delius kicked him again, nudging him closer to the pool.

I turned to Delius. "You were the man who took those boys across the lake, weren't you, when Nero's death threw everyone into a panic?"

He nodded, his sword now hanging limp at his side.

"I know something of your origins—including how you made this signet ring." I raised my hand. "How did you get involved in this unspeakably vile business?"

"When I was eighteen," Delius said, "I fell in love with Leucippe, a slave on your father's estate."

"She's now the wife of Nereus."

"Much to my regret, and hers. She came into the goldsmith's shop with her mistress, the lady Plinia, wife of Caecilius."

"My mother."

"That's right. Well, whenever they came into town, Leucippe would manage to come by the shop or arrange to meet me at a *taberna*. As often as I could get away from the shop, I went to visit Leucippe. To my amazement, she returned my love, the first person to do so since my mother died.

"One day a customer brought in three pounds of gold for us to make some jewelry for his wife. I knew this would be my one opportunity to break free. I got a message to Leucippe to be waiting for me. It would take us several days to design the pieces and get the customer's approval for the designs. The next night I took the gold and headed north.

"When I got to your father's estate, Leucippe wasn't the only one waiting for me. Her brute of a father, Barbatus, and your father himself stood between us. Caecilius told Barbatus he could deal with me in any way he liked. He held Leucippe and made her watch while Barbatus beat me badly, breaking two of my teeth, and sent me away. I will never forget Leucippe's wailing as he drove me off, bleeding from his attack. I intended to go down to the lake and drown myself.

"But Fortune has a funny way of dealing with us, doesn't she? As I escaped from Barbatus, I saw a man I knew, Marcus Livius. I had made a false tooth for him and a brooch for his daughter. That night I hid because he was drawing a boat up onto shore and kept looking around to make sure no one saw him. What caught my attention was his cargo—two boys about six or seven years old.

"I followed the three of them. Livius kept giving the boys treats and telling them how much fun they were going to have. They finally arrived at this place. I had no idea it was even here."

"Hardly anybody does, I gather," I said.

"I climbed a tree so I could see over the wall. In the garden of the villa was this large pool." He waved his sword toward the water. "There were five men in and around the pool, all nude, and eight or nine little boys, also nude. What the men were doing to those boys still nauseates me. I recognized three of the men as customers from the shop.

"Suddenly three pounds of gold seemed a pittance. I knew I couldn't approach any of the men at that time. They outnumbered me, and I would disappear if they knew I was there. But one by one I could deal with them. If anyone knew what they were doing, they would become a laughingstock and forfeit any hope for political advancement. Their fear would be my fortune. I hid out around here for a while, keeping an eye on this villa and robbing some of the customers. They couldn't admit where they'd been, you see. Then I made my way back to Comum, repaid what I had stolen and made abject apologies to the owners. They had to take me back because people liked my work so much, but they kept an eagle eye on me, not that I blame them.

"One day Marcus Livius came into the shop to buy something for his wife. We were alone, so I asked him if he might like something for a little boy. At first he tried to pretend he didn't know what I was talking about, but I mentioned the names of the other men I'd seen at the villa whose identity I knew.

"Livius asked me what I wanted. I told him I wanted a job that would get me out of the goldsmith's shop. He took me to meet two other men, Pompeius and Romatius. Pompeius had been one of the men at the villa whom I did not know. I told them I had written an account of what I had seen and hidden it where it would be found if something happened to me. In exchange for never saying anything, I wanted to be given a position in one of their households.

"Livius didn't like the idea of being blackmailed. Pompeius here almost wet himself at the thought of his dirty, secret life being exposed. He said his wife would divorce him, and most of 'his' money is actually hers. Romatius was close to tears during the conversation. 'Give him what he wants,' was about all he had to say."

I turned to Pompeius, who had recovered some of his composure. "Is this true?"

Pompeius nodded. "We had to take him in, since he knew Livius and he'd seen the boys that Livius was bringing ashore, and he recognized some of the men in the villa. We needed someone to live in the villa and manage the place for us. None of us could be here all the time. Delius wasn't afraid to enforce discipline, among the boys or among the customers."

"You and Romatius were cowards," Delius sneered. "Not a pair of balls between you."

"I can't deny that," Pompeius said. "Things went well for several years. Then Livius got greedy. He said he was taking a larger share of the risk than the rest of us, finding the boys and bringing them over, so he wanted a larger share of the profits—half to him, the other half for the three of us. Romatius and I met with him at the villa, to try to talk some sense into him."

"But you ended up killing him."

"That was my doing," Delius said. "There's no point in denying it, since you two aren't going to live to tell anyone. One night at the villa Livius drank too much and got into an argument with Pompeius and Romatius about the money, like the old man here said. Neither Pompeius nor Romatius was worth anything in a fight, so I had to step in. After all, my job was to keep order at the villa. There were no customers there that night. Livius was strong and determined but drunk. I didn't really mean to kill him, but I hit him on the head with a rock."

"So Livius is the man we found in the wall. Why put him there?"

"We were in a bind," Pompeius said. "We couldn't risk leaving Livius' body anywhere on our premises or just burying him in the woods. Animals dig things up, you know. Romatius suggested putting him in his boat and setting him adrift, but the blow to his head would make it clear he had been killed. I knew that your father was building a wall, so we took Livius there."

"And my father just agreed to this? Why?"

"Your father had to agree to hide the body, since he was a member of the *collegium* and his name was on the agreement that we had all signed."

So this was the document about an "investment" that my steward Decimus had been unable to explain. "Why was one of Livius' teeth removed?"

"I insisted on that," Delius said. "I had made the tooth."

"And it had your mark on it, DEL, like my ring and my wife's brooch."

Delius nodded, with a touch of pride. "At the goldsmith's shop I gained a reputation for being able to carve or cast anything a customer wanted—a signet ring, a brooch, even a false tooth from ivory. People took pride in having a piece with my DEL on the back of it. I had to remove Livius' false tooth, just in case anyone ever did find the body."

I faced Pompeius, resisting the temptation to kick him. "My father made you sign another agreement, didn't he?"

"Yes. He insisted that Romatius and I sign and seal a document exonerating him from any guilt in Livius' death. He promised it would remain sealed and hidden. We didn't see any alternative. Livius' body had to disappear. I take it you've found that document."

"Yes. He hid it with Lutulla."

"But her *taberna* burned," Delius said.

"It was under the pavement in the courtyard, so burning the place and killing her did you no good, Delius."

"I was acting on his orders." He waved the sword dangerously close to Pompeius' head and pushed him closer to the pool.

"Why was it so important to have that document?" I asked Pompeius. "No one even knew who the man in the wall was."

"When I heard what you'd found," Pompeius said, "I thought we could ignore it. But my sister has talked so much about her son-in-law's cleverness, and that night when Livia barged in on Tertia, she kept saying you would never let it rest until you'd found out who it was. I couldn't take that chance. I had to get that document and destroy it. Kidnapping Livia was the first plan I could come up with."

"You told me you were going to look for her, but you knew where she was."

"No, I didn't. I handed the plan over to Delius. He said he wouldn't tell me where he was taking her because he didn't trust me to keep the secret. And he was right. But when your driver was killed, I knew things had gone too far. There had to be some other way to get that document."

"I still don't understand why it was so important."

"Livius was a schoolmate and friend of Domitian. In that summer when Otho, Vitellius, and Vespasian were fighting for power, Livius and his aunt, Pompeia Paulina, a cousin of mine, hid Domitian in her house in Rome. Livius and Domitian were students there. If Domitian ever found out that we had anything to do with Livius' death… well, you know what would happen to us. Probably to you, too, Gaius, since he was found in the wall of your house. What would Regulus do with that information? Think about that for a moment before you condemn me."

His words played on my worst fear, but they were true. Marcus Aquilius Regulus and I hate one another. My uncle had hated him, and he hated my uncle. Under Nero, Regulus had made a fortune digging up information with which to ruin people. Vespasian and his son Titus were decent men and paid no attention to Regulus, but Domitian welcomed him back onto the Palatine Hill. Regulus was making up for lost time by reviving charges that Vespasian and Titus had refused to listen to. Domitian took it all in, like a baby bird with its mouth gaping, waiting for its mother to drop something into it. I could say that I was only a child when Livius was buried in the wall of my house, so I couldn't be held responsible. But what about my mother?

"I can see why you were worried," I said. "So you buried Livius in the wall, but his boat sank. My father said he saw it go down."

"It did," Delius said. "We punched a hole in the bottom of the boat. Then we plugged it with Livius' tunic. I rowed it out a ways and removed the tunic so the boat would sink far enough from shore that no one would find it. Caecilius would put out the story that he had seen the boat go down in the storm that came up that night. Then I swam back and let go of the tunic close enough to shore that it was sure to wash up in a day or two."

"It was an excellent plan," Pompeius said, "worthy of a fox. A man trying to save himself from drowning might well slip off his tunic. All that wool makes the things soak up water like a sponge. We thought someone could identify the tunic."

"That is, in fact, what happened," I said. "Pompeia recognized the stitching around the neck."

"When she did," Pompeius said, "we couldn't believe our luck. She became an important witness to our story."

"But you left Pompeia and her daughter in a very vulnerable position."

"I know, I know. I urged Livius' brother, Quintus, to marry Pompeia. I think he made her happier than Marcus ever did. At least he liked women. Your father told me that he would agree to have Livius' daughter marry you, to make certain she was taken care of."

"And, ironically, because of that marriage and because of Livia's demand for more space in my villa, I tore down the wall where her father was buried."

"Fortune does have a way of making fools of us, doesn't she?"

"I've seen the mosaic in your *triclinium*, Pompeius, and heard your favorite saying."

"About Fortune having us by the balls? Yes. It surely seems that way. Those of us here at the villa weren't doing anything that Nero wasn't doing in Rome, but we weren't the *princeps*."

"Be honest with yourself," Delius snarled. "There was the matter of what happened to the boys on those return trips. Nero wasn't dumping his playmates in a lake when he was done with them. Even if he had been, no one could prosecute him for it."

"You came up with the idea of the masks that covered the top half of the men's faces, didn't you?" I asked Delius.

"Yes. I hoped, if the boys couldn't identify the men, we might be able to get them out of here without killing them. I was sure that's what Livius was doing. He would take only one boy at a time on those 'return' voyages, and he always went at night."

Pompeius nodded and appeared about to cry again. I turned back to him and tried to keep him focused. "I'm not sure this is the end of your story, though."

"You're right." Pompeius cleared his throat. "About a year after that horrible night, your father was having financial problems. That estate never has been very productive, you know."

"So I'm learning. And he drained off some of the income to support Lutulla."

"Exactly. He told Romatius and me that we would have to pay to preserve his silence. He called it 'rent for Livius' quarters.' He said he had made certain the document we signed would remain hidden and that you would know where it was. Romatius and I talked it over and decided we were safer paying the blackmail, even after your father died."

"Were you paying two separate types of blackmail, disguised as interest on a loan?"

"No. He named one sum we had to pay. A third of it we paid directly to him as interest on that imaginary loan. The other two-thirds we paid through an odd system—"

"You left the money in the storerooms of his unfinished temple. Lutulla told me."

Pompeius sighed. "It has been a burden on us for all these years. Romatius' son has never had the money to qualify for the equestrian class, something he dearly aspires to."

"Did you kill my father?"

"I swear to you, Gaius Pliny, I did not. What Delius here might have done, I can't say. He never got over his resentment of having the girl he wanted taken from him and the beating he got, but that was the work of your father's stable man, wasn't it?"

"It was," Delius said, "but Caecilius stood there, egging him on. I hated them both. When Caecilius demanded blackmail, I thought I might get my revenge and pin it on Pompeius and Romatius. I came up to the estate one night to formulate a plan of attack and found your father in the stable, looking after a sick horse."

"You struck him, I imagine, and left him for the frightened horse to trample."

"Yes. I wanted to get Barbatus, too, but I decided I would have to come back another time."

"That leaves me just one more question."

"Ask all the questions you want," Delius said. "You can go to your grave knowing all the answers."

Because of something I had heard and a flash of movement I'd seen behind Delius, I had some confidence that my life wasn't going to end here, so I persevered. "Once Livius was dead, how did you get rid of the boys who had gotten too old to interest your customers?"

"We didn't have to worry for a couple of years," Delius said, "because the boys we had at that time were young. But we were getting close to that dilemma when Nero fell. Some of our customers panicked. They said armies were marching south. They knew this villa would fall and they would be doomed. We had only five boys at that time. I got them together one night and took them to the lake. I stole a boat and took them across. I pointed them in the direction of Old Comum and told them I was sorry I couldn't do more. Then I sailed back across the lake."

"You must have been angry at him," I said to Pompeius.

"We were, but we couldn't do anything. He claimed he had hidden a list of the people who had visited the villa. We couldn't take the chance that he was telling the truth."

"And he still works for you?"

"I can't get rid of him, Gaius Pliny. He knows too much about me, and I know too much about him. You've seen a monstrous birth, I'm sure, when two animals failed to separate completely in the womb. That's what Delius and I are. In a sense, I need him. Because of the way I live, I am threatened now and then. At those times, the Fox becomes useful. I've never asked him to do something which he found too distasteful."

"Even kidnapping your own niece?"

"No one was supposed to get hurt. I gave strict orders about that. And it wasn't Delius who killed your driver. With the short notice I had given him to hire someone, that dolt Aurelius was the best he could find. I'm truly sorry. I hear the fellow has been dealt with."

"Decisively." The image of Aurora plunging her knife into Aurelius sprang up from wherever it had been hiding in my mind since that moment.

"Well, your questions have been answered, Gaius Pliny," Delius said, "and this is getting tiresome." With a final push of his foot he shoved Pompeius into the stinking pool. "Find out what it felt like for those boys, you filthy old bastard!" Pompeius sank beneath the leaves and garbage covering the surface of the water.

I lunged at Delius, trying to disarm him. He was a wiry man, much stronger than he looked, and I couldn't get firm footing on the slick paving stones around the pool. As much as I hated to do it, I put my strength into pushing him into the water. He dragged me with him, but at least he let go of his sword.

The water came up to our chests as we exchanged blows. I was desperate to finish him so I could rescue Pompeius. Delius had his hands on my throat when a woman's voice screamed, "Gaius!"

Delius looked up at Aurora standing on the edge of the pool and his grip loosened. That gave me the instant I needed to slam his head back against the edge of the pool. He collapsed and sank under the water.

"Are you all right?" Aurora cried.

"Yes. I need to find Pompeius." I floundered around in the water until I got a grip on Pompeius' arm, but I knew as soon as pulled him to the surface that he was dead.

I spent a few minutes sticking a finger down my throat to make myself vomit. Water that vile could sicken me, I was sure. Aurora held me as my heaving subsided.

"A gruesome ending, isn't it?" she said.

"Yes, but perhaps the best possible. I believe in justice and courts of law, but airing all of this evil in a court would have done more harm than good to the families of everyone involved."

As we loaded the bodies of Delius and Pompeius onto their horses, I was relieved that they had met an appropriate kind of justice. My bastard cousin and brother-by-adoption had killed my father and my wife's father. I felt like the avenger in a Greek tragedy. I wondered if the Furies would pursue me, as they often do in those stories, for killing a member of my family. Perhaps it was retribution enough that I wore a signet ring he had made and would feel his DEL against my skin for the rest of my life.

"Why would you go off by yourself like this?" Aurora asked as we plodded back through the woods toward my villa. "If I hadn't decided to come down here—"

I touched the Tyche ring.

XVI

Refrain from asking what will happen tomorrow;
every day that fortune grants you, count as gain.

—Horace

TWO DAYS LATER, in midafternoon, we came within sight
of Livia's villa in Umbria and drew to a halt. The house is on the
east side of Lake Trasimene, off the road to Perusia. We had stopped
on a rise in the road and could see the entire estate. Most of the land
was given over to growing olives. Tacitus and I were on horseback,
along with several servants riding with us as guards, while Felix drove
a wagon, with Aurora fidgeting at his side. She can't be around a horse
without wanting to ride it or drive it. Julia sat more patiently in the
back, playing with one of the macabre skull masks we had taken as a
kind of booty. She and Tacitus had decided not to continue to their
estate in Gaul. The rest of their servants would pack and return with
their wagons to Rome.

"Shall we wait here for you, my lord?" Felix asked.

"That won't be necessary. Go on into Perusia and see what kind of
accommodations you can find us. I don't expect to be here long. She
may not even let me in the door."

"Do you want me to come with you?" Tacitus asked.

I pondered for a moment. "That's probably a good idea."

Julia gave a short laugh. "Somebody may have to carry your body
out."

I decided to take a couple of the servants along for protection on
the road. By the time we reached the front of the house, the servants we

passed along the way had relayed the news of our arrival. Livia's steward was waiting for us. I had met the man on my one trip up here shortly after our wedding but could not remember his name.

"This is an unexpected pleasure, my lord," he lied. "Shall we prepare rooms for you?"

"No. I was passing by on my way back to Rome and wanted to see how my wife is doing. I won't be staying."

"Very well. I'll let her know you're here, my lord. Please, come into the garden and have some wine while you wait."

Tacitus and the servants stopped in the atrium while I continued into the garden, where I waited for probably a quarter of an hour. At least the wine was good and the garden had some charm, with a fountain in the center and a pleasant variety of vegetation. I stood when Livia came into view, accompanied by Procne and two other servants. She wore a white gown with a red mantle. Her hair was loose and damp, as though she had just washed it, and her eyes appeared dark and sunken from lack of sleep.

"Thank you for sending my father's bones to me," she said without any prelude or warmth. "In your letter you didn't explain what happened to him."

"I didn't want to put anything in writing that might fall into the wrong hands. I thought I would tell you in person."

"Then let's sit down."

We seated ourselves on the shady side of the garden and, at my request, she dismissed her servants. As succinctly as possible, I told her that Pompeius had confessed to arguing with her father over sharing the money from a business deal, and one of his henchmen had killed Livius.

"What sort of business deal? You're being evasive, Gaius."

"The details are complex and unnecessary. I don't fully understand it myself." Better evasive than lurid. I had no desire to destroy her perception of her father. Nor did I want to tell her that her brooch—the prized gift from her father which she was wearing at that moment—was made by the man who killed him.

"So, *your* father didn't actually kill *my* father," she said when I finished.

"No, thank the gods. He was complicit in covering up the murder, though, and he blackmailed Romatius and Pompeius for years. He set up a complicated arrangement by which they had to continue paying long after he died. I'm going to have to see what I can do to make it up to their children."

"Well, then, it sounds like that's all settled." She folded her hands in her lap.

I nodded. "Pompeius and his henchman are both dead. No one will be bothering you anymore."

"Thank you for coming to tell me all of this." Her voice brightened slightly. "Are you on your way back to Rome?"

"Yes."

"I wish you a safe journey, and I'm sure you want to get back on the road." She might as well have pushed me toward the door.

"There is one more reason for me to be here," I said.

"What is that?" Her voice, now flat again, revealed how unhappy she was that she had to talk to me any longer.

"I wanted to find out how you're faring."

She drew back and studied me before she said, "Why do you even care?"

"Livia, you're my wife. Of course I care."

"Well, I managed to sleep through most of last night," she said. "Dreams of being in that cave woke me only twice."

"I'm sorry that it still troubles you so much."

"Troubles me? Gaius, it horrifies me. I can still see all that blood and can feel the sword at my throat. No matter how many times I bathe, I still feel that animal's hands all over me and his blood in my hair and on my face." She wiped her hands over her body and face.

"Those memories will fade, I promise you. It has been only a few days."

"It feels like a lifetime. I even considered shaving my head and wearing a wig." Her tears welled up, and I suspected they were real. "Tell me, how can you lie with a woman who has killed a man?"

I didn't bother denying that Aurora and I had coupled. I wondered how Livia would react if I told her that, by saving her life, Aurora had lost my child—our child. But that would only give her another weapon to use against me. "People might ask the same question if I were to lie with you."

"Liburnius' death was an accident." She said it slowly but with less vehemence than before, like someone who's tired of repeating a lie but determined not to tell the truth. "I told you. He slipped in the bath and hit his head."

"Do you still expect me to believe that? He violated you in what you considered a particularly vile way, and you took your vengeance. You admitted as much in your hysteria at Eustachius' quarry."

She drew her mantle more tightly around her. "A woman can say anything when she's hysterical. You can't prove a word of it."

I took a sip of wine. "So, what are you going to do? Are you going to continue to live here?"

"I cannot risk my life by living with you, Gaius. Livilla was right about that. You attract danger. You've settled this business, but something else will come up. Sometimes I think you seek out trouble."

"If you want a divorce, I won't stand in your way."

"No. We both know that you won't initiate a divorce because of what it would cost you, and I won't do it because I would be left with only this estate. I can't live on that. Before we married we agreed on how much money you'll provide for me. I'll just have to keep a safe distance from you—and from your knife-wielding paramour."

"Are you expecting me to keep to that bargain when you aren't fulfilling your obligation as my wife?" Not that I wanted her to in the least.

"You know, don't you, that I could inform on you and…her for that knife. Slaves can't run around armed, killing people."

"And what would you gain if I lost everything?"

Livia pursed her lips. "Some satisfaction at seeing what happens to her. But, don't worry, I won't do that. Ruining you would cost me more than I'm willing to pay. All I'll say—and then only if I'm asked—is that she helped you and Tacitus rescue me when I was kidnapped. It was dark in the cave. I was frightened and everything happened so fast, I suppose I'm not sure who did what."

"And what about Procne? She was there, too."

"Procne was only half-conscious. She doesn't know what happened. All she remembers is the pain of having her wound cauterized."

She stood and I did as well.

"I'm sorry I cannot love you, Gaius, and even sorrier that you cannot love me. But, then, I doubt that any man could."

"That's not true."

"Well, no, not entirely. My father did love me, and not just because he had to."

For the first time I felt sympathy for her. The one person in her life whom she cherished had been a brutal, perverted monster who, frankly, deserved to be killed and stuffed in a wall. "Livia, you are my wife. If you give me the chance, I will honor and protect you as a husband should."

She touched my arm and almost smiled. "That's a very pained expression on your face, Gaius, the expression of a dutiful husband, but not a loving one. Now, you need to leave. I'm sure she's out there, not far away, and you want to get back to her." She gestured toward the door.

I didn't know what to say.

"Is that so-called husband of hers with you?"

I nodded.

"As long as she remains married to him and in the background of your life, I won't stand in your way. *Just don't humiliate me.*"

We found rooms in a very nice inn in Perusia and sent a servant to watch at the city gate and tell Gaius and Tacitus where we were. The other servants were given rooms on the top floor, while Tacitus and Julia, Felix and I, and Gaius got rooms on the second floor. Felix understood, of course, that I would be spending the night in Gaius' room. "I'm unaccustomed to sharing a bed with anyone else," he said as I gave him a kiss on the cheek and went out the door.

Gaius and I did not make love. I knew I wasn't ready for it, and Gaius was too considerate to insist on anything. It was such a relief to lie beside him, knowing that, with the servants on another floor, no one would be surprised, or dismayed, to see me walk out of this room in the morning. He stretched out on his back, with his left arm around me, drawing me close to him. My head rested on his shoulder.

"Do you think Livia is really going to let us be together?" I asked him.

"She said she wouldn't stand in our way. I do feel an obligation to make

it up to her that my father was involved in the murder of her father and the hiding of his body. I can never divorce her or embarrass her the way her first husband did."

"You wouldn't do that anyway, you dear man." I kissed him on the neck. "Our relationship can never be more than it is. I understand that."

"I could emancipate you and—"

I put a finger on his lips. "Then how could I be yours?"

"She does expect that you remain as unobtrusive as possible and married to Felix."

"That would be the best arrangement," I told him.

Gaius ran his hand through my hair and kissed my forehead. "I'm surprised to hear you say that. It wasn't how you felt when I told you that you were going to be married."

I punched his chest playfully. "That was because of the clumsy way you handled it. Felix is a nice man. I actually enjoy his company. He's more like a father, except he won't sell me. And, if I should be with child again, it will seem perfectly natural to everyone else because I have a husband."

We lay quietly for a while, listening to a storm build up and unleash its fury outside. I snuggled closer to Gaius. "Do you remember that night, when we were eight…"

EPILOGUE

Gaius Pliny to his friend Romatius Firmus, greetings.

You and I were born in the same township, were schoolmates together, and have been friends since childhood. Your father was a good friend of my mother and my uncle, and a friend to me as well—given the difference in our ages. These are compelling reasons why I ought to help you advance in your career. The fact that you hold the office of *decurion* in Comum shows that you have a fortune of 100,000 *sesterces*. In order that we may have the pleasure of seeing you not only as a *decurion*, but as a Roman knight, I am giving you 300,000 *sesterces*, to enable you to qualify for equestrian rank.

We've been friends long enough to guarantee that you will not forget this favor. I don't have to urge you to enjoy the equestrian dignity which this gift will allow you to attain, because I'm sure you will do so from your own innate nature. People ought to guard an honor all the more carefully, when, in so doing, they are taking care of a gift bestowed by the kindness of a friend.

Farewell.

—*Pliny, Ep. 1.19.*

CAST OF CHARACTERS

HISTORICAL PERSONS

Caecilius Pliny's biological father. Pliny never mentions him in his letters, but since his name, after adoption by his uncle, was Gaius Plinius Caecilius Secundus, we know his father's family name (*nomen gentilicum*) was Caecilius. Inscriptions from around Comum mention men named Caecilius, but we don't know if any of them was Pliny's father.

Julia Daughter of Julius Agricola and wife of Tacitus. All we know about her is that she and Tacitus were still married in the late 90s, when Tacitus wrote the *Agricola*, his encomium of his father-in-law.

Lutulla I'm not sure where to put Lutulla. Her name appears in an inscription from around Comum, and she seems to have had some connection with a Caecilius. Whether either of them have anything to do with Pliny, we don't know.

Plinia Pliny's mother and the sister of Pliny the Elder. Pliny mentions her in only a couple of his letters, particularly 6.16 and 6.20, those describing the eruption of Vesuvius. We have no idea when she was born or when she died.

Pompeia Celerina In several letters Pliny mentions or writes to his mother-in-law, Pompeia Celerina, but he never mentions the name of her daughter (his wife) or her husband's name. Relations between Pliny and his mother-in-law seem to have been cordial later. In this book they are off to a rocky start. Pompeia owned an estate at the town of Narnia, northeast of Rome, which Pliny enjoyed visiting.

Romatius Firmus A childhood friend of Pliny's. Several letters are addressed to him (see Epilogue). He apparently stayed on in Comum as an adult.

FICTIONAL CHARACTERS

Aurora Pliny's servant and lover. After a brief first appearance in *The Blood of Caesar*, she has become a more and more important character and her relationship to Pliny has deepened.

Barbatus The stablemaster on Pliny's estate near Comum.

Delius Illegitimate son of Pliny's uncle, born to a mistress thirty-five years before the narrative date of this story.

Livia Pliny's wife. Pliny was married two or three times, but the only wife he mentions by name is the last one, the youthful Calpurnia. The anonymous wife who was the daughter of Pompeia Celerina seems to have died about A.D. 96. Pliny mentions his affection for her in one of his letters.

Livilla Younger sister of Livia, first engaged to Pliny. She does not appear in this book but is referred to several times. If a man was named Livius, all of his daughters would be named Livia, the feminine form of his family name. Putting *-illa* on the end of the younger daughter's name would serve to distinguish her from her older sister.

Naomi Servant and confidante of Pliny's mother, and one of my favorite characters. She is Jewish and has had some influence on Plinia's thinking.

Phineas Son of Naomi, and Pliny's chief scribe. He's a couple of years older than Pliny. He and Naomi were taken captive at the capture of Jerusalem in A.D. 70.

Pompeius Brother of Pliny's mother-in-law, Pompeia Celerina.

Tertia Her name would have been Pompeia Tertia, since she was the third daughter of a man named Pompeius. To avoid some confusion, I have called her Tertia, as she would have been called by her family.

GLOSSARY OF TERMS

Also see glossaries in previous books in this series.

aedile Roman magistrate whose duties included public works (roads, sidewalks, etc.), staging games and shows, and overseeing fair dealing in the marketplaces.

clientela Every Roman aristocrat was a patron and had lower-class persons who were dependent on him. The root *cli-* means to lean on, or rely on, someone. It's also found in *triclinium*, where three people reclined on a dining couch. Clients were expected to be at their patron's house early in the morning to greet him and receive a small donative to get them through the day and then accompany him as he went about his affairs in town. The size of a man's *clientela* was an unmistakable measure of his wealth and prestige.

collegium A business partnership, usually among wealthy equestrians. The term could also cover a group of people, even a religious sect, who needed authorization to act as a corporation. Being recognized as a *collegium* gave them the right to own property, to establish a treasury, or to inherit when someone died.

equestrians The class of wealthy Romans just below the senatorial class, originally so called because they could afford to ride a horse into battle. Senators were forbidden to engage in any business, which left room for ambitious men from the lower classes to make fortunes. To qualify for equestrian rank, one had to have a total fortune of 400,000 *sesterces* (1,000,000 for the Senate). Periodically the censors would go over people's accounts. If one's fortune had slipped below the required mark, one would lose the equestrian status. Members of this class wore a narrow purple/red stripe on their clothing, the same color as, but not as broad as, the senatorial stripe.

hipposandals A kind of Roman horseshoes, strapped over a horse's hooves when the animal had to pull a particularly heavy load or travel over rough terrain.

municipium The Romans established towns with various degrees of rights. A *municipium* was originally a settlement in Italy, but the term is later used of towns across the empire.

pankration A type of "mixed martial arts" practiced by the Greeks.

papyrus/parchment Papyrus, made from a plant that grows along the Nile, was the favored type of writing material in antiquity. Pages were glued together to make scrolls. Parchment, or animal skin, was known as far back as the fifth century B.C., but was considered an inferior material. Both are labor-intensive to make. Parchment won out because it works better in the codex, or book form, which we now use.

Perusia Ancient name for the city of Perugia, one of the major towns of Umbria, founded about 300 B.C. It is near Lake Trasimene, site of one of Hannibal's major victories over the Romans in the Second Punic War.

Tanagra figurines Small terra-cotta statuettes depicting people, usually women, engaged in daily tasks or sitting and chatting. They were typically 4–7 inches high and originated in the Greek town of Tanagra, north of Athens, in the late fourth century B.C.

tunica rustica The gown traditionally worn by a Roman bride. It was white, with a saffron belt and veil.

AUTHOR'S NOTE

When I wrote the first Pliny mystery, *All Roads Lead to Murder*, I did not envision a second, let alone a sixth. I'm grateful for the encouragement that readers and reviewers have given me. I also need to express my gratitude to my writers' group, the West Michigan Writers' Workshop, which I began to attend in 2001. The make-up of the group has changed over the years, but our facilitator, Steve Beckwith, keeps us focused on the craft of writing. The group has established a web site: https://sites.google.com/site/westmiww/.

In the rest of this note I want to address three unrelated topics: the change in publishers, confusion about Pliny's family, and the epigraphs at the beginning of each chapter.

PUBLISHERS

In the interest of transparency, I would like to explain why the Pliny mysteries have been issued by different publishers. Ingalls Publishing Group published the first three, while the fourth and fifth were published by Perseverance Press. Several years ago Ingalls decided to focus on southeastern regional books, and ancient Rome didn't seem to fit that profile. I was fortunate to connect with Perseverance Press right away and enjoyed working with them on *Death in the Ashes* and *The Eyes of Aurora*. It was helpful to have a different editor's perspective for a couple of years. I learned quite a bit from Meredith Phillips and John and Susan Daniel.

In the world of small-press publishing, we usually work one book at a time, so when Bob Ingalls called and asked if I would consider returning to Ingalls, I agreed to give the offer some thought. I knew I would gain something either way, but I would also give up something, no matter which publisher I went with. It wasn't as though I had St. Martin's and Random House bidding for my services, but... Several factors led me to return to Ingalls—primarily my long and excellent working relationship with Judy Geary and Ingalls's willingness to consider publishing some of my non-mystery projects, as they did a few years ago with *Perfect Game, Imperfect Lives.* (Perseverance Press is strictly a mystery publisher.)

Sadly, Bob Ingalls died early in 2015. His wife decided to shut down the publishing business. I posted on the DorothyL online list, asking if anyone could suggest a publisher. I was considering doing the book myself when Meredith Phillips contacted me and invited me to come back to Perseverance Press, which I was quite happy to do. I owe Perseverance a lot. They have kept my publishing career—insignificant as it is—going when I thought I might be done.

PLINY'S FAMILY

In this book, and in earlier ones, there are references to Pliny's biological father, a Lucius Caecilius, and to a possible sibling. Pliny never mentions his father in his letters, nor is there any reference to any siblings. He always refers to his uncle (his adoptive father) as his uncle. Questions have arisen because of two inscriptions, both from the area around Comum (modern Como), Pliny's hometown. One refers to a Lucius Caecilius Secundus, who began building a temple to the Eternity of Rome and Augustus in honor of his daughter, Caecilia, who scholars believe was deceased. The temple was completed by Caecilius Secundus *filius*, possibly our Pliny, but part of the name is missing.

Another inscription mentions a magistrate named Lucius Caecilius Cilo and two sons (or possibly brothers) and a concubine, Lutulla the daughter of Pictus. The Caecilius and Plinius families were numerous around Comum and the name Secundus is by no means rare, so we can't be certain that either of these inscriptions has anything to do with Pliny the Younger. They do, however, provide just enough grist for the mills of a historical novelist.

Pliny was married two or three times, but we know the name of only his last wife, the teenaged Calpurnia. He writes letters to his mother-in-law, Pompeia Celerina, but he never mentions Pompeia's daughter by name or the name of Pompeia's husband. A wife of Pliny's, presumably Pompeia's daughter, died about the time Domitian was murdered (September A.D. 96), and he seems to have been married to her for some time.

The Pompeius family had many branches, so I don't think I have stretched the bounds of possibility too far to suggest that Pliny's mother-in-law may have had some connection with Pompeia Paulina, the much-admired wife of the philosopher Seneca.

Aurora is, of course, a fictitious character. She appeared briefly in the second book in the series, *The Blood of Caesar* (named by *Library Journal* one of the Five Best Mysteries of 2008). In each succeeding book she has come to play a larger role. In this book I have again given her a chance to speak in her own voice, as I began to do in *The Eyes of Aurora*. Sections written from her point of view are in italics. It is a challenge to write from the p. o. v. of a young, wealthy, slave-owning Roman aristocrat, since I am none of those things. It is an equally daunting challenge to write from the p. o. v. of a young female Roman slave, since I am not any of those things either.

CHAPTER EPIGRAPHS

Working on a novel with Fortune as its theme, I was impressed by how much the Greeks and Romans had to say on the subject. I have put epigraphs from various writers—all of whom could have been known to Pliny—at the head of each chapter. Some have more connection with the chapter than others. Once I got started, it was hard to stop. Perhaps someday a graduate student, desperate for a thesis topic, will try to figure out what the epigraphs have to do with the chapters. As Freud allegedly said (but probably didn't), "Sometimes a cigar is just a cigar."

ABOUT THE AUTHOR

ALBERT A. BELL, JR. is a college history professor, novelist, and weekend gardener who lives in Michigan. He and his wife have four adult children and two grandsons. In addition to his Roman mysteries, Bell has written contemporary mysteries, middle-grade novels, and nonfiction. Visit him at www.albertbell.com and www.pliny-mysteries.com.

More Traditional Mysteries from Perseverance Press
For the New Golden Age

K.K. Beck
Tipping the Valet
ISBN 978-1-56474-563-7

Albert A. Bell, Jr.
PLINY THE YOUNGER SERIES
Death in the Ashes
ISBN 978-1-56474-532-3

The Eyes of Aurora
ISBN 978-1-56474-549-1

Fortune's Fool
ISBN 978-1-56474-587-3

Taffy Cannon
ROXANNE PRESCOTT SERIES
Guns and Roses
Agatha and Macavity awards nominee, Best Novel
ISBN 978-1-880284-34-6

Blood Matters
ISBN 978-1-880284-86-5

Open Season on Lawyers
ISBN 978-1-880284-51-3

Paradise Lost
ISBN 978-1-880284-80-3

Laura Crum
GAIL MCCARTHY SERIES
Moonblind
ISBN 978-1-880284-90-2

Chasing Cans
ISBN 978-1-880284-94-0

Going, Gone
ISBN 978-1-880284-98-8

Barnstorming
ISBN 978-1-56474-508-8

Jeanne M. Dams
HILDA JOHANSSON SERIES
Crimson Snow
ISBN 978-1-880284-79-7

Indigo Christmas
ISBN 978-1-880284-95-7

Murder in Burnt Orange
ISBN 978-1-56474-503-3

Janet Dawson
JERI HOWARD SERIES
Bit Player
Golden Nugget Award nominee
ISBN 978-1-56474-494-4

Cold Trail
ISBN 978-1-56474-555-2

Water Signs
ISBN 978-1-56474-586-6

What You Wish For
ISBN 978-1-56474-518-7

TRAIN SERIES
Death Rides the Zephyr
ISBN 978-1-56474-530-9

Death Deals a Hand
ISBN 978-1-56474-569-9

Kathy Lynn Emerson
LADY APPLETON SERIES
Face Down Below the Banqueting House
ISBN 978-1-880284-71-1

Face Down Beside St. Anne's Well
ISBN 978-1-880284-82-7

Face Down O'er the Border
ISBN 978-1-880284-91-9

Sara Hoskinson Frommer
JOAN SPENCER SERIES
Her Brother's Keeper
ISBN 978-1-56474-525-5

Hal Glatzer
KATY GREEN SERIES
Too Dead To Swing
ISBN 978-1-880284-53-7

A Fugue in Hell's Kitchen
ISBN 978-1-880284-70-4

The Last Full Measure
ISBN 978-1-880284-84-1

Margaret Grace
MINIATURE SERIES
Mix-up in Miniature
ISBN 978-1-56474-510-1

Madness in Miniature
ISBN 978-1-56474-543-9

Manhattan in Miniature
ISBN 978-1-56474-562-0

Matrimony in Miniature
ISBN 978-1-56474-575-0

Tony Hays
Shakespeare No More
ISBN 978-1-56474-566-8

Wendy Hornsby
MAGGIE MACGOWEN SERIES
In the Guise of Mercy
ISBN 978-1-56474-482-1

The Paramour's Daughter
ISBN 978-1-56474-496-8